Cryptic Heartbeat

CIERRA GARDNER

NORTHWEST PINES PUBLISHING

CRYPTIC HEARTBEAT

Paperback Cover by **Kellie Cover Designs**
Hardback Cover by **Ruby Spark**

Published by Northwest Pines Publishing

This book is dedicated to my dear friend Sal. A man who taught me so much and gave so much of himself to help others including me. For over a month I thought I lost you, I mourned you. But you came back from the dead and I am forever thankful.

Author's Note

This book contains the following elements:

- Kidnapping, torture, stalking
- Guns, shooting, threats, violence, blood
- Mention of death, death, family death,
- Military flashbacks, tactical scenarios, PTSD
- Mention of homelessness
- Sexual harassment, harassment
- Hospitalization, medical scenes
- Adult language
- Explicit sex, including BDSM aspects (breath play, knife lay, electricity play, restraints, blindfolding, whips)
- Workplace conflict
- Mention of MM
- Mental health decline
- Mention of Down syndrome
- Childbirth

And let's be honest there is probably more so… enjoy.

Chapter One

REN

The Emergency Department at Silver Heart Medical Center was always busy, and, of course, today was no different. People moved in and out, some waiting for hours, others giving up and leaving. When they left, my curiosity would often get the best of me by the end of my shift and I'd glance at their chart.

Let's just say some people need to learn what is truly an emergency. Not to mention if they were leaving, they weren't that sick, and dying people don't generally walk out of ERs. This hospital was the best one in the area, to the point that patients came from other states to get their care here, thus making the ER always busy.

Despite knowing most people who came in could wait to be treated by their primary care doctor or an urgent care physician, I still worried. Some serious illnesses can present with mild symptoms. Not only that, but people are inherently stubborn and can minimize symptoms.

Dr. Internet didn't help.

It either went to the *OMG I'm dying* to *oh, it's nothing,* and people wound up dead due to lack of treatment. The internet could be a useful tool if used correctly, but unfortunately it was filled with false information.

As I watched people leave before being seen, I often worried that something bad could happen and we wouldn't get to them in time. It had happened before, and Lord knew it would happen again.

Despite my specialty being cardiology, I worked in the ER at least two or three times a week. Let's be honest, I was already overworked, but Dr. Thompson, my best friend, was the head of the Emergency Department. Naturally, I would cover for him sometimes when he had family matters, or I would even work alongside him when one of his staff called off. What are friends for?

The sudden loud sound of heavy items hitting the floor drew my attention behind me. Dale slept restlessly in the chair, and his belongings, which I assume had been in his pockets, were now spread about the floor.

Over the years, I had treated Dale. Life came down on the man and he found himself homeless, then as a result, he developed heart and lung issues. When he came into the ER the night I met him, he was in rough shape and his X-rays were concerning.

From the second my pager had gone off for a man in his sixties, I fought for him. Dale was found unconscious inside the homeless shelter bathroom. When Thompson ran his tests, his B-type natriuretic peptide levels were off. Drugs were quickly ruled out, and I was called as he got his X-rays and ultrasounds.

When the results came back, he had pneumonia and an enlarged heart. After ordering his meds, I admitted him immediately.

That's when I had gotten to know him. My lunch was mostly spent in his room, and we would talk about anything and everything. He told me about his daughter, who worked for the government, and that he lost his true love years ago.

I dragged out his stay as long as I could but made sure that he had a place for a couple weeks. Unfortunately, his living conditions were not great, so he would come back every few months, and this would continue until he either died or found housing.

The man felt like family, so seeing him sick was rough. Not to mention knowing that he would be here less if people didn't steal his meds, a frequent occurrence among the homeless community.

God forbid if he came in on my day off. They would treat and turf as the saying goes, but not for me.

I snapped back to the present when Nurse Celeste grabbed my arm and moved me back to the closed doors separating the ER waiting room from the treatment rooms, essentially bringing me back into chaos.

"Dr. Doux, I know we are busy today, but you can't just see the patients in the waiting room. They need to be seen in their own rooms. You have plenty of patients that need your attention."

She was correct; there was far from a shortage of patients waiting to be seen. Hours ago, they diverted ambulances, and I was pulled to work after my already full day in cardiology. However, my mind wandered to Dale. Was he here resting, or was he feeling unwell?

"Do we know why Dale is here?" I asked.

Celeste smiled warmly at me. We had both grown to love and care for him. If I wasn't having lunch with him while he was here, she was. Every time he came in, we both tried to call his daughter, who I don't think even knew her father was homeless. But we never got an answer. Hell, whenever we tried to call her, it went straight to voicemail. It truly broke my heart.

He never said it, but you could tell he missed her and was worried about her. The stress of his worry was not helping anything. As a friend, I was angry for him. As a doctor, I felt like she would be helpful to his health...if we could just get ahold of her.

"Looks like some chest discomfort. EKG was normal."

"Can we order a cardiac ultrasound, see if his heart is getting worse?"

"Of course, Doctor. I'll do that right away," she said as she closed out the patient program and headed to the nurses' station. In my opinion, she was the best ER nurse there was.

Feeling determined, I logged into the tablet and looked for his daughter's number again. Without a second thought, I pulled out my personal phone, not the hospital's, per protocol, and dialed her number. I nearly dropped the damn phone when it rang after being sent straight to voicemail all this time. The utter shock when she answered was enough to make me lightheaded.

"Hello?"

Holy shit.

"Hello, my name is Dr. Doux. I am trying to reach Rosalina Conrad."

I heard rustling in the background and wondered what she was doing.

"This is her. What is this regarding?"

"I work at Silver Heart Medical Center in Spokane, Washington, and your father is a patient under my care," I said, pausing momentarily when I heard her sudden intake of air. "Your father came in to be seen, and I suspect his living conditions are making his heart worse."

"Living conditions?" she asked. I could hear the concern in her voice. She clearly had no clue.

"Dale is homeless, ma'am."

"He is what?" she yelled. "Oh no, this will not do. Shit. Sorry, I am on assignment and can't get away right now. Text this number or call the number I sent to the number you called from. I will be there as fast as I can," she said. Then, before I could even respond, the line went dead.

Assignment? What the hell did that mean?

4

Shaking my head, I slipped my phone back into my pocket and went to find Celeste. When I found her, she had a large stack of files and looked frazzled. "I got some good news."

She looked up at me as I got close. "And what is that, Doctor?"

"I was finally able to reach Dale's daughter."

Her head snapped up, and the files fell. Most landed on the counter, but a few crashed to the ground.

Shit.

We both squatted down, and I helped her pick up everything and place them on the counter to be sorted later. It wasn't surprising to see Nurse Melody move from behind the desk and start grabbing the files and frantically trying to reorganize them in the correct order. OCD for the win.

"You mean the phone was on?"

"Yep. She said she was on assignment but would come when she could. I'll make sure Dale is here when she gets here. I need to run tests on him anyway, so it wouldn't be that much of a stretch. Unless it's too long, then I don't know. Maybe have him live with me for a bit."

"I'd run that up the chain to make sure it's okay and not jeopardize your medical license. I'll put the order in. His new ultrasound results are back." She handed me a tablet with everything already pulled up. I scrolled through the written results and the images. My grip tightened on the tablet, and my heart felt like it would shatter.

Fluid... Fuck.

He was getting worse. Hell, he was dying, and I didn't think I could save him. Unless he suddenly got a home, I couldn't help him more than I had already. It was truly terrible since I knew he could someday be off meds and healthy if he wasn't on the damn streets. The lack of a warm place to sleep every night, his diet, the days he may go without water, and exposure to the elements were taking their toll. I could only increase his meds so much.

Yeah, this was definitely the part I hated.

As I approached his room, I took a deep breath. I only hoped his daughter got here soon, wherever she was coming from. And maybe, just maybe, she could help him get a place, so he no longer had to fight this battle on the streets. I needed to bring him home with me one way or another.

Chapter Two

ROSE

I was able to get away for a check-in with my handler, and I turned on my personal phone after letting it charge. When it rang within minutes, I was in shock.

Who the hell?

The man's voice sent a jolt of electricity down my spine. When he revealed he was a doctor and was calling about my father, I dashed into the storage closet like some sort of scared schoolgirl ditching class. I couldn't risk getting caught on the phone. My boss could be a hardass and hated when we took personal calls at work or on assignment. Well, ever really, to be honest. But I deserved a few damn minutes after spending all my time making him look good.

My dad was sick. Not only that, but he was homeless.

How the fuck did that happen and when?

And why didn't he say anything?

After I finished this assignment, I was entitled to some time off. My father needed me, and I wasn't going to let him suffer or die alone if he was that sick.

God, I hoped not. I wasn't ready to let him go.

I called my handler as soon as I hung up.

"I need this wrapped up. I made plans for you to go to Afghanistan in three days," he quipped.

"I'm sorry, sir, but I need some personal time. My father—"

"I don't pay you to concern yourself with your father, Rosalina. I pay you for results."

I gritted my teeth, trying to hold in my anger. To say I wanted to smack this asshole in the head through the damn phone was an understatement. This job used to mean everything to me, but when Hank Barks became my boss, I started to hate it. The smug man had no family or life outside of the CIA, so no one on his team could either. I was about to speak, probably say something I'd regret, but the line went dead.

Damn.

As soon as I could, I was getting a message to the director. I respected the hell out of the director. Having served under him in the Navy was an honor, so I jumped all in when he recruited me here at the CIA to work with him. And if the doctor ever called the number I gave him, he would make sure I got home ASAP.

Chapter Three

REN

After the phone call, I had to do something. I didn't want to call the number just yet, so I held on to it and got to work on keeping Dale in the hospital as long as I could. I texted the number every day and never received a response. Hell, I had no way of knowing if she was actually getting them.

I sat at the doctors' station and stared at the number.

"You may as well call it, you know you are dying to," Celeste said.

She wasn't wrong.

My finger tapped the screen and the phone rang.

"This is Richards," a deep male voice echoed in my ear.

"Um, hi, a woman named Rosalina Conrad gave me your number when I notified her about her dad."

The man remained silent so I went on to tell him everything, hoping I was not violating the next of kin's wishes.

"I will see that she gets home after this assignment. Give me the name of your hospital's director, and I will see that he can come home with you. Unfortunately that's all I can do for the sake of national security. But I promise she will be home as soon as we can do so safely. She checks in with me regularly, so if there is anything urgent please call me."

"Thank you, sir," I said, and the line went dead. I texted him the name he asked for, then looked up to meet Celeste's curious eyes. "That was by far the most unnerving call ever, but I think it was a good one to make."

I filled her in on what he said and she smiled.

"Fingers crossed he comes through for Dale."

My pager beeped, and I saw my presence was needed in admin. I swallowed hard. Could he have made it happen that fast?

I entered the doorframe of the director's office and he smiled. "You made a friend in the government, I see." His tone was relaxed so it was fairly safe to assume he wasn't mad.

"No, sir. My patient—"

He raised his hand and silenced me. "I know all about it. I also know you are seeking permission to bring a patient into your living quarters until we get word that his daughter is, in fact, coming home."

"Yes, sir."

"Well, we received a generous donation for our cooperation so I am granting you the permission. But only for this case."

"Understood." It took everything in me not to jump up and down like a child.

"Use tonight to get things ready, discharge him at the end of your shift tomorrow."

I nodded and headed to Dale's room to tell him the news while I texted the mysterious daughter with friends in high places.

"Hey Dale, I come with some news."

"And what's that, Doc?"

"I was finally able to reach your daughter." As the words left my lips I could see a brightness come into his eyes. "She isn't able to come today, but she did pull some strings. You will be here until my shift ends tomorrow, then you will get to come home with me."

"Rene, you don't have to do that."

I placed my hand on his shoulder and squeezed gently. "No, I don't, but I want to. You will stay with me until she can get back."

"Okay, son."

My heart felt like it swelled to twice its size. He called me son. Coming from a man that I took care of on a daily basis for days and weeks at a time, it truly meant the world. "I'll have Celeste bring you some cookies. I have to finish up for the night, but tomorrow at five we will leave here together."

As the door closed behind me I opened my texts.

> Everything is a go. Tomorrow he will be with me at my place.

> Take care. He looks forward to your return.

AFTER I GOT HOME, I cleaned my place for my long-term guest. Then I crashed on my bed. Now I was wrapping up at work and everything was good to go with Dale's release into my care. I had his meds and belongings in my bag and just needed the man himself.

"Ready to go?" I asked as I walked into his room.

"Yes I am."

I was glad to see him looking well and standing. It took us a bit but we got to my car, grabbed some Greek food, then went to my place. We ate our dinner and watched *NCIS* together and talked about his life raising Rose.

She sounded like a badass.

Once I settled him for the night, I texted her, telling her all was good and he was resting. She sent a voice text back, and I swear she sounded seductive. Or was that my sex deprived dick putting thoughts in my head?

Only time will tell, I guess.

OVER THE NEXT SEVERAL MONTHS, Dale was either at my place or at the hospital, depending on how he was doing. Even with my care, he would get sick and have to come in. I texted his daughter regularly, and she called a few times.

If I was being honest, her voice had me spellbound. Sometimes she would call while Dale was asleep and we would talk about her dad and what was happening stateside. I found myself getting to know her and wanting to know more every day.

I stood at the end of Dale's bed and looked at the chart. She needed to get home. Stress and heartbreak were not helping him. I picked up the phone and called her, hoping she would answer.

"Hey Ren," she said.

"Hey Rose. Are you any closer to coming home? I think your dad needs you." *I need you.* My cock twitched and I held back a moan.

"I'll see what I can do. I think I can get home now."

"Please hurry."

"For my dad or you?"

Both.

I cleared my throat, but before I could answer, the line went dead.

Chapter Four

ROSE

Ren seemed like he truly cared for my dad. He had stepped in when I couldn't. Every chance I had, I was in communication, and I was finally back at the office. Now to go to the boss and get my time off. I already texted my SEAL buddy Richards to tell him I was back. Especially since he was my director.

I walked into Barks's office, and he barely acknowledged me. "Rose, I need you to go to Africa tomorrow."

"Sir, I need time off for a family matter."

"I pay you to do a job, I expect you to do it."

"Barks, we talked about this. Our assets need a break from time to time. Some are not married to the job like you. Give her six weeks off. She earned it after single-handedly taking down Volkov," Richards said as he walked into the room.

As much as I hated Richards taking care of my issues with Barks, because believe me there were plenty, this time I didn't mind it.

Barks straightened up and said, "Yes, sir."

"You go take care of your dad. Call me if anything comes up," Director Richards said.

"Yes, sir."

Walking quickly, I headed back to my desk. I grabbed the necessities and went to the elevators. While the elevator descended, I scrolled through my phone and booked a flight for tonight, leaving just enough time to pack some clothes and make it to the airport.

Traveling was not my favorite, but I always made it better by packing light and upgrading to first class. As I made my way to security, I flashed my badge and security personnel pulled me to the side to check my firearms. Being an agent, I had to do a lot of things. I was a jack-of-all-trades, if you will. Most of my weapons were in my carry-on. The security officer checked my credentials and nodded for me to continue. I didn't pack all my guns, but I definitely brought a few.

I wore a business suit, which was definitely not comfortable for travel, but I wasted no time getting to the airport. As the plane took off, I looked out the window. Despite loving my job, it took a lot out of me. Hell, I wanted a husband and kids but spent months, and even years, on assignments and in very dangerous situations. Honestly, I was beginning to think about a career change, maybe even starting my own business in investigations or perhaps recovery. I loved Richards to death, but if my dad was sick, I needed to be with him, not thousands of miles away in a foreign country like I have been since I was eighteen.

My mom passed away when I was seventeen, and I enlisted right after, coping by serving. After five years of hard work, I became the first and only female Navy SEAL. Five years after that, when Richards retired, I decided I was done too. No one could lead like him. I knew Richards would be sad to see me leave the CIA if that was the route I picked, but he would also support me. There was lots to think about, that's for sure.

When we finally landed, I waited for everyone to push their way out of the plane. It was annoying how impatient people could be. Didn't we all have somewhere to be? There really was no need to hurt anyone while trying to get there. We were all trying to get to baggage claim, anyway.

Once I had my bags, I headed to the shuttle to pick up my rental car. Despite being just me, I opted for the black SUV since I usually drove one for work. While my primary employer was the CIA, I did liaison work for the DOD, DEA, FBI, and Secret Service on a case-by-case basis. With multiple specialties that put me in high demand, I got tossed around a lot for the "security of our country." It also helped that I was fluent in fifteen languages. It was unusual for people to be fluent in more than five but I have been studying since I was in diapers. That combined with schooling and my auditory memory played a role in the number of languages I knew.

I pulled up to the hospital and handed the keys to the valet. "It's a rental. Be careful."

With a quick nod, he got into the car to park it. As I walked through the automatic doors, the smell of disinfectant hit my nose. My ears were assaulted with beeps, coughs, and even some yelling. Looking around, I noticed just how busy the waiting room was.

Jesus.

There was a line leading up to the desk. As I took my place at the end of the line, I noticed there were no open chairs in the waiting area. People sat in the hall, some were standing, or, hell, sitting on the floor waiting to be seen. A nurse came around and asked who I was checking in. "I'm here to see my father, last name Conrad."

"Oh, you're here to see Dale." Her voice was filled with admiration and even love. I couldn't help but let my lips curve upwards. It seemed my dad was still a charmer.

"Yes, ma'am."

"Let me show you to his room. He is on the sixth floor."

I wasn't sure if it was standard for an ER nurse to escort me to a room, but I was not complaining. Shit, I didn't even remember the last time I'd been able to come home.

Fuck, it was five years ago. How much of that had he been homeless?

I took a deep breath. "You had no way of knowing," I whispered to myself. "You are here now, and that's what matters."

"Here we are," she said as she stopped in front of a door.

"Thank you."

"I will let the doctor know you are here," she said before leaving. I slowly opened the door, and my heart fell when I saw my father. His skin was pale, his face sunken, and there were wires everywhere.

When did he get so damn sick?

Fuck Barks and his phone rule.

My father turned his head as I clicked the door shut behind me. He blinked a few times before recognition set in, and a smile stretched across his face. It almost looked painful, but the brightness shone in his eyes.

"Rose," he said weakly, reaching out for a hug. I moved in and embraced my father, holding him close and trying to keep my emotions in check.

"I missed you, Dad," I whispered roughly.

"I know, my little warrior. But you serve and protect, and I am proud to call you my daughter." My dad's words made me almost smile, but also filled me with pain. He was proud of me, yet here he was in a hospital and homeless because I left him here alone.

Chapter Five

REN

The day was coming to an end, and I went through my files for tomorrow's clinic patients. Being the head of a department was never easy. Add in the fact that our hospital had one of the best cardiovascular departments in the nation, and it became even more complex.

My door swung open, making me jump as I looked up to see who had barged into my office. Typically, people knocked. To my surprise, it was Celeste. I raised an eyebrow in question.

"She's here. The daughter."

I could tell she ran here because her breathing was sporadic at best. The realization of what she said hit me, and I stood before heading down the hall briskly. When I got to Dale's room, I took in a deep, calming breath before opening the door to see the elusive daughter.

When I walked in, the business-dressed woman stood, holding her father's embrace as she whispered in his ear. I cleared my throat. "You must be Rosalina. I'm Dr.—"

"Doux. I know, you have a unique voice. That and the nurse said she was grabbing the doctor and since you called me, I assumed it would be you," she said as she faced me. Not going to lie, I was impressed. I had barely spoken to her, and she somehow remembered my voice.

Who the fuck is this chick?

My eyes had a mind of their own as they looked her up and down. She said mission, but she was dressed for business.

Interesting.

When my gaze reached her face, my breathing grew more rapid. She had strong cheekbones, and her hazel eyes were a perfect blend of green and blue. Her hair was up in a military-style bun. A slight smirk spread across her lips as I found myself staring at them.

"Doctor, are you going to inform me about my father's condition?" Her voice trembled with amusement.

"Yes…um…my apologies." I shook my head, trying to clear my garbled and, dare I say, lustful thoughts. "Your father has heart and lung issues. It started with a severe case of pneumonia a couple of years ago and has gone downhill from there. He came in last night for some chest discomfort, so I ordered some tests. He appears to be in the beginning stages of heart failure. It is treatable at this stage, but his eating and living conditions are not conducive to a great outcome."

"I will get him housing as soon as possible." She looked at her dad as she spoke. I could only imagine what thoughts were going through her head. One thing was for sure, though, her love for her father was evident in her eyes.

"I want to keep him here until we get the meds stabilized. He will need a caregiver once he is out. I will have my nurse bring you the options for that. His insurance should pay for most of it."

She looked over at her father and smiled slightly before bending down to whisper in his ear. He nodded, and her eyes locked with mine. "Can I speak to you in private?"

"Of course." I opened the door so she could walk out. I

couldn't help but wonder what she wanted to tell me that she didn't want to say in front of her father. She brushed against me, and my cock responded immediately to the tingling that spread across my skin.

Good lord, this woman was having an effect on me.

"We can meet in the family room."

"Do you have something more private? Like an office?"

Holy shit. Was there seduction in her voice? I internally slapped myself. *Snap out of it, you desperate idiot.*

"Yes, of course. We can go to my office."

She followed me in silence as I made my way to my office. Her fingers brushed the letters below my name that spelled out "Department Head."

"I didn't realize my father was under the care of the boss."

"Yes. There are a few patients I follow. Your father is one of them. The night I met your father, I was working an ER shift when he came in. I treated him, and we talked for a few hours since it was an abnormally slow night. He is well-loved by our staff. Even when he is well, he will come in, and I will pull out my cot for him to get some shuteye," I said, motioning to the cot in the corner. The edges of her lips curled upward.

"Thank you for being here for him."

"It's my job, miss," I said respectfully.

"No. You go beyond your job. Most doctors would dismiss a homeless man, and even give up on them, but not you." Her voice almost sounded seductive again, or maybe it was the fact she was attractive and I hadn't gotten laid in ages.

I smiled warmly at the compliment. She wasn't wrong. I do tend to get overly passionate about patients. With a motion of my hand, she entered my office. I closed the door behind me and sat at my desk. I watched intently as she scanned my shelves, which displayed my awards and accomplishments. As I did, I propped my leg on my knee and leaned back in my chair with my hands in my lap.

My eyes roamed to her perfect, round ass, and my mouth

watered, my cock jumping slightly. I closed my eyes and counted to ten. When I opened them, she stood before my desk, looking at me. Something flashed in her eyes before she schooled her reaction.

What was that?

Never breaking her gaze, she sat across from me and mimicked my position.

"Despite what you may think or what it might look like, I love my father dearly. He is my whole world. My job has taken me from him far too much and now I'm trying to navigate that. I know my father needs me, and I want to be here."

"I never questioned your love for your father. Honestly, I figured you were somehow busy. Based on how your father talked about you, I had a feeling you weren't estranged. Your dad mentioned the military and the government, so I figured you were stationed overseas or something."

She smiled slightly. "Something like that. I work for the government but left the military eight years ago. I visited regularly for three years until I got my new boss. Then, all I could do was work. Believe me when I say I prayed nightly and wanted to reach out, but that was dangerous for him and me as well."

All I could do was listen. I don't know what she did exactly, but based on her outfit and what she said, I guessed something intelligence-related.

"I need you to be honest, Doctor. No sugar-coating anything."

"Of course."

"Should I take an extended leave, maybe a career change? How sick is my father?"

I took in a deep breath, dropping my leg and leaning forward on my desk. Again, she matched my position. "He is very sick. With proper care, we might be able to get a few good years, maybe even get him fully out of heart failure, but the heart is unpredictable and can change rapidly. His best chance is being stress free and not on the streets."

All she did was nod and look back at my awards. "Harvard grad, huh?"

"Best cardiovascular program in the country," I said proudly.

Chapter Six

ROSE

I wasn't going to lie. I was impressed as hell as I saw the various awards, degrees, and certifications the doctor held. The man clearly took his education seriously, and I noticed the large number of President's List commendations. One thing that really caught my eye was the fact that he had his grades on display.

Who does that?

I was disciplined and a fighter, trained to be calm under pressure, yet for some reason, my heart fluttered wildly in the confines of my chest around this man. If I wasn't careful, I might just go into cardiac arrest.

Hmmm, then maybe he'll give me mouth-to-mouth.

Good Lord. I have issues.

My tongue brushed against my bottom lip, and I inhaled deeply. My nostrils flared as the scent of cinnamon and leather hit me, dampness following as my arousal became evident.

Seriously, I needed to get my shit together, and quickly. This man was my dad's doctor. It was clear I needed a sexual release and fast. Hell, he probably wasn't even interested and even if he were, my job would make sure to kill that vibe quickly.

I took a deep breath, stood, and centered myself back on the present conversation. "Impressive, Doc. Especially your grades. I must say doctors saying they were top of class and actually seeing the grades are two very different feelings."

I turned to him again as I leaned against the wall, needing some distance to defuse my libido.

"As of right now, I am off for six weeks. I need to gather a few things, then I will be looking into what to do after that. For the most part, my time will be spent here. If I am not here, you need to call me if anything happens, no matter how small. The number you called me on was your personal cell, right? Caller ID said Rene Doux not Silver Heart Medical Center."

He stood there in silence. The man was at least a foot taller than my short five-foot-two frame. People underestimated me regularly, especially in the military. But instead of letting it consume me, I embraced it and used it to my advantage. If anything, I swear I saw a sparkle of admiration in his gaze.

"The first order of business is I need to call my director. Second, I need to find a place for my father. I trust that he will be taken care of while I run those errands."

My mind kept wandering to what the hot doctor would be like throwing his strength around. How much control he could have as I writhed underneath him. Dominating me, choking—

Jesus.

I needed to find out if this man liked me even a little bit, because just looking at him was going to give me the equivalent of blue balls for women. "Now, is there a Realtor that you know of that can help me find a place quickly?"

"Yes. I have a good friend who sells homes. He buys them and fixes them up. You could move in as soon as the money goes through. Are you looking for a mortgage, or will you be paying cash?"

"Cash."

I hated loans. Debt was no joke, and my father would have none of it. My savings account was healthy, so I could buy us a home with no issue. Dr. Doux reached in his pocket to retrieve a business card from his wallet.

"I will tell him to expect a call and to make it happen. He owes me."

All I could do was nod my head slightly. Was he seriously calling in a favor for me? He just met me.

"Thank you, Doctor," I said before walking toward the exit.

I retrieved my rental and headed down the hill to a small park. It was lit up with Christmas lights, and I had to admit, it was enjoyable to look at. The number of hours this must have taken to set up and remove had to be astronomical. Not to mention the number of people involved. Reaching into my back pocket, I pulled out my cell and called Richards.

"Hey Fire, how's your dad?" he answered. My lips curled slightly at my nickname from our service together.

"He's not the best, but he could be worse. I'm not calling you as my boss, but as my friend. So shoot straight only."

"Alright," he said, drawing out the word in almost a question.

"My gut is telling me I need to stay here, leave Langley, and pursue the private sector, but I don't know where to start or what to do."

"Hmmm. You have excellent skills, and with your background and training, you can do a lot. You could be independently contracted by agencies and work for private entities as well. Since you specialize in computers, finding people, decoding, and negotiations, you can monopolize on that. I can even call a buddy of mine to work for you. He is a gadget guy and smart as a whip. His boss doesn't appreciate him, so he's actually looking for a new job. We served together when I first commissioned."

"What would I even call it?"

"I have no clue, Fire. But I will say this. I'll call him and you two can work it out. He will help with the legal stuff as well since he is almost done with law school. He doesn't actually plan on practicing unless he really wants to help someone, but thought it would be fun to do."

"Barks isn't going to like this," I muttered.

"Let me worry 'bout him since I am his freaking boss. Let me know once you are ready to go and I'll get you the work. I will visit when I can. Complete your leave to max your money, then resign. As much as I will miss you, I have your six. Always will."

"Thanks, Tank," I said, chuckling. The man truly was a great friend. I hung up the phone and pulled out the business card the doctor handed me. I took a deep breath and dialed the number.

"This is Corey Blacksmith. How can I assist you today?"

"Hey, I was told you could help me find a house. Doctor—"

"Ah, yes. You must be Rosalina. Ren told me you would be calling. You are in luck. I just finished a place. It's a single floor, four bedrooms, two baths with a fully finished basement made into a studio. It has its own entrance at the back of the house, so there are no stairs. I am asking three fifty for it."

It was a bit bigger than I was expecting, but honestly it gave me a place to rest my head and my father his own space. "I'll take it. When can we sign the forms?"

"I can meet you right now at the house. I will text you the address."

After about two seconds, my phone alerted me to the text. "I got it. I'll be there in twenty."

When I arrived, a man was standing against a black Volkswagen, and he straightened as I approached. He shook my hand.

"Once you see the place, we can sign all the forms, and then you can move in three days. Normally it would be at least two weeks for your papers and payment to process, but I trust your money source."

"Sounds good." Honestly, I was already impressed. The house was visually appealing and had a beautiful porch. It looked brand new, not remodeled. Once inside, I was even more impressed. Everything about the house screamed home.

When it came time to sign the papers, I didn't hesitate. I

pulled out my phone and wired the money from my government-issued secured account. He handed me the key, and I looked up at him, confused.

"I know I said three days, but honestly, you can start moving in now. I saw the account type your money came from. But best believe if the payment drops, I will come after you."

I held back a laugh at the man's attempt at a threatening tone.

If only he knew.

Using the key, I locked up and pulled up Google on my phone. I found a local furniture store and headed in that direction. The house needed furniture, and I would have Richards ship my belongings to me as soon as possible.

Chapter Seven

REN

After she left, I locked my office. I needed a minute. My cock was painfully hard, and no amount of palming it down was going to fix the tent in my damn scrubs.

Fucking hell.

Something about this woman was turning my mind into mush. Worst part was I couldn't say I minded, though I could do without the erection at work. Hours later, my phone vibrated with a text from my buddy, Corey.

> Hey bro. She came by and bought the place. Thanks for the reference, man. I'd say we are even, but I feel like this favored both of us.

I smiled. The fucker was a pain in the ass at times, but I loved him to death.

> No, bro, we are even.

Something told me that I wouldn't end up winning that battle, but to me, we were even. I found myself happy that Rosalina had a place and seemed to be making plans to stay for a while. This would be great for Dale, but if I was being honest, I had my own motives. I desperately wanted to bring this woman on a date and then have her beneath me. Hell maybe even submit to me if she was even into that, and I was definitely getting hints that she just might be.

A knock on my door sounded. When I opened the door, I smiled, seeing it was Celeste.

"How is our favorite patient?" I asked.

"He looks to be in better spirits. His levels also seem to be improving. His daughter is good for him."

My lips curved up into a slight smile. "That's good to hear. From what my friend said, she got a place, so he won't be on the streets anymore."

Celeste raised her eyebrow with an amused and shocked expression. "You're telling me you sent her your buddy's information? You never do that unless you have known them for years. Hell, I practically had to beg you to help me find a place a few years ago."

She wasn't wrong. It wasn't just out of character for me to pawn someone onto my friends. I collected a favor for a stranger. I knew my friend had this place about done and the fact that it had an apartment in the basement. Not going to lie, I wanted her to have this place so maybe someday I could visit.

I know, wishful thinking.

My apartment wasn't the best. I sent most of my money to my mom so she could live comfortably in the facility she was in.

Luckily, I didn't have loan debts, but my mom had lots of debt and could no longer work, so I paid for all of it. I still had plenty to live on but cheaped out on my place of residence to build savings and have money for the unexpected without getting a loan.

I HAD SEEN my patients for the day, including Dale. He looked loads better and was looking forward to his daughter's visit after his procedure. We had more tests to run, which meant Celeste had let Rosalina know her father would be unavailable for a while. It saved her a trip and kept her from having to sit around here until he was done.

Now I was in my office signing paperwork and looking up a proposal for a new study that looked promising. A new kind of artificial heart that was just as good, if not better, than a transplant, a heart made of your own cells and grown in a lab. To say I wanted in was an understatement. I was a finalist on the list of MDs being considered.

The sound of knuckles hitting my door made me look up, and I couldn't stop the deep smile that engulfed my face at the sight of Rosalina.

"Rosalina, what can I do for you?"

"Please call me Rose, Dr. Doux. My father considers you family, and I don't feel right having you call me by my full name."

"Of course, Rose. Please call me Ren."

"Ren, may I ask how that nickname came about?"

"Honestly, it's a name my mom gave me. My dad named me, wanting the traditional French name. My mom is also French but thought Rene was too feminine. When I was born, my mom had an emergency C-section and was asleep when the paperwork was filled out. So she just called me Ren."

I had no idea why I went into the whole damn story instead of just saying my mom gave it to me, but here we were. Her lips curled into a slight smile, and the sight took my breath away.

Holy shit.

Even my cock noticed, and I needed a subject change or I would be sporting a hard-on the rest of the day. "Were you able to get settled?"

"Yes, actually. I wanted to thank you for that. The place he showed me was perfect. A little big, but since I am starting a business, I need office space, so thank you."

Starting a business? Was she actually planning on staying?

"It was no problem."

"Furniture is being delivered tomorrow, so I am getting a hotel for the night. My dad is tired and after my last…work trip I need a comfortable bed, not a cot. No offense."

It was like she knew I'd offer my cot. Could she read me already?

"None taken." My thoughts screamed to offer her a room at my place. I had a spare room and this time of year, hotel rooms were hard to find. "Have you already booked a hotel?"

"No, actually," she sighed. "All the ones I have called are booked so far, but I have a few more places to call. Do you have any recommendations?"

Just like I thought.

Lord, help me with what I am about to do.

"This time of year is hard." I looked into her eyes for a moment, then continued, "Look, don't take this the wrong way, but I have a spare room. You are more than welcome to utilize it until you get a bed in your home."

Chapter Eight

ROSE

Honestly, I was shocked about his forward offer to his spare room. But I would be lying if I said my immediate response was no. My body desired him, and being in his spare room might make things interesting.

It's only one night, not a damn week, calm yourself.

"That's a mighty generous offer."

"Look, nothing will happen that you don't want to happen. I can promise that. If you say no, there will be no hard feelings. I can try to call a few people and find another place or a room. But this would save you money as well. Even if you did manage to find a room, the price would be astronomical," he rambled, probably thinking he made me uncomfortable. And he did, just not in the way he was thinking.

Well, here we go. May as well dive in.

"Okay. I'll stay at your place tonight," I said. A smile took over his features and a sparkle in his eye accompanied it.

Is this attraction?

There was no way. I had to be seeing things.

"I am actually about to leave. You can follow me to my place if you give me a moment to gather my stuff. It's not far from here. I will warn you, though, it is on the small side."

Small, what does he mean by that?

He is a doctor, so shouldn't he have lots of money and a nice place?

Oh well, it isn't my business.

He quickly gathered his belongings, and I followed him out the door. The valet brought me my car, and I met him at the small park just below the hospital. It only took us twenty minutes to get to an apartment complex further north into town. "Tumble Spur Apartments" the sign read. I parked in a spot close to him and the leasing office, then looked around.

This place was not state of the art or even close to new. It did look like they had been trying to make improvements, but it was clearly in a rough area as I noticed a group of homeless people making a mess near the dumpster. Suddenly, the hairs on the back of my neck stood up. Trouble.

Shit.

"We need to get inside. Something is about to go down," I said in a tone that left no room for argument.

Without a word, he picked up the pace to his apartment. As I followed, I rested my hand on my firearm, ready for anything.

Once inside, I relaxed a bit, but quickly drew my weapon when I heard the sound of gunshots.

Fucking knew it.

Pointing my gun down, I looked out the window in time to see a car peel off. Despite its hasty getaway, I was able to get a partial plate. My eyes continued to roam the area for any further threats as I pulled out my phone and put it on speaker.

"Nine-one-one, what is the location of your emergency?"

"My name is Agent Conrad. I am at the Tumble Spur Apartments. There was just a drive-by, no injuries visible from my current position. Three white males who appeared to be in their teens took off going east in a black Escalade. Partial license plate

6794 out of Washington," I said as I continued to look outside while listening for signs of victims. There were none.

Thank God for small favors.

"What Agency do you work for, Agent Conrad?" the dispatcher asked.

"CIA."

I noticed Ren shift, and a look of shock was on his face. I'd have to deal with his questions later. Right now, the shooting needed to be dealt with. But I wondered if he would have an issue with my occupation. There was a lot to do. The job demands all of your time, and so do relationships. Being an agent's partner is not an easy task.

"Are you certain all the shooters left?"

"To my knowledge, yes." I knew better than to guarantee that, especially since I was not out there but in an apartment.

"Where are you right now?"

"I am in apartment 202 in building D," I said as I looked to the left and saw police vehicles arriving.

"Stay where you are. An officer will come and speak with you when they are ready. Police have arrived."

No shit. I can see that.

The line went dead. I placed my gun back in its holster and tucked my phone back in my pocket before I turned to look at Ren.

God, I hope he didn't freak out.

Chapter Nine

REN

My eyes almost bulged out of my head when she pulled a weapon from her hip. Don't get me wrong, I owned a gun due to the area I lived in, but the fact it was on her and I never noticed was kind of a turn on, if I was being honest.

Lord, help me.

When I registered the gunfire, part of me wanted to get my own firearm, but I also didn't want to make any sudden movements since I didn't know how she would feel about it. Not only that, but she was clearly the professional in this situation. My legs went weak when she identified herself to the 911 operator. She was the fucking CIA.

Fucking hell.

No wonder she was hard to get a hold of. She mentioned using one of her extra rooms as an office, so did that mean she was leaving the agency? So many questions, but fuck if I wasn't rock hard.

Her eyes locked with mine. My lips tried to form words, but

nothing came out. I was having an issue wrapping my head around the CIA thing. Did she seriously stun me speechless?

Mother fuck.

As an Army vet myself, I could confirm it wasn't the gunfire that had stolen my ability to speak. At this point I was used to it. Shootings happened here regularly, though a little less since we got security. They did a good job removing people who didn't belong here off the property. But once they left, the troublemakers would come back. Not to mention, they could only do so much about the residents who were nothing but trouble. However, they did get a lot of them evicted quickly with their reports and photos. So that was a perk as well.

My mind was overwhelmed with thoughts and questions that made themselves known, seemingly all at once. She had mentioned just getting back from a mission. How long was that mission? Was it five years long or multiple back-to-back? Then I remembered it didn't matter. Now, she sounded like she was leaving her job for something new and close to home. I wasn't going to lie, I liked the sound of that. I wanted to get to know her. I wanted her company.

After she hung up and secured her gun, she looked at me. I didn't speak; I just stared into her hazel eyes.

"Cops are here." Her voice was so calm and seemingly unaffected by the adrenaline-fueled situation we just experienced.

Impressive.

She was definitely trained for this. Since I couldn't speak yet, I just nodded. Her lips curved upward slightly in response. "Cat got your tongue?" she mused.

In an effort to clear my mind, I shook my head and took a deep breath. "No, I guess I didn't realize you were——"

"CIA?"

"Yeah," I breathed. She kept eye contact with me, almost like she was trying to read my unspoken words through my eyes. It was intimidating but also hot as hell.

"I might not be able to answer all of your questions, but I can answer some. Though not right now, the police will come to speak to us soon and get our statements."

All I could manage was a quick nod. A loud knock filled the room, and I jumped.

Jesus.

Why am I so jumpy? Did this woman seriously have me that much off my game? Honestly, that had to be it, but why? I noticed a slight smirk on Rose's face, likely at my reaction.

Without a word, I moved toward the door and looked through the hole. I was aware of Rose behind me, resting her hand on her holstered gun and at the ready. When I realized it was a uniformed police officer, I sighed in relief, and Rose dropped her hand. Slowly, I moved my hand to the doorknob and twisted the door open, just in case. Especially since I couldn't see the cop's face.

My lips tugged up on the ends when I recognized the cop standing before me. Officer Brian Cobb had been a close friend since grade school. To tell the truth, I was glad it was him. He was damn good at his job. He was late to the police force and secretive as hell at times, but I knew he could be trusted.

"I thought I recognized the address, though dispatch said it was a woman who identified herself as CIA," he said as he looked at me up and down, probably checking to see if I was okay.

I didn't respond. Instead, I opened the door wider, revealing Rose standing just out of view. His jaw slackened and his eyes darted between her and me. Questions were evident in his eyes, but he was a professional. He would question me later, probably at our usual Monday lunch.

Joy.

"Oh, hello, ma'am. I am Officer Cobb. You must be Agent Conrad," he said smoothly, with no evidence of any shock he may have had.

"Yes sir," she said, her tone reminding me of a soldier in boot camp.

Cobb asked her questions and then asked me a few about my recollection of the events. I usually stayed out of it or wasn't home when it happened. He received a radio call about a potential match to the vehicle, so once he was done with us, he left to go to that. Before he left, we heard SWAT was en route. At least our part of this was over, until court, that is.

Once we were alone, Rose turned to look at me. "Do you know Officer Cobb well?"

I cleared my too dry throat.

Fuck, it felt as if a desert had invaded my esophagus.

"Yes, been inseparable since kindergarten." My voice sounded rough as hell. I may have served four years in the Army, but I was a desk soldier, a nerd. They put me in the infirmary as I completed my pre-med classes at the military's expense. So, unlike her, I never saw any action, especially not the kind she appeared accustomed to.

"Would you like to sit and ask me some questions now?"

"Yes," I whispered as I locked up and headed to the couch. I only had a two-seater and no chairs, so Rose was close when she sat beside me. My body tingled with anticipation of her touch, but I would not dare make the move. That was up to her. But once she did, I could not promise I would be able to control myself. She turned slightly to face me and smiled a warm and reassuring smile.

Shit, what do I ask first?

My mind whirled with all my questions, but one thing kept coming to the forefront. Dale. "Why have you been gone for five years? You said that you just got back. Was the mission years long?" As I asked, I hoped I didn't offend her with a potentially sensitive subject right off the back.

She took a deep breath. "No, I have had twelve missions in the last five years. Some were a month-long, and the longest was about a year. My direct supervisor doesn't believe in life outside of the agency, so neither do we. And because of that, my missions have been back to back. Recently, I did a big job and was able to return to Langley, which was when you called. My friend and director permitted me to come, overruling my boss." Her tone was filled with emotion, and I wanted to pull her into a hug and rub out her tense muscles.

As she explained, I didn't speak. I just took the time to process everything she was saying. Luckily, it wasn't quiet for long. "I am leaving the agency. My dad needs me. My director is helping me start a private-sector business using my skills. Don't get me wrong, I love my job and serving my country in any way I can, but my family is my everything."

Relief washed over me. Dale would have his family, but I would be lying if I said I didn't have my own selfish reasons to be happy about this.

Maybe we have a chance?

I had to keep myself from rolling my eyes. That was wishful thinking at best.

"Your father will love having you around again," I said. Her plump lips turned up slightly. I tried to avert my eyes, but they stayed locked on her lips until I closed them.

Lord, help me.

Chapter Ten

ROSE

Sitting next to Ren as he asked questions was nice. He seemed mindful to avoid types of questions I couldn't answer. Though one question took me a moment.

"What do you do for the CIA?"

I couldn't fully answer that, but I wanted him to know so badly.

"In a nutshell, I find people and information. No one can evade me."

I appreciated he didn't push hard, though I could see the curiosity in his eyes. But it wasn't just curiosity. Multiple times, I caught him looking at my lips with longing in his eyes.

Could this man really be interested in me? Surely not.

Desperate to break the tension, I eased off the couch and looked out the window, watching the last police vehicles leaving as security pulled in. I huffed a laugh at their impeccable timing.

Figures.

As I stood there, I became aware of two things simultaneously: one, I was tired as hell, and two, Ren was standing directly behind me.

Carefully, I turned and let out a gasp at just how close he was to me. I looked up into his eyes, which were boring down into me. The clouds in his eyes were mesmerizing and seemed filled with desire. His hands lay on the wall on either side of my head, his body so close I was pinned.

Fuck, why did I like this so much?

I fought the urge to squirm and pull him closer.

"I really want to get to know you more," he whispered, his lips grazing mine ever so slightly as he spoke. The sensation sent bolts of electricity through my body, settling in my center in a pool of wetness.

Jesus Christ.

As much as I craved his touch, I barely knew the man, and he was my father's doctor. The last thing I wanted was for my father to get less than the best care so I could get some dick. I cleared my throat.

"I am exhausted. Can you show me to my room for the night?"

He blinked a few times before answering. "Of course. It's the room to the right."

"Thank you," I said as he pulled himself off the wall, allowing me to leave his personal space. A feeling of loneliness overwhelmed me for a moment, but I pushed through it.

Once in the room, I flopped dramatically on the bed and groaned into my pillow.

Ugh.

So much was happening all at once, and now I was desiring a man who seemed interested but also not. Then, the whole being my father's doctor. Why does my life have to be so damn complicated?

My job didn't exactly allow me a man's touch. Hell, I don't even remember the last time I was touched by a man. I craved it, yes, but where I worked, it was not wise. Don't get me wrong, some agents sleep with people to get close and gain rapport, but that wasn't my style. The furthest I'd go was a kiss and maybe a well-placed hand, but the clothes never came off in any way.

Ren was hot as hell. He was fit, but not overly muscular. The idea of him controlling me, making me do what he knew I needed, was appealing, to say the least. He checked all the right boxes so far, and if I wasn't careful, I'd lose control soon.

With a sigh, I stood up and got ready for bed. I slipped into my shorts and tank top before brushing my teeth. The sound of knuckles tapping on the door caught my attention.

"Yes?" I inquired.

"Hey. I'm sorry about the, um, thing I did. I didn't mean to make you uncomfortable."

I opened the door and looked at Ren in nothing but his boxers. My eyes raked up and down his perfectly toned body.

Good lord.

Okay, so now my self-control was breaking down. I wanted so badly to tell him I didn't mind, and that he could do so much more whenever he wanted. "You're fine, I'm just not used to close contact."

That wasn't a lie, but it damn sure wasn't the whole truth, either. He raised an eyebrow. I sat at the foot of the bed and patted the space next to me, inviting him in. As he sat down, he faced me.

"In my line of work, we don't exactly have time to socialize, let alone have a relationship. And since I don't sleep with assets, I don't get touched often," I confessed. I felt safe with Ren. Something told me he wouldn't judge me, nor would he push me.

He didn't say a word, just placed his hand gently on my knee. I tensed a moment, then relaxed under his warm contact.

"Rose, I won't lie to you. I am attracted to you and would love nothing more than to bring you on a date and truly get to know you. But we can go at your pace. You have a lot going on with the new business, your current job, and your father. Just know if you need an ear to listen, I'm here. If you need physical touch, I'm here." His tone was soft and understanding but somehow stern.

I placed my hand on top of his, and I squeezed it gently. "Thank you," I whispered.

My body moved automatically, leaning into his side. His arms wrapped around me, pulling me into him. It felt natural, as if we were two puzzle pieces that fit perfectly together.

Fuck, I could get used to this.

After several minutes, Ren broke the silence. "I'll let you get some rest," he said as he stood to leave.

He gave my hand a gentle squeeze, one last time, before exiting, pulling the door closed behind himself. Feeling restless, I hopped under the covers and pressed my eyes closed. Maybe if I tried hard enough, I could will myself to sleep.

Chapter Eleven

REN

I couldn't believe I told her how I felt. The words just came out like I was being controlled by a puppet master. To my delight, she seemed okay with my confession. None of what I said was a lie, but part of me hoped it would happen sooner rather than later. That part definitely included my cock, which seemed to be in a permanent state of hardness.

A scream woke me from my dreams of Rose under me, and I jolted upright. My brain quickly realized it was Rose. Before I could think about it, I was moving like the apartment was on fire and flung open her door. My heart broke seeing her sitting up, clenching her chest as she heaved, her body sweating from whatever nightmare she had.

Not giving anything a second thought, I was by her side and pulling her to me, kissing the top of her head.

"Shhh. It's okay, you're safe."

She relaxed instantly into me, and soon her breathing slowed to normal.

As I held her, I didn't ask what her dream was about. It

wasn't my business unless she wanted to tell me. Knowing what she did for a living and that she was in the military before that, I assumed she must have seen or done horrible things. It was no wonder she would suffer from nightmares. All I could do was be there for her in whatever way she needed, and right now, she needed my touch.

After a few minutes, she tilted her head up to look me in the eye, and I locked my gaze with hers. The words she said with her eyes told me she was thankful and, dare I say, wanted more. I leaned down so our foreheads touched, our breaths mixing between us. Her hands pressed down on my thighs for leverage as her lips got closer to mine until we were almost touching. I didn't dare move, not wanting to jump the gun and make her uncomfortable again, while hoping she was, in fact, going to kiss me. But I would only take the kiss if she gave it. Nothing more, not in her current state.

Her hand moved behind my neck and pulled me in until our lips touched. A wet, hot tongue brushed my lips, asking me to open. A low growl escaped me as I granted her request, allowing her to dive inside. The kiss grew in passion, and soon she was straddling me. My hands rested on her hips as I struggled to control myself, stop myself from rutting against her.

Oh fuck.

The way she tugged my hair made my cock harden in my boxers. I had no doubt she felt it pressing against her sweet ass. Out of breath, I pulled back and nestled my nose into her neck, breathing in her scent.

"Sorry," she whispered.

I stood and laid her down and leaned over her, my erection brushing her thigh. "Don't apologize. As you can feel, I enjoyed what we just did." My voice was husky with desire, and her eyes clouded with her own lust. Her soft whimper made my cock twitch against her thigh. I closed my eyes, struggling for control.

Fuck.

"You had a nightmare, and I won't take advantage of you

while you are in a vulnerable state—no matter how much I want to bury myself deep inside you."

As much as it pained me to say it, I knew it was true. Our first time would not be in haste and mental instability. It would be special and intense. I pushed up and stood as she lay on the bed, looking up at me. The sight was one for the movies. She would look so damn good under me.

"Please, don't go," she breathed. "Just stay with me, be close to me. Please." Without a word, I moved the sheets and got under them, letting her settle into my side, resting her head on my chest.

Hmm.

Her soft snores filled the empty room, and I had to palm my hard cock to make it chill out.

This was going to get uncomfortable fast if I didn't get a release soon. But that was tomorrow's issue. Tonight I had a gorgeous woman in my arms seeking my comfort, and that was more than I thought I would ever get, especially with her.

Chapter Twelve

ROSE

As I gradually woke up, I became very aware I was snuggled into Ren with my leg flung over his thighs. My eyes opened slowly as I took in everything around me. Based on his breathing, he was awake but waiting for me to move and respond. I subconsciously licked my lips when I noticed the sizable bulge protruding from his boxers into a tight tent. It looked uncomfortable as hell.

"Morning," I said. My voice cracked with the word, and I cleared my throat.

"Morning," he replied. His growly morning voice made me soak my shorts with arousal.

Holy shit.

Fueled by lust for this man, I reached down and brushed my hand against his cock before gripping it firmly. Which was rewarded by a deep, seductive moan. From what I could feel and see, he was well-endowed, and I wanted to feel him deep inside me, filling me.

A loud beeping pierced the sexual air, snapping me back to

reality and away from my lustful thoughts. Ren growled as he twisted to grab his pager and silenced it before pulling out his phone. He let out a long, exasperated sigh before sitting us up.

"I got to deal with some business at the hospital. Do you want a ride? We can have lunch and you can visit your dad, then I will take you where you need. I have the afternoon off."

I mean, I was capable of driving myself, but I was intrigued by the idea of spending time with Ren. "Yeah. I'd like that."

He definitely appreciated that as his lips curved into a smile that reached his eyes, and I loved seeing it on him.

Once he left the room, I changed into a button-up baby blue shirt and my dress slacks. It was winter, so I wore a warmer blazer. One of these days I needed to find what my style was outside of work clothes. I secured my gun to my hip and headed out to the dining room where Ren was standing, holding out a cup of coffee in one hand and drinking his own with the other.

"Thank you." I caught him looking at my outfit and noticed he bit his bottom lip slightly. "I got to get some non-work clothes," I mumbled.

"We can stop by a place after lunch. Though I don't mind you in this outfit." His tone was thick with desire, and I couldn't help but look down at his bulge.

My lips curled into a smile. It felt so natural and right. Not my usual fake one. "I'd like that."

We each grabbed a muffin and headed out to his car. His vehicle was nice, but it wasn't flashy, like most doctors. Probably a good thing, considering the neighborhood he lived in. He had a regular Jeep Wrangler with a hard top. I was pleasantly surprised when he came around the passenger side and opened my door. Chivalry was not a common thing in today's society, so it was refreshing, to say the least.

The drive was quiet, but not in an awkward way. We both needed time to process last night and this morning. Had we not been interrupted, I likely would have pleased him with my mouth until he shot his warm seed deep down my throat. I bit my lip at the thought.

God, yes.

He pulled into the doctor's parking lot and quickly found a spot. Again, he walked around and opened the door, even offering me a hand as I stepped down. We approached the doors, and he turned to me. "This is where we part ways. Meet me in my office at eleven?"

"Yeah. I'll be there. Go save lives, Doc."

With a quick smile, he turned toward the boardroom where a young man was waving him in.

Wonder what he had to do there?

I'd ask him later. I checked in at the front desk. Once I had my visitor pass, I headed up to my father's room.

In just a day, my father looked ten times better. He was brighter, happier. When he noticed me in the doorway, he moved his food tray and opened his arms for me to come in for a hug. Without hesitation, I moved into his arms and he just held me.

After a bit, I pulled back and settled into the chair next to him. I moved his tray back in front of him, encouraging him to eat.

"I know that look. It's the look of love. Who is it?" he said as he picked up his fork.

I rolled my eyes. My father was too damn observant some-times. Though love, no—a crush, maybe. Mom always said he knew things about her, even though she hadn't realized yet. I inherited that ability. It was why I was so good at what I did. Though with Ren it seemed foggy at best.

"Dad," I warned.

"Don't 'Dad' me, young lady. I can see it all over you and how you walk. You met someone. Now I don't think you let him take you, but you sure the hell want him to, so who is it?"

I knew I had to tell my father, but I also thought it was too soon. For heaven's sake, I didn't even know what was happening.

"Yes, I met someone. I don't know where it is going, but I do know I want it. I want him. Just trust that I will tell you who when I know what it all means," I pleaded. His eyes softened, and he looked at me for a moment.

"Okay," he breathed, and I relaxed back into the chair. "So, what are you doing about work? I'm getting the feeling you aren't going back to your current employer."

I huffed a slight laugh.

Damn, he was good.

"No, Dad. The job is demanding, and my supervisor is a damn nightmare. It's time I come home and stay. My former commander knows a guy and is helping me open a practice here. I would be doing what I did in the military and for the agency, but in the private sector. I'd keep my clearance as well so I can contract with the government, but I dictate what contracts and jobs I take."

"That sounds amazing. I know you will be successful and do good." His words made my heart feel warm. "Other than seeing me, what are your plans for the day?"

"I have a lunch date, then I meet with my potential business partner this afternoon. I got to get some more normal clothes and make a few calls. The furniture should be delivered today." As I spoke, my phone buzzed in my pocket and I pulled it out. I noticed an email from the furniture company.

My apologies. One of our drivers is out sick. We will have to reschedule your delivery for first thing Monday. Again, our apologies, and we will refund the delivery cost for your troubles.

Well, damn. That complicated matters.
Or did it?

Pretty sure a certain doctor would allow me to stay at his place without hesitation.

That idea was quite intriguing. My mind wandered to last night and my nightmare. They didn't happen often, but when bullets flew, it brought it all back. It brought back the night I lost my best friend, my brother-in-arms, Jasper Killian.

THE INTEL I received was good. It had all been triple checked. My team and I were heading in to retrieve our man. We always tried to reduce casualties as much as possible, especially the innocent bystanders. The connections I had formed with the women were vital and because of that, no innocent civilians were hurt that day.

Jasper was my second. He often helped where I wasn't able. As a woman, I would hit roadblocks and that was where Jasper came in. He made the relationships and contacts I couldn't.

My team breached, and everything was going well until it wasn't. When I rounded the corner, I saw Jasper with a gun to his temple and Charlie chained to the floor next to him.

I grew up with Jasper, so we had a way of communicating without speaking a word. Charlie had a son on the way, a wife. Jasper only had me. Jasper was the kind of man who would do anything for anyone, including risking his own life. Dropping my gaze, I noticed Charlie had picked the lock, and he was waiting for my cue. The sound of gunfire told me the rest of the team was a bit occupied, so this was on me.

"Ora, guerriero." The words cut through the silence, and I knew that was the cue. I dove and retrieved Charlie, yanking him behind me as I watched Jasper struggle with the man. "Vattene, amore."

As I turned to hightail it out of there, a loud bang filled the room, and my heart dropped. I turned in time to see Jasper's limp body hit the ground. Anger filled my entire being and in a flash, I was on top of the now disarmed man, beating his face in with every ounce of energy I possessed. My knuckles were bleeding from the force, bone cracking beneath them. Firm, warm hands grabbed my shoulders, yanking me into their chest. Richards just held me while the others checked the bodies—both DOA.

"Hostage secure, two dead, one hostile, one SEAL." The officer's voice *cracked with emotion as he radioed the update.. No one spoke or moved for a moment, as Richards worked to calm me. The others grabbed Jasper's body and carried him to the humvee. We would make sure he made it home, so he could be buried by my family since we were it for him. And I would never be the same again.*

OVER THE YEARS, my flashbacks decreased—with a lot of help. Only one other person had been able to comfort me through them, and that was Richards. But now it appeared the doctor had the ability as well.

"Your anchor is your lifeline. One to be loved and cherished. Don't run from it, but embrace it." Richards always said this to me, whenever I resisted his touch, his help. He always said there would be a day I find another anchor.

Is this it?

I looked at the time and realized I had a lunch date to get to. With a quick goodbye to my father, I headed to the doctor's building to see my date. Nerves racked my body.

Was this really a date or two friends having lunch?

God, I hope it is the first option.

He was my anchor. I needed him, all of him.

Chapter Thirteen

REN

The transplant team meeting was long and honestly pointless. Not much got done, and we didn't discuss any new patients. But when the president of the hospital calls a meeting, you show up, especially if you hold any power..

As soon as the meeting was over, I was out the door and to my office. I rubbed my temples as my mind replayed last night and her nightmare. Her distress was heartbreaking, and I wanted so desperately to fix it. Her eyes looked so damn haunted.

What had she seen? What had she been through? I was thankful I was able to bring her peace with my closeness, but I wanted nothing more than to take the pain away from her all together.

Looking in the small mirror in my office, I adjusted my tie. A soft tapping came from the door.

"Come in," I said as I finished fixing my collar. The door squeaked softly and my eyes locked with Rose's before they raked up and down her body.

She was somehow more beautiful than when we left this

morning. I could see the stress in her eyes and I wanted desperately to know the reason, but that was a later issue. Right now, she needs a nice lunch and good company. The rest could wait.

"Where is the good doctor taking me for lunch?" Her tone was laced with desire, and I suddenly wanted to take her home and bury myself inside her warm channel. I swallowed roughly before speaking.

"I hope you like Italian," I said nervously.

"I do. Where do you have in mind?"

"In the time you have spent here, have you ever gone to Tomato Street?"

"I can't say that I have. However, if I recall, we drove past it on the way to your apartment."

Holy shit, she remembered that?

Who am I kidding, she noticed that?

This woman never failed to impress the hell out of me. "You would be correct. It's also close to a shopping mall, so after that we can buy clothes," I said as I offered her my arm, and she took it.

"Sounds good."

The whole drive there, my hand was firmly on her thigh. It seemed to ease her somehow. So, until and unless she told me otherwise, that is where my hand would stay. Tomato Street didn't take reservations, but it was a weekday, so the lunch rush was small. We got a table right away, and I watched in fascination as Rose took in the environment.

"I grew up here. This restaurant does summer field trips with the largest district in the area that has an after-school-program-slash-daycare called Express. Kids come and guess how many cans of tomato sauce are in the building, and if you guess right, you get a free meal. The pizza is fired in a brick oven, and the pasta is to die for. The wait staff wear hats to be silly and easily recognized by patrons. Hell, they even write their name upside down and backwards on the table."

As if right on cue, a young lady with a top hat that had a

dove sitting on it came up to the table and introduced herself while writing her name upside down to her but right way up to us. I ordered a couple of waters for now since neither of us had a chance to glance at the menu, though I knew what I was getting already. Steak myzithra with extra sauce and myzithra. It was no longer on the menu, but they would make it when asked.

"What's good here?"

"Everything," I said honestly. She rolled her eyes, and my cock twitched at the sight. If she kept doing that, we were going to end up in the bathroom while I fucked her until my cock was the reason she rolled her eyes as she screamed my name. "I know that's not helpful. My second favorite is Uncle Tony's pasta with extra sauce on the side. It can be dry sometimes."

She placed the menu down. "I'll get that then."

I couldn't help but smile. Part of me got the vibe she wanted the choice taken from her. She wanted to be controlled in some ways.

Fuck.

I liked the idea of that. And that was something I could definitely do.

It wasn't long before our waitress came back and took our orders, my eyes never leaving Rose's. Her hazel eyes, leaning toward blue in the dim lighting, were mesmerizing, to say the least. They kept me captivated at all times. It was almost painful not to look at them.

Fuck, I had it bad already.

Chapter Fourteen

ROSE

The feeling of his eyes on mine was like nothing I had ever experienced before. It was somehow erotic, and I loved it. When the waitress brought our food, my mouth watered at the aroma. My plate looked fucking delicious. White sauce smothered the baked pasta, topped with cheese. I looked at his dish, and it also looked delectable to the point that it made my mouth water even more. The slight curve of his lips told me he noticed my stare.

I diverted my eyes, and a warm sensation covered my cheeks.
Shit, was I blushing?

His hand rested on my thigh, and his other hand cupped my chin, forcing me to look at him.

"I don't mind sharing," was all he said before waving at a passing waiter, never breaking our contact. "Can we get two extra plates?"

"Yes, of course." The waiter moved quickly through the tables and came back in about a minute. Ren split our plates. I tried mine first, and it was almost orgasmic. My tastebuds danced even more when I tried his dish. This was the best pasta I've had since Italy. I couldn't help the moan that escaped my lips.

"Sounds like you approve."

"Oh, hell yes. This is some of the best pasta I've had in years."

His lips curled up into a knowing smirk. "That's good to know," he said, with a hint of something in his tone.

What was that?

Managing to finish everything on my plate was a surprise to even me. Though I thought I might have to roll to the store at this point.

Once he paid the bill, we got in the car and drove about a mile. The large building was clearly a mall with multiple large store fronts including a Barnes & Noble. I followed him inside the large glass doors. My eyes wandered around and took in all the stores and the large map.

Oh, thank God.

No need to wander aimlessly until I found a store I liked. I could see all of them and how to get to them right here. My eyes roamed the business names until I found my favorite. Torrid. I wasn't a big girl, and I wore their size 00 or 0, but they had great style and, let's just say, under this suit, I was gifted in the chest department. Once I figured out how to get there, I began walking. Ren was right behind me. He sat on a bench outside the store and motioned for me to go in.

The fact that he didn't come in made me slightly sad, but we weren't an item, and I would prefer to give him a fashion show in private. That thought sent a heat so strong through my body I thought my clothes would melt off.

I ended up grabbing a silver off-the-shoulder top and a pair of jeans, along with several black pants, skirts, and even more shirts. Of course, I grabbed some regular pants and T-shirts for relaxing. When I got to the mini lingerie section, I couldn't resist and grabbed some matching sets. I snatched a few shoes to complete the looks I was going for.

I placed the items on the counter, and the saleslady rang everything up. The total almost made my eyes pop out of their sockets. Of course, I had no personal wardrobe, so it was needed, but a thousand bucks was a bit much. Fighting the urge to pout, I sucked it up and slid my card to pay.

When I walked out of the store with five of their large bags filled to the max with clothes, I saw Ren's lips curve up into a smile.

"I said I didn't have any clothes."

He shook his head and chuckled softly. "Did you have to buy the whole damn store?"

I glared at him, earning me another laugh as he reached to grab my bags.

Such a gentleman.

Chapter Fifteen

REN

I doom scrolled TikTok trying to distract myself. My mind tortured me with images of Rose underneath me. Hell, I wanted to follow her into the store, but didn't want to make her feel rushed. The sound of paper crinkling caused me to look up, and I caught sight of Rose with several bags of clothes.

Typical woman.

And of course she took offense to the assumption before I even said anything. Which only made me tease her before I took the bags from her and we headed to the car. After the bags were placed in the trunk, I opened her door again.

Since we had stuff in the car, I decided to go back to my place. This way, she could change if she wanted to. I carried her bags up the stairs and placed them on her bed. "You are welcome to change if you want. I'll be in the living room. Then I can drop you off wherever you'd like."

"I can drive myself, you know," she said with amusement in her eyes.

"Oh, I know, but like I said, I have the afternoon off." I shocked myself with how rough and husky my voice sounded.

Her eyes sparkled at the words as she turned to close the door behind her. I moved to the fridge and opened flavored water before plopping on the couch. When she came out, I looked up, nearly choking on my water.

Holy shit.

The silver brought out the blue in her eyes, and I had to admit those jeans hugged her in all the right ways.

Fucking yummy.

It was refreshing to see her in everyday clothes, and I was excited about the idea of seeing her in sweats and a T-shirt. The shorts she wore last night would not do much to keep her warm in the winter, though they did give a nice view. She completed the look with a full-length coat and a small purse.

Damn.

She looked amazing. Even my cock noticed as it pressed uncomfortably against my zipper.

It took a lot of effort to swallow; my throat was as dry as a desert.

"I have to meet with my new potential business partner at the Atticus Coffee & Gifts off Howard," she said, her voice seeming a little lower than normal.

Was she sensing my arousal?

I cleared my vocal cords and looked into her eyes. They seemed to sparkle with mischief and I wanted to tame her wild side so damn bad.

"Yeah, I know where that is. I'll drop you off, then go down the road and grab some groceries. Just text me when you are ready to be picked up, or if I'm done, I'll find a place nearby to wait." My voice sounded rough, but judging by the way she clenched her thighs, I'm pretty sure she liked it.

As discreetly as I could, I pushed down on my erection, not wanting to let her see just how much she affected me. Once I had my keys, I motioned her out the door and locked up before opening the passenger door for her to get in.

The drive took less than thirty minutes. "I'll be at the fresh market just down the road a bit. Shoot me a text if you don't see me and I'll be here as quick as traffic will allow."

"Thanks Ren. I appreciate this. Parking looks like it would be horrible down here."

I grinned widely. "That's downtown for you."

She rolled her eyes, making my cock re-stiffen in my suddenly too-tight jeans.

Damn.

This woman was seducing as hell, and it didn't even seem like she was trying.

Chapter Sixteen

ROSE

As I got out of the car, I took in the brick storefront and smiled. It was quite beautiful. Richards had sent me the location and time after he called his friend. All I knew is he served in the Navy like us and was a nerd. Apparently, he helped us on a few missions, though I don't personally recall it, but the voices in our ears were just that. Most of the time, I never knew who it was, just trusted them as my brother-in-arms. So now I wondered which voice in my ear he was and which missions he was on. Richards said it was his story to tell or for me to figure out.

Damn riddles.

My phone chimed as I was about to open the door. I stepped to the side so a woman in a business suit could go inside. Tilting my phone so the sun wouldn't glare, I saw the message from an unknown number.

> I'm here in the far corner wearing leather.

Well, okay then.

I opened the door and scanned the room until I noticed a man sitting in front of three laptops sipping a large hot drink. His leather coat almost looked like it would rip if he moved wrong. He was a bit more built than I'd prefer, but he was good looking. I approached and his eyes left the computer.

"You must be Rosalina."

It took me a moment to collect myself. His voice was huskier than I thought it would be.

"Please, if we are potentially working together, call me Rose."

"Very well, Rose. I'm Weston, but please call me Wes."

"Okay, Wes." I sat down across the table from him, careful to avoid his computers. "Alright, I got to ask. Why three computers?"

He looked up, and the corner of his mouth lifted into a smirk. "You really don't remember me, do you?" he asked, with a bit of humor and emotion.

Interesting.

"No. I'm sorry. Richards said that you helped us, but I can't place you."

His eyes fell, and he fidgeted with his hands as if he didn't want to say what he was about to. "You might remember me as Wiz."

My mind flooded with memories. He helped secure details and was Jasper's lover whenever they had a chance. He was also the voice on the other end that was thick with emotion as they acknowledged the death count. Neither of us spoke as both our minds whirled with memories.

As the images and flashbacks calmed in my mind, the question of could I work with him came to the forefront. I took a deep breath and closed my eyes.

Yes, yes, I could. No one would be better for the job.

"I understand if this is too much for you. I w—"

"It may have taken you a moment to remember me, but I knew who you were right away. If I didn't want this, I wouldn't be here. Maybe being around Jasper's sister will help me be more at peace, but at the very least, I know you will treat me with respect and I will keep busy."

A slight smile spread across my lips and I went straight to business. "Okay, so first step. We need a name."

"It should be something to honor Jasper."

"Agreed." I thought hard for a moment. "What about Killian's Eye?" The name felt so right as I said it. His name was Eye, because he saw everything, even the smallest of details. I glanced up to see a tear running down Wes's cheek and a smile on his face.

"Perfect," he whispered roughly.

After a few moments of catching up, we got back to business. We decided we would help find missing people, whether it be convicts or everyday people. For a side hustle, we'd take on big money bonds as well. Then, of course, decoding, hacking, and translating for the government. Wes was going to handle all the paperwork and licenses. We would hire eventually, but for now, it would be just us.

"I should have everything ready to open in about two months. Some stuff will be faster, but we can start looking for cases. It might take a while to get the clearance part, but since you have it already and I still have mine, it should be faster. Plus, our connections." As he spoke, I just nodded. "Well, I guess that's all for now. I'll work on a logo and once you approve it, we can make business cards."

"Sounds good." I stood up and shook his hand. "I'm glad it's you and not some random guy."

"Same. I wish we could have done this sooner. I wanted to but didn't know how." The way his voice cracked, I knew he was still grieving Jasper. I could only hope this was a step toward his healing.

All I did was smile before stepping out of the coffee shop. When I got outside, I noticed Ren's car across the street. He got out of the car, and without even thinking about it, I embraced him, resting my head on his chest. His breathing hitched a moment, then he nestled his nose in my neck. The sensation of his breath sent jolts of electricity through me.

"Does this mean it went badly?" he asked cautiously.

"No, it went great. We knew each other, some of the memories were hard, is all." I knew he needed and deserved more than that, but here on the street was not the place. "Let's go to your place and I'll explain."

He didn't speak, he just nodded, giving me a kiss on the top of my head, then opened the door for me before heading toward his apartment.

Chapter Seventeen

REN

We didn't speak as I drove us to my place. The memories must have been rough because the sparkle was gone from her eyes. Every part of me wanted to do anything to get it back and I would, but for now, the only thing I could do was to be here for her. In an effort to comfort her, I placed my hand on her thigh. Once at my place, we headed up and sat on the couch. I didn't push. She was in charge here.

"You remember my nightmare?"

Of course I did.

Wanting to keep my words to a minimum, I just gave a slight nod.

"Right before I left the SEALs, I lost my brother. He wasn't biologically my brother, but he was in every other sense of the title."

Holy shit.

My head spun with emotions. I've lost patients before, some I had even grown to love like family, but that was far different from this. My body grew heavy as the sadness of her words set in.

"Jasper and I met when we were kids. He would come over when his dad would get drunk and angry. Soon he was at our place more than he was at home. To us, he was family, though never in the eyes of the law. At eighteen, he made a choice and joined the military. When he told his parents, his dad got angry, more angry than ever before. So much so that he tried to shoot him. His mom stepped in between and was shot instead, killing her. Needless to say, his dad went to jail. His mom was no angel, but despite the haze of her drugged mind, she saved him, and I am thankful for that. We took him in and he focused his energy on the military. I joined soon after he did for my own reasons. So last night the gun shots brought back the memories of the day he was killed in front of me. Hence the nightmare," she said, then took a deep breath.

"What is your favorite memory of him?" I didn't want to ask about what happened. There was no reason to make her relive that. And saying "I'm sorry for your loss" like everyone else didn't seem right. She seemed taken aback, but a slight sparkle appeared in her sorrowful eyes, followed by the hint of a smile. My heart fluttered in my chest.

"Jasper was crazy," she laughed, as if she remembered something funny. "He got us into sticky situations all the time. One time he threw a water balloon at a cop and we had to run five blocks to lose him. He was quite the clown."

My lips curled in response. I had a friend like that growing up. Little did she know she had met him already. I repositioned myself and invited her to snuggle into me, and my heart soared when she moved in without a second thought.

"And the man you met with today?"

"He was his lover."

"Oh."

Well, I didn't expect that.

My face expression must have been quite funny since Rose laughed as she looked at me. I cleared my throat, trying to compose myself. Though hearing her laugh was like angels singing hymns, beautiful and full of grace.

"So, are you two going to start your business?"

"Yes. It's hard to reconnect, but honestly, Jasper didn't trust very many people, and Wes was one of the few he did. We want to honor him so we are calling ourselves Killian's Eye. His call sign was Eye."

God, that was beautiful.

I loved it. Even though I didn't know Jasper, from what I did know, I figured he would, too.

Chapter Eighteen

ROSE

Talking to Ren felt so right. He never once said "I'm sorry for your loss" or seemed uncomfortable. He only asked for my memories. The way he held me calmed my body and my mind. His soft voice was the icing on the cake. After my meeting, my heart was heavy, but within a short time, I was lighthearted and carefree again.

I hadn't realized I had fallen asleep until Ren shifted beneath me. I opened my eyes slowly and looked up, meeting his soft eyes.

"Sorry, I didn't mean to wake you. I just needed to use the restroom and planned to move you to your room."

The sentiment of what he said made my lips curve into a smile. We weren't even a couple, and he was taking care of me. I mouthed, *Thank you.* His returning smile made me feel warm inside.

When I slowly sat up, he moved and headed to the bathroom, like he said. Part of me didn't want him to leave. My heart ached with the knowledge that I would likely have another nightmare tonight. They generally lasted a week or so, but I couldn't possibly ask him to hold me for the next week.

After a few minutes, he came around the corner, concern on his face. He looked into my eyes for a minute, then twitched his lip slightly upwards.

"I mean, if you wanted to be carried, all you had to do was ask," he said as he scooped me up bridal style and carried me to my room before tossing me gently on the bed. My breath caught as he leaned over me, his bare chest touching my chest as he untucked the blankets to place over me. As he went to pull away, I gripped his arm.

"Stay," I whispered, the sound so low I almost didn't hear myself. His eyes met mine as he seemed to search my soul for the meaning of my words. I didn't hide anything. With a slow nod, he slid under the covers and I cuddled into his chest.

This was home.

Chapter Nineteen

REN

Having Rose in my arms lying next to me was like nothing I could have imagined. Last night we had fallen asleep quickly as I rubbed my hands down her back. As soon as I woke up, I ran my hand down her body. After a few minutes, she turned slightly before pushing back against my chest, looking into my eyes.

"Hey," she whispered.

"Hey back."

She pushed up until her lips brushed against mine. My breathing became more rapid with anticipation. Her hand grabbed the back of my neck and she pulled me into her kiss. A deep, animalistic moan escaped my lips as I dove my tongue into her open mouth.

In a swift motion, I was suddenly on my back and she was on top of me, our lips never breaking contact. My cock was as hard as concrete and kept brushing against her round ass. The sweet friction drove me absolutely crazy.

Jesus Christ.

She pulled away slightly as we both tried to catch our breath. As she ground her ass against my painful erection, I growled and flipped us so she was under me.

"Dove, don't start something you don't want me to finish," I said, my tone a dominating and deep growl. She squirmed and moaned as she pulled me back into her kiss.

Fucking hell.

My hands wandered down her body and cupped her ass, pulling her close to me, settling her just right underneath me, my cock now rubbing against her belly. With a quick swat of my palm on her ass, she gasped. My knee was now damp with her arousal.

Never breaking the kiss, my fingers brushed her folds beneath her thin lace panties, making her arch her back as she groaned. I broke the kiss.

"Do you want to continue?" I asked, desperately hoping she would say yes. She nodded. "I need you to say the words, Dove."

"Yes," she whispered. Her body shook with pleasure as I plunged my fingers into her core. Her moans made my cock leak in my shorts. As much as I want to relieve the pressure I was experiencing, I would make this moment all about her and her pleasure.

She deserved this.

My thumb held pressure on her clit as I moved my fingers in and out of her. My lips only parting from hers for a breath every now and again. I found her sweet spot inside and focused on that as my thumb continued its small circles. Her cursing and moans told me she was deep in ecstasy.

"I'm about to—" She couldn't finish the words as I felt her walls tighten around me, her clit throbbing beneath my thumb as her cum coated my fingers.

After she rode out her orgasm, I pulled my fingers from her and licked every last drop as she lay there, sated, watching my every move. Once I was clean, I leaned in and kissed her, making her taste herself on my mouth. Her moan told me she loved it.

Fuck me.

Chapter Twenty

ROSE

H*oly fucking shit, that was intense.*
    The orgasm had made my body one with the bed. To say I was satisfied was an understatement. The man never even used his dick, and he had me moaning more than a whore in church. If he could make me come this hard with his fingers, I can't imagine what he could do with his cock.

"How are you feeling, Dove?" he asked.

Dove.

I liked that. It made me feel…special. He wasn't just calling me babe, sugar, or honey like everyone else. Doves are also beautiful animals and represent peace, freedom, and…love. I laughed at his question.

"I feel like a blob in this bed. My body is still tingling. Not to mention now I want a nap despite the fact I just woke up," I retorted.

He chuckled softly next to my ear, and I turned to snuggle into him. He pulled me so I was flush with his body.

"Sleep, Dove, it's the weekend. We got all day to see your dad."

We?

Fuck, why did I like that so damn much?

I didn't respond. I just snuggled deeper into his chest and dozed off.

I WOKE up to the smell of garlic filling the room. My stomach growled in response. My hand reached for my phone and I checked the time. When the screen lit up, my eyes bulged. It was two in the afternoon.

Holy shit.

Who knew your first orgasm in a decade would wipe you out so damn much? I slid off the bed and slipped on his shirt, which had been lying on the floor. It came down just past my ass, but considering what we did this morning, I don't think he would mind. Now to follow the delicious smell coming from the kitchen.

When I rounded the corner, my eyes refused to leave the view of Ren shirtless in gray sweats, standing at the stove. His back muscles were relaxed and inviting. Before I could second-guess myself, I walked up behind him and wrapped my arms around his waist.

"It smells delicious," I hummed into his back.

His hand wrapped around mine before he moved us until I was sitting on the counter and he was between my legs.

"I'm making garlic Parmesan," he whispered against my ear.

I turned into him until his lips met mine. The kiss was slow, but still filled with passion.

Hmmm. Yes.

"I know I already showed my feelings for you and told you the other day when I fucked you with my fingers, but you never told me yours. I hope what we just did means what I think, but I want to clear it up so there isn't a misunderstanding," he said.

Shit. Showed me indeed.

There was no mistaking my feelings for him. I wanted this, but again, he was my father's doctor.

"My father…"

"Is my patient, yes I know. I just have to report the relationship, but everything will be fine with my job and your father's care, if that is what is stopping you."

"I haven't been in a relationship in years. I don't know how to do this, and with my new business, my time is limited," I said.

Ren's hand tucked some loose hair behind my ear and brushed his lips against mine, then moved down my jaw until he reached my neck just below my ear.

"I am a very patient man, and I can make the best out of whatever amount of time you can give me. I just want time with you, want to get to know you, and"—his eyes dropped and so did his voice—"devour all of you."

My body responded with a pool of wetness between my thighs and a small moan. Ren placed his hand on the counter between my thighs as he bent so his face was in front of my aching pussy and licked the wetness he found.

"Be my girl, my dove, and I will rock your world. I can promise you that," he said, his tone deep, husky, and so dominating.

Oh, fucking hell.

"Yes," I breathed. His lips crashed into mine, and I wrapped my legs around his waist as he deepened our kiss. A loud banging interrupted us, making him pull away.

Motherfucker.

We both struggled to catch our breath. His eyes traveled up and down my body as if he just noticed my attire. A cocky smirk consumed his face.

"Go put some pants on, Dove."

I got off the counter, headed to my room, and grabbed my shorts before coming back to the living room to see who interrupted us.

Chapter Twenty-One

REN

I swear to God, whoever is at the door better be important. The sight of Rose in my shirt was fucking hot as hell. Now she was mine, and I wanted to make her come undone in every way possible.

Fuck.

I wanted to be balls deep in her sweet kitty, making her scream my name.

Once I got to the door, I looked to see Brian.

Of course. Fucking bastard.

I opened the door, and he eyed me suspiciously. "Hey brother, is Rosalina here?"

"Yes, she should be out in a second. What do you need?"

"I have some follow-up questions about the shooting she called in," he said.

"What can I do for you, Officer Cobb?" Rose asked as she snaked her hand around my waist. I pulled her in and kissed the top of her head, which got an eye bulge out of Brian. It was a look straight out of a cheesy cartoon, and I had to hold back a laugh.

Yep, definitely going to be interrogated on Monday when we have lunch.

I motioned Brian into the apartment, and the two of them sat on the couch while I finished up the food. During their talk, I managed to catch bits and pieces of the conversation. They had found the teens involved, and she confirmed the car as the one she saw. After a while, Brian stood up and shook her hand.

"Thank you for answering my questions."

"It's no problem. I'm just glad you were able to catch them."

"It was all thanks to you," he said with clear admiration in his tone.

Once he left, Rose turned to me and smiled. Her eyes flashed with hunger, but not for the food I was dishing up.

Oh hell.

She practically floated as she walked to me. I wrapped my arms around her, leaning down for a kiss.

After a minute, I pulled back. "As much as I want to devour you right here, right now, you need to eat and visit your dad." The sigh that escaped her lips almost sounded like disappointment. I tilted her chin up with my hands before nipping at her ears.

"When we get back here, I will lick that little kitty of yours until you are screaming my name for everyone to hear and your cum is all over my face," I growled, making her whimper.

I pulled out the chair and placed the plate in front of her as I took my place across the table. She took a bite and her eyes closed.

"This is really good," she practically moaned.

My lips curved up into a smirk. "I'm glad you like it. An old Army buddy taught me how to make it."

"You served?"

"Yes, four years. I was in the infirmary while I went to school."

"I never would have pegged you as the military type."

I chuckled softly. Well, she wasn't wrong. "Honestly, I wasn't. I joined for the GI Bill and my family legacy. I hated every second of it. It just wasn't me."

"It's definitely not for everyone." She put her fork down, chewing her last bite. I picked up her plate and placed both in the sink. She stood up, and I moved in close to her, stealing a kiss from her perfect lips.

Fuck, I wanted to pound her so damn bad.

"Now go get dressed. No one else needs to see your sexy ass from beneath my shirt. That is for my eyes only," I ordered as I cupped her ass and squeezed.

Chapter Twenty-Two

ROSE

His dominating tone made my body tingle with desire. The idea of having him control me in every way possible was a turn-on I never knew I had. Being as young as I was in the military, I didn't exactly know much more than vanilla. Through the years, I learned more through stories from my brothers-in-arms, but never experienced most of it myself.

While in the military, I had a few partners, but nothing special. Then in the CIA I never had the time, really, not to mention my options would have been some not-so-savory people, most being criminals, and that was not going to happen. Especially after a female agent I knew got pregnant, and it complicated the mission and put a huge target on her back. Absolutely not.

I slipped into some black ripped jeans and a white shirt with a SWAK that said "Feeling Smutty." To complete the look, I threw on a leather jacket. The look gave off motorcycle girl vibes, and I fucking loved it. One thing I always wanted was a Harley. Now that I was working stateside, I could get myself one. The thought alone made my body tingle in anticipation of the vibration beneath me.

When I walked out of my room and looked at Ren, he was biting his lower lip and his eyes were cloudy with lust. Hell, I was pretty sure I heard him growl. One thing I knew for sure, he liked what he saw. I noticed he was now in dark-wash jeans and a Jeep T-shirt, with his own leather jacket on. The man looked like a piece of dessert.

He reached out his hand and I grabbed it, then was yanked into his chest. I let out a gasp at the sudden impact of his body, and he chuckled.

"You look so fucking delicious I almost don't want to let you leave," he hummed in my ear, making my knees buckle slightly. The vibration of his laugh heated my body. "Love how I make you Jell-O with just the smallest things. The power you give me is intoxicating." He flicked his tongue over my ear.

Oh hell.

My boyfriend was something else, and I fucking loved it.

"Only for you, Alpha," I breathed.

In the blink of an eye, I was pinned against the wall as Ren nipped, kissed, and licked my jaw down my neck. I whimpered from the lust filling my core.

Oh, fuck me.

He almost seemed to growl as his hand ran up my torso to my throat, where it tightened slightly, just enough to give an erotic feeling like I've never experienced.

Fuck yes.

The moan that came from my lips was loud and filled with need.

"Yes Dove, I am your Alpha, and I will show you just what that means later…after you see your dad like the good little slut you are," he growled.

Oh fuck.

The pool of wetness that formed told me I definitely liked what he just said, and I wanted, no, needed more.

Chapter Twenty-Three

REN

When Rose called me Alpha, I almost lost it. Lust overpowered me, and it took everything in me not to rip her brand-new clothes off her body and take her right there against the wall. But fuck if I didn't plan to do just that later. As we walked out of the apartment, I had to palm my cock to get it off my zipper before it was permanently dented with the imprint.

I opened her door, allowing her to get in, then closed it before I climbed into the driver's seat. When we got to the hospital, I planned to report my relationship so it could be processed first thing Monday, but I also needed to clarify the plans for today.

"Obviously I am bringing you to the hospital, then I am taking you out on a date. But I want to know if you want me to accompany you to see your father or not."

She looked lost in thought for a minute and leaned into my side as much as the car would allow. "My dad already suspects something. I don't want to hide anything from him. My old jobs came with a lot of secrets, and I don't want this to start that way."

I pulled her closer as I crushed my lips against hers. "While we are there, I will file the paperwork declaring my relationship to you, thus to your father."

She didn't speak, only nodded. I reached for her hand and just about jumped for joy when she intertwined her fingers with mine. As I drove, I would pick up her hand and kiss it as I looked at her suggestively, making her squirm. This was a fun red-light game. Utilizing my parking pass to park in the doctor's garage, we entered through the side entrance with my badge.

"This won't get you into trouble, will it?"

I loved how concerned she was about me. "No, staff use their passes all the time when family or friends are in the hospital. This is no different. Plus, I am here to file paperwork, so technically, I am here in an official capacity."

She smiled softly, and I reached for her hand again, hoping she would take it since we were now in public and at my work. My heart soared when she clasped my hand just like she had in the car.

We stopped at the desk and the volunteer looked up and smiled when recognition hit. "Doctor Doux, what brings you in on your day off?"

"Suzie, I need two visitor passes, and I need the relationship declaration form," I said in my professional tone. Her eyes widened slightly, then she looked at Rose, then back to me, her mouth forming an O. She pulled out the form, and I quickly filled out the single-page document, then handed it back. I placed the pink sticker on myself, then turned to Rose and placed hers just above her left breast, my hand lingering for a moment, as I stole a kiss and a quick touch.

"Oh. My. God. Doctor. Doux. Are you kissing Dale's daughter?" Celeste's playful tone said from behind me. I chuckled softly and almost laughed hysterically when I saw the deer-in-the-headlights look on Rose's face.

"It's okay, Dove, she is a close friend," I whispered for only her to hear. I was pleased to see her relax, and thankful the volunteer had left to file the form before Celeste came out. Grasping Rose's hand, I turned to face my friend. "No, I was kissing my girlfriend, who happens to be Dale's daughter."

I gave her a wink. She shrieked like a damn teenager, and I fought the urge to cover my ears as she jumped up and down.

Good lord.

"About damn time, Rene. I thought you would die single!"

I rolled my eyes and heard a slight laugh escape Rose's lips. "As much as I would love to tell you about this all right now, we have someone to visit."

"Of course, don't let me get in your way," she said, then moved out of the way.

Rose and I walked at a slow pace, not in any rush to go anywhere, just enjoying each other's company. I pulled her to me just outside her father's door, ignoring all the looks from my staff as most of them just now got to see me in my normal clothes.

"Do you want to go in together, or do you want me to wait out here?" I asked.

"Together," she whispered as her lips brushed against mine. The sensation drove me wild.

Lord help me.

Chapter Twenty-Four

ROSE

As I was opening the door to my father's room, I was so nervous about what he would think. Having Ren's hand in mine helped calm my nerves a bit. Don't get me wrong, I knew my dad liked Ren as his doctor, but would he like him as more than that?

Only one way to find out.

My father looked away from the small TV on the wall and smiled as he saw me, then despite how impossible it seemed, his smile grew wider as he saw the man at my side. His eyes zeroed in on our joined hands.

"Oh, I knew it. I knew it was you, Doc."

But how?

Before I could speak the words, Ren said, "And why do you say that, Dale?"

He huffed slightly, as if he was insulted. "My daughter never kept anything personal from me, so when she hesitated to tell me who she met, I knew that in her mind it was a gray area. I damn well knew it wasn't anyone from work, but you, that I could see."

I couldn't help but smile at my father's approval because that was what this was.

After my dad did his fatherly interrogation of Ren and his intentions, we all just talked and laughed like we had always been together, like family. Seeing the smile on my dad's face was every-thing I needed to see to know this was where I was meant to be.

My dad yawned. "This old man needs to sleep. You two go have fun and enjoy each other."

Oh, we will.

In more ways than one.

Ren stood and held out his hand to help me up. Our fingers twisted together on their own accord. We turned to leave, and I swear I saw my dad wink at Ren.

What the hell?

It didn't take us long to get back to the car. Ren pinned me against the door and his lips brushed against me.

"Dove, I want to show you something just as beautiful as you," he whispered, his tone filled with unspoken promises that made my body shiver in anticipation.

"Well then, show me," I said, nipping at his jaw. He growled as his hand wrapped around my waist before he squeezed my ass.

"Don't be a brat, or I will punish your kitty so hard you won't be able to walk."

"Promise," I gasped.

"Promise," he snarled.

Oh hell yes.

Chapter Twenty-Five

REN

My erection was becoming quite the problem, especially after Rose decided to be a little brat. That would be corrected tonight, and boy, was I looking forward to that. When I pulled up to the park, I watched her reaction to the scene before her.

Trees and flowers were everywhere and the sound of rushing water from the river filled the air. People's Park was an excellent hiking park, with a gorgeous waterfront, which was why I brought her here. Before meeting Rose, this was the most beautiful thing I had ever seen, and now seeing her here surrounded by nature's beauty was like nothing I had ever experienced before.

So fucking gorgeous.

"Wow," she breathed as she stepped out and took the view in. "I've traveled the world, but this, this is beautiful."

"Not as beautiful as you," I remarked and watched as her cheeks turned a cute shade of pink. In a swift motion, I pulled her into my chest and kissed her. My kiss lingered in passion as my mind whirled with images of what I wanted and planned to do to her. My cock hardened even more, and she let out a gasp as it twitched against her body.

Fuck, I wanted to take her so damn much.

Homeless people did it here. Would it be farfetched for me to claim her here?

Ugh. She deserved better than a quick fuck in the park, but that didn't mean I wouldn't please her in other ways while we were here.

When I opened my eyes, I noticed the knowing smirk on her perfect lips. The effect she had on me was so damn intoxicating. Just her kisses made me feel drunk. She stood on the tips of her toes and nipped at my ear.

"I want you deep inside me, giving me that punishment you promised. But first, I want you to show me your special spot." Her whisper was seductive and made my cock harden even more, which I wondered how the hell that was possible. It already felt like concrete. A low growl escaped my lips when she added a soft, "Alpha."

"If you keep calling me that, my self-control is going to break."

"Hmmm, tempting."

Jesus Christ.

I took a deep breath, trying desperately to cool the fire in my balls. "You are going to be the death of me, Dove."

A slight chuckle made my stomach flip. "Show me so we can go back to your place." Her tone was suggestive as fuck, and I thought I was going to cum right there without a single touch.

Without a word, I grabbed her hand and moved her down the path to the river. I sat once we got to the old tree along the shore, and she settled between my legs. My body wrapped itself around her, mimicking a cocoon.

The view was always amazing and the sound relaxing. A

place of peace made even better with her body against mine. After a bit, she turned and kissed me softly, the movements of our lips growing more frantic. When her hand brushed my bulge, I let out a deep, needy growl and, without a word, I scooped her up and carried her up the hill and to the car.

I was done waiting.

Chapter Twenty-Six

ROSE

Ren practically kicked the door in when we got back to his place. He didn't touch anything as he carried me to his room and tossed me on the bed.

Oh, fuck yes.

His eyes shone with desire and dominance, and my panties almost caught fire from the heat. The rough, hard grip he had on my breast sent a thrill through my body. Don't get me wrong, I didn't mind a gentle touch, but with him I needed his domination, bad.

I stared as he stripped off his shirt before climbing over me, covering me with his whole body. His lips crushed mine as his hard cock brushed against my inner thigh, making me moan. When his lips left mine, I whimpered, wanting more, wanting all of him.

"Dove, I want you so damn bad."

"Then take me," I pleaded. The responding groan followed by my shirt being ripped off my body made an intense wetness pool between my legs.

A million times over, fuck yes.

His lips crushed mine again as I felt the rest of my clothes get stripped off me, then the sensation of his now-naked body rubbing against mine. I bucked my hips up, seeking more.

My hands moved up and down his toned body, feeling every curve. As my touch neared his swollen cock, he moaned, closing his eyes. I wrapped my fingers firmly around his shaft and tugged. He let out a growl, and next thing I knew, my hands were pinned above my head and I heard the sound of foil, then latex.

Oh shit, this was happening.

His tip brushed against my aching pussy, and I squirmed.

"Do you want my cock deep inside that pretty little kitty of yours?" he growled.

"Yes," I breathed. "Fuck me, Alpha. Fuck me like you own me."

I screamed in ecstasy as he plunged his full length into me. The slight pain was intoxicating, and I loved it. The feeling of his cock inside me, filling me, was like nothing I could have imagined.

Fuck.

I was so damn full it bordered on pain, and I relished it.

I squirmed in his grip as he kept my hands pinned above my head. A moan escaped me as he nipped my nipple.

"So fucking perfect," he moaned.

He moved his hips back, then plunged into me, making me arch my back from the pleasure. His smooth hand roughly grabbed and pulled at my breast and nipples, inflicting just enough pain.

Who knew I would find pain so erotic?

The feeling of my hands being pinned and the way it made my body open and vulnerable was like nothing I ever experienced before, and I loved it. I also wanted more of his hands all over me. Shit, I never thought I'd like the idea of being restrained, but here I was loving every second of it.

I almost seemed to be constantly leaking my wetness as the sounds of us together got noisier, wetter.

"Your kitty is so slutty and I love it," he growled as he plunged roughly into my core.

"Fuck me harder," I pleaded, and his response was immediate with a hard, fast thrust that hit me deeper than I thought he could, sending shockwaves of pleasure through me.

My body tingled, and I was getting close. He freed one of his hands that wandered up my curves as his fingers wrapped around my throat and applied pressure. I screamed out as I convulsed, my eyes rolling back as I came hard around his throbbing cock, his own grunts of release filling the room.

His thrusts slowed as we came down from our orgasms. In a swift movement, the condom was off and in the trash, and he pulled me into his chest. Neither of us said a word, our breathing too rapid and my mind in too much bliss. Ren ran his hand through my hair and down my body until I looked up to meet his gaze.

"Dove, you are something else. That was—"

"Something out of a romance book."

"Yes, that, but real and so much more," he said. I couldn't help the smile that formed on my lips. He leaned down and kissed me softly. "Get some rest."

I closed my eyes and snuggled in, listening to the sound of his heartbeat as it told me just how much Ren enjoyed being with me.

Chapter Twenty-Seven

REN

Fuck, that was the best sex I'd had in years. Hell, maybe even ever. When her wetness splashed with every thrust, I almost came right there, but I wanted so much more. I wanted to please her like no one ever has. Hell, I wanted to lick up every last drop of her wetness, but the need to be inside her was stronger. But believe me, it was going to happen. I was going to drive her wild with nothing but my tongue.

When I knew I couldn't hold off anymore, I reached for her throat, knowing just how much she liked it before. I wanted to do so many things, but without my rope or cuffs, I had to pin her hands. Though she didn't seem to mind, the opposite actually.

Nonetheless, a trip to the sex store was needed. I hated reusing items for the bedroom between partners. To me, it felt wrong. Everything should be for the person you are with. If that means spending a few hundred bucks every time, then so be it. This way, everything is custom to the person you are pleasing and is only theirs.

Waking up after that was like a pleasant hangover, if that was even a thing. I felt alive and, dare I say, satisfied. Plus, the fact she was still snuggling into my chest just added to the bliss. When she shifted slightly, I kissed the top of her head. She hummed, then looked up at me.

"How are you feeling, Dove?"

She moved and let out a groan. "Sore."

I couldn't help but chuckle. "Hmm, I can imagine why. I'm not exactly on the small side and you took it hard and rough."

"And I loved every second of it."

"Hmm, good, cause now that my cock got a taste of the little kitty of yours, I won't be able to stop myself from devouring you."

Her response was erotic as she rubbed her now-soaked pussy against my bare thigh, resulting in a possessive growl.

"Dove, I will claim that kitty right now if you do that again."

I could feel the smirk against my chest as she rubbed against me again. A deep snarl escaped my lips as I flipped her so she was on her hands and knees. The need to tie her up was strong, so I reached down and grabbed her destroyed top and used it to tie her hands behind her back. Her responding curse told me she liked it.

After I slipped on another condom, I positioned myself at her entrance, taking in the view. Her perfect starfish called my name, begging to be plugged. I definitely needed to go to the store so I could explore that part of her. With one hand at the base of my cock, the other gripping the material binding her wrists, I plunged into her, pulling her into my thrust.

"Fuck yes," she yelled.

My movements were animalistic as I plunged hard and deep into her. I could have sworn my cock hardened with each thrust. With a twist of my wrist, I tightened the material on her hands as my other hand smacked her perfect, round ass. Her resulting groan was exhilarating. I moved my hand across my body and smacked her other side with the same force.

"Hmm, yes. Punish me, Alpha."

Oh hell.

I rammed into her so hard I thought we would launch off the bed. My balls tingled, warning me of my impending orgasm. I pulled back on the cloth until my thumb was pressed against her back hole, while my other hand pulled back on her ponytail as I sucked and bit at her neck. Honestly, I loved how fucking flexible she was. Not everyone could do this position, and the fact my Dove could was erotic as hell.

"Ren," she screamed as she went limp in my hold. Her core squeezed my cock, making me explode with my own orgasm.

"Rose," I growled as I bit down on her shoulder, which gave her orgasm a second wind as she cried out and tightened around me again.

Holy shit.

She was a kinky little thing.

Fuck.

A woman after my heart.

Chapter Twenty-Eight

ROSE

To say the rest of the weekend was spent sleeping and fucking was an understatement. He made sure that I ate and prepared a bath for me while he ran to the store. When I asked what he was getting, he said, "You will know when I want you to know."

Oh hell.

Those words made me so goddamn horny, I almost jumped him right then and there. Today he had to work, and I had to see my dad, meet with Wes to find an office location, and get my furniture this afternoon. Originally they were set to come first thing, but once they did the route it became afternoon. Honestly, I didn't care. I like being with Ren at night. Hell, the guest room was where I kept my clothes at this point.

Maybe I could convince him to come stay at my place tonight. You know, break in the furniture.

I got dressed in my go-to black jeans with a soft blue T-shirt and leather jacket. I really needed to buy my bike soon. Nothing like the sweet vibrations of a Harley between your thighs.

Well, other than Ren, that is.

We were walking out and heading to our cars when a woman came out of the office. "Mr. Doux, do you have a minute?"

He stopped in his tracks and turned to face the woman. She was dressed professionally but somehow still provocatively. I barely kept myself from rolling my eyes at how flirty she was with him.

"You never called me. You said you would," the woman whined.

His temples bulged as he gritted his teeth. "Ma'am, I said I would call if I needed anything else." His tone was hard but polite.

Was this woman sexually harassing him?

Hmm, that just won't do.

I moved in closer and grasped his hand, happy when he returned the gesture.

"Babe, you are going to be late for work. Surgery waits for no one."

I knew he didn't have surgery today, but it held urgency, so I knew it would help him get away. The woman's eyes almost fell out of their sockets in her shock.

"Thanks, Dove," he whispered to me so only I could hear, then turned back to the woman. "If you will excuse me, my girl-friend is right. I have to get to work."

He headed to his car and got in. This time, I held the door for him.

Once the door was shut, I leaned in the open window and kissed him.

"Don't worry about her. She is obsessed but has never crossed a line," he said.

"Well, she was pretty close today. I can be possessive just as much as you can, Ren. She better not test me."

"Fuck, I love the sound of that," he hummed.

"Good," I said with a wink. "Now go to work, maybe come

over to my place tonight, so we can..." I paused and looked around. "Break in some of the new furniture."

"Hmm. I think I will take you up on that, Dove."

"Good, I'll text you when I get to the hospital to see my dad, but you mentioned you had lunch with Cobb, right?"

"Yes, but I will try to see you. We normally eat at the cafeteria."

"Okay." With another kiss, he drove off to go to work. I turned to see the woman still looking my way. As much as I wanted to give her a piece of my mind, I held off, giving her an evil smirk instead.

Chapter Twenty-Nine

REN

The way Rose handled the office lady was hot as hell. She read that situation so well and handled it like...like a professional. Which made me feel stupid about the fact that I worried she would take the interaction the wrong way. Others had, but she wasn't like them, not in the least.

But I also knew people like Clarrissa and knew she would soon become a problem. She was a ticking time bomb of unwarranted jealousy. When Rose asked me to come over tonight, I jumped at the opportunity. For one, I loved spending time with her, and for two, it gave me time before I'd have to deal with Clarrissa.

As usual, I entered the hospital through the ER so I could check in with Celeste and see if I had any patients in the ER. When I rounded the corner to the nurses' station, Celeste beamed at me while looking me up and down. The rest of the nurses were away tending to patients. "Okay Rene, you looked well fucked."

I rolled my eyes. She was always observant. "Well, having a girlfriend will do that," I retorted.

She giggled as she jumped up and down. "You two are so damn perfect for each other. I'm so happy for you."

"Yeah, she is pretty great. She is"—fuck, what's the word?—"special."

"Well, I'm glad to hear it. I don't have any patients here for you, well not currently. Room 7 needs a consult. But I did hear from the overnight doc that they want to release Dale in the next few days."

"Who did they put on his case until the meeting with the board?"

"Doctor Charles Rain."

Oh, thank God.

I trained him from the time he was a med student, so I knew he was competent. I would still be Dale's lead doctor, but due to my relationship with his daughter, most medical calls had to be reviewed or done by another doctor to ensure unbiased and unemotional decisions.

"Glad to hear that. I can't think of anyone better for the job."

"You meet with the board at ten. So you just got to do rounds until then," Celeste said.

"I really need you in my department, you know. You are great with the patients," I said fondly.

"Rene. You know my heart is in emergency medicine."

"I know," I sighed. "But you can't blame me for trying."

She shook her head at me with a smile on her face. "You are something else."

I couldn't help but laugh at that one. "I best get to my rounds, starting with the consult."

Celeste led the way to Room 7. "Mrs. Thornton, this is Doctor Doux, the head of cardiology," she said.

I looked intently at the woman in the bed. She appeared to be in her sixties and in shape.

"Good morning, ma'am. What brought you into my hospital

today?" I asked as I started reading her chart. My memory wasn't photographic, but close. If I read it, I remembered it and I was a quick read.

"I was doing my yoga, and I got a sudden pain in my chest followed by pain in my left arm. My father died of a heart attack, so I came right away."

I listened to her words while looking over her test results. To say the results were not good was an understatement. She had experienced a pretty significant heart attack and her heart was now struggling.

"I'm glad you did. You did have a heart attack and, by the looks of it, it was a big one. We will need to admit you while we run some tests on your heart so we can devise treatment."

"I did everything right. I eat well, I exercise, I watch what I put on my body and take in." Her words were filled with shock, confusion, and sadness.

"Unfortunately, you can do everything right and genetics or bad luck can show their nasty hands. But trust that we will do everything we can to give you a good, long, and healthy life, Mrs. Thornton."

She let out a sigh and nodded. "Thank you, Doc."

"Now get some rest." I headed out the door with a look at Celeste. "You know the tests."

"Sure do. I will get her admittance going as well."

When Celeste left, I swiped my hands through my hair and took a deep breath.

Time for rounds.

Chapter Thirty

ROSE

As I walked into my father's room, he sat up and smiled warmly.

"Okay, now you have the 'I just spent the weekend getting fucked' look about you," my dad remarked. Heat rushed to my cheeks, and I looked away, avoiding his knowing eyes.

"Dad, must we talk about this?"

"Yes, daughter. I am happy that you are happy. But I guess we can talk about your new business plan instead."

Okay, that was a subject I could talk about. "We should be up and running in the next two months or so."

"I am so happy for you, love."

We spent the next hour talking about the plans for the business, the name, and so much more. He was excited about his own apartment, and he expressed an interest in working for me, answering calls.

To be honest, I loved the idea. He would need an official background check and some level of clearance, but that should be easy enough. My father served the country for years and had carried clearance in the past, though not as high as mine.

Our conversation abruptly ended when I heard the door open behind me. I didn't have to turn around to know who came in the door. His unique footfall gave him away. One of my many talents was identifying voices and sounds with ease.

"How is my favorite patient?" Ren asked as he closed the door.

"I'm assuming you are responsible for my daughter's sexed-out look?"

I looked at Ren to see his cheeks were just as red as mine. "Well, I, um…"

"You don't have to answer that, Ren." I reached my hand out to pull him closer so I could lean into him. Once he came over, I did just that, and he rubbed my shoulder.

"Well, I do come with good news. It looks like they will release you in the next couple of days. Meds are doing their job, and once the furniture comes, it will be safe to send you home. Celeste secured a home care aide for you. She is a close friend. Her name is Rebecca. She is great at what she does and is in school to be a nurse with goals to be a cardiac nurse. Bonus is she is close to Doctor Rain, his niece to be exact, and will be able to contact him easily."

Rain.

Could it be?

Impossible.

"Ren, can I speak to you in your office?" I whispered, my voice sounding hoarse. My dad glanced at me, but I masked my reaction as best I could. I would explain it to him later, but right now, I needed answers.

"Of course, Dove," he replied, his voice thick with concern.

I stood up and gave my dad a quick kiss before following Ren to his office. Once inside, he locked the door and sat on the couch, inviting me to join him, which I did.

I loved how he didn't push me, though I imagine he had a lot of questions. He just held me and waited until I was ready. In an attempt to calm my nerves, I took a deep breath. "What is Doctor Rain's first name?"

"Charles."

Shit.

"Did he serve?"

It was quite a moment, and I almost twisted to look at Ren when he finally answered. "Yes, Navy."

My heart clinched, and a quiet whimper escaped my lips.

Chapter Thirty-One

REN

The noise she made was one of pain. With quick but gentle movements, I was out from under her and kneeled on the floor between her legs, looking at her. Again I didn't push, I just rubbed small calming circles on her thighs. Her fingers twisted into my hair as she laid her head on mine, seeming to breathe me in.

"The day Jasper was killed..." She sucked in a hesitant breath, and I cupped the side of her cheek with my hand. "Charlie, Charles Rain, was who we were sent to rescue."

Fuck, what were the odds of that?

I had so many questions, but that was not what she needed at this moment. Only one question needed to be answered right now. "Are you okay with him being your dad's doctor?"

There was a moment of silence, then she whispered, "Yes...it just took me by surprise, is all. I haven't seen him since...since the debrief."

Fuck.

I wish I could take away her pain, but I couldn't.

"I can have him come in here, so no one is watching when you meet again."

"I'd like that," she said, and I pulled out my phone to text Charles. I got up to unlock the door, then tugged her back onto my lap. The sound of knuckles on my door filled the small office.

"I got to go warn him. I'll be right back," I whispered.

She nodded before lying on the couch, seeming to want nothing more than to disappear into the cushions. And I didn't blame her.

I slipped out into the hall, which got me a raised eyebrow from Charles, probably since I normally just let him in.

"The patient you were assigned, the one whose daughter I'm dating."

"Dale Conrad, yes. Is he alright?"

"Yes, he is fine, but his daughter, his daughter, knows you."

Now the man looked really confused.

"I don't know the whole story, but she said something about a rescue gone wrong." I watched as all the color left his face and I wondered if he would pass out.

"She was a SEAL?"

"Yes," I breathed. "I know it must be a lot to fathom, but I think the two of you reuniting is best done in the privacy of my office."

He cleared his throat and nodded. "Yes, hell, we may even need the chaplain."

"If you need him, I'll call him, but you should go in there and talk to her. Knock twice if you need me, if she needs me."

With a quick nod, he opened the door to my office and went in.

Chapter Thirty-Two

ROSE

When I heard the door open, my back stiffened. My body ached like I had the flu as I slowly sat upright. Charlie never knew the names of me or my team members but had seen our faces. Every detail about that mission was need-to-know. Not to mention this never even crossed my mind as possible. I mean, what are the odds? He was a medic and was with his own unit when he was taken hostage, which got us called in.

For years, I blamed this man for the death of Jasper. If he hadn't been taken, Jasper would still be here, alive and being a clown. But even then, his unit failed to protect him.

Who knows?

Only the higher-ups are privy to that information.

Fuck, I miss Jasper.

I stared down at the ground as my mind prepared itself to look at the man I had blamed for so long. The man Jasper died to save. The couch shifted as he sat on the opposite side of me. After a few deep breaths, I looked up to face the man, tears threatening to break free at any moment. When I saw tears falling down his cheek, I let go of the ones I held too.

"No words will ever make what happened right. I wish so much it turned out differently," he blubbered.

"Me too," I whispered.

"You, your team, and Jasper gave me the chance to be a father. Jasper was never forgotten after all was said and done. My wife and I named our son Jasper, in his honor. He is a great kid, you know, and because of your team, I got the chance. Though my marriage didn't work out, I am still able to be a father to my boy."

Shit, his marriage failed.

"What happened?" I asked, knowing it wasn't my business, but I was curious nonetheless.

"PTSD," was all he said, and it was enough. PTSD was a huge contributor to divorces and the downfall of any type of relationships. "I'm better now, but the damage couldn't be undone. We are friends and co-parent well together, just can't be together. It was all just too much for her."

Well, shit.

Saying I'm sorry seemed like something everyone said, so I wouldn't say it. "I'm glad you guys can still get along," I said as I turned to him and saw the pain in his eyes.

"I feel like you and your team saved me and I made it for nothing."

Oh no. This was not healthy for him to think. Not to mention far from the truth.

I reached out and grasped his hand in mine. "Charlie, I went through years of therapy. At one point, I blamed you for everything until I worked through it. Saving you was our job, and we did it well. But no matter how much training we had there is always error or unforeseen circumstances. Jasper was a good man, and he knew what he was doing, what he was signing up for when he gave the cue. Yes, things didn't work out for you and your wife, but *you* did get to be a father. PTSD is part of military life, but you got out, became a dad, and a damn heart doctor. That wouldn't have happened if Jasper hadn't done what he did. Losing him hurt like hell, yes, but he would have it no other way."

The words were hard to say, but they were the God's honest truth and everything in my gut told me he needed to hear it, and hear it from me, Jasper's sister.

I held open my arms, inviting him in for a hug, which he accepted. He sobbed briefly against my shoulder for a minute before pulling away.

"I will take care of your dad like my own family. Between me and Rene, your dad will come out on top of this. If it's the last thing I do."

My heart warmed at the words. "Thank you," I whispered.

"No, thank you."

Chapter Thirty-Three

REN

I leaned against the wall just outside my office while I gave Rose and Charles time alone. It was not my place to eavesdrop. My hand nervously ran through my hair, which was a little long on the top. The protective part of me wanted to take all this away from her, but I couldn't. This was something she had to do herself. All I could do was take it all away from her, alone, in our bed.

Our bed.

My mind already wanted us to be together, live together, but shit, it was way too soon, right?

"Ren," Rose said.

I practically broke down the door to get in. Looking between the two, I could see signs of crying, but they seemed in good spirits now. Charles stood up and gave me a half hug.

"Thanks Ren, you have no idea what you just did for me, for both of us."

"Of course, brother."

"I am going to go check on my patients, then go to lunch," he said. I gave him a quick nod as he directed his attention back to Rose. "It was nice seeing you again. And under better circumstances."

She smiled warmly in return.

Once he was out of my office, I sat next to Rose and she immediately snuggled into me, clearly needing my touch to comfort her, and that made my heart skip a beat.

"Do you need me to cancel my lunch?"

She sat up and looked at me, bewildered. "N-no, I just need you for a minute. I need a distraction to balance me."

Oh, I could do that and so much more.

I gripped her jaw and pulled her face up to mine before teasing her lips. She opened immediately as I dove in to taste her.

"Hmmm. Does that help?" I hummed.

She whimpered, giving me my answer, so I deepened the kiss as I pulled her onto my lap until she was straddling me. My cock pulsed in my scrubs and the sound of my door opening made us pull our lips apart. She went to move, but I held her there. She was the only thing blocking my erection from being seen by whoever came in uninvited. Her head fell onto my shoulder and into my neck as she attempted to hide. I chuckled slightly, then looked to see who had come in.

"Okay, so now I need the damn tea. First, she was at your house and is CIA. Now you are practically fucking her in your office. I thought we were friends, man," Cobb practically whined. I rolled my eyes at his childlike tantrum.

"Nice to see you too," Rose remarked, sarcasm heavy in her tone.

I fought the urge to laugh, but failed. Which was made worse when Brian glared daggers at me. Rose's soft chuckles vibrated through my chest, and I loved it.

I had to take a few deep breaths before I was able to speak. "Brian, Rose is my girlfriend."

When his eyes widened and his face morphed into one of

complete and utter shock, I had to hold back my laugh, but failed so I ended up snorting like a damn pig.

Fucker.

"And you call me the pig," he retorted with a smug grin. At least I knew he wasn't broken since he was still his smart-ass self.

"You are the popo, so yep."

"Asshole."

"Yes, I have one, Mister Piggy."

"Ugh."

"Sweetie, I don't know why he is shocked, he caught me in your place twice, and one of those times I was in your shirt with shorts on and now this," she teased, making me laugh even harder as the look of being insulted morphed into Brian's face.

This woman is a kinky freak.

I fucking love it.

"Dove, you are something else."

"Oh, I know, and I plan to do so much more, but first I'll let you get to your lunch while I go see my business partner."

I gripped her hips harder, not wanting her to go. She leaned into my ear and whispered, "If you don't let me go, I will fuck you right here in front of Cobb."

Oh fuck.

The threat turned me on beyond what I thought it would, hell, what I thought was even possible. Which, of course, made my cock twitch. She chuckled against me, but I released my grip, crossing my legs as she stood to hide my now sizable and painful bulge. With a quick kiss, she left me in my office with a somewhat baffled man.

Chapter Thirty-Four

ROSE

When Officer Cobb came in and whined about needing the tea, I lost it. We weren't exactly secretive about it. Hell, you had to be blind after the second day. I swear men could be so damn clueless.

I went to the bathroom to right myself before heading out to my car. Pulling out my phone, I texted my dad.

> Hey dad. Sorry about earlier. Everything is good now. The doctor Ren mentioned is someone I know from my time in the Navy, and it just brought back some stuff with Jasper. We talked, and all is good. I'll be by later if I can, but furniture is being delivered tonight.

If I didn't have a meeting, I would just go see my dad, but a text would have to do for now. I headed to the same little coffee shop as before. When I walked in, Wes smiled and stood to give me a short hug.

"Hey," I said.

"Hey yourself."

We sat down, and he looked at me. "Okay, what's up? You look like you did some crying recently. Is your dad okay?"

I smiled at his concern and took a deep breath. "Do you remember the soldier we were rescuing the day we lost Jasper?" He didn't answer, but gave a quick nod. "Well, he is now one of my dad's doctors."

"No, shit. Damn. How do you feel about that?"

"I'm actually okay with it. It was a shock, but we talked and all is good."

"I'm glad to hear."

"Now let's get to business," I said, needing a topic change. With a smile, he pushed a file to me and I opened it. The drawings were stunning. Each option was more beautiful than the next. "These are amazing, Wes."

"Thanks. I have a passion for art. These are possible logos, but I want your input since we are partners and all."

I looked down again, spreading the photos out so I could see all of them. My eyes wandered to a shield with an eye at its center with guns on the edge with Bound by Honor at the base. It was perfect.

"This one," I said, pushing the photo toward him.

His smile stretched to his ears. "That was my favorite, too."

Reluctant to reflect too much more on Jasper, I redirected the conversation before we could get all sappy again. "How are the permits and stuff going?"

"Good actually. I was able to get everything filed, and I sent the clearance stuff in and emailed Richards so he could work his magic. Now it's a waiting game, but I have some connections in the government and should be able to pull some strings. So I think a couple weeks until we can fully run. That being said, based on local laws, we can start doing certain things right away."

"Awesome. Did you find anything in particular?"

"Yes, I did, but we need to contact law enforcement on this one."

"Why is that?" I inquired as I looked over the file we did have.

"It's a cold case for a missing woman. It would be easier to get the file from them if we can."

My mind immediately went to Cobb. "I might know someone. I'll see what I can do."

He slipped me a file, and I looked inside. It was a filled-out form with Killian's Eye on the top.

Brittany Slade, age 21
Last seen 02/22/2020 leaving a party.

So young. I knew the odds she was alive at this point were small, but I would do my best to find her and bring her family closure. I would bring this up to Ren tonight at some point. The last thing Wes slipped to me was a file with possible office locations.

"Look this over and let me know your top pick."

"I'll get back to you on this tomorrow," I replied. The rest of lunch was catching up and some more strategy talk.

My phone rang, and I answered it. "Hey this is Cole. I have a furniture delivery for you. I was calling to give you a heads-up that we will be there in about thirty minutes."

"Alright. Thank you. I will be there."

After some quick goodbyes, I headed to my car and drove to my house. The men were super helpful and put everything together and in their spots. I ended up with a bed in each room, minus my office, several dressers, a desk, a couch, dining room furniture, and lots of small tables. By the time we were all done, it looked like a home.

Once the delivery people left, I flopped on my sectional and pulled out my phone. I noticed a text from Richards.

> Hey stranger. I miss you. Hope everything is going well. Might be able to visit soon. Also, your items are being shipped and should be there in the next few days. The flight leaves today and if it goes right, you should have your stuff tonight, but it depends on the pickup at the airport.

I smiled and texted back.

> I look forward to your visit.

Next, I opened a text to Ren.

> Is my Alpha ready to play and break in some furniture?

I felt so damn slutty sending that, not to mention naughty, but hell, I'd be lying if I said I didn't like it, and clearly he did, too.

> Fuck, Dove. I'm still at work, though I might bail a few minutes early, hmm I'll bring some stuff I want to try with me.

The text was complete with emojis, and I laughed.

> Hmm. What kind of stuff?

I was about to put my phone away when I got a reply.

> That's for me, your Alpha, to know and you, Dove, to find out.

Oh, fuck me.

I must have dozed off because I jumped up at the sound of knocking on my front door. My hand instinctively reached for my waist.

Who the fuck?

Slowly, I made my way to the door and looked to see who it was. I relaxed instantly when I saw Ren looking back at me.

Fucking finally.

Chapter Thirty-Five

REN

To say Brian interrogated the shit out of me would be an understatement. I felt like I was being questioned about a crime, not my girlfriend. But I knew he was just looking out for me. Then when Rose started texting me, I was desperate to leave early. Luckily, I thought ahead and had the stuff I had bought for us still in my trunk, ready to go.

Now I was on her porch, staring at her. Her hair was untamed and looked like she had been asleep. I wrapped my arms around her waist, claiming her mouth with mine. She moaned into my mouth and my cock twitched.

Jesus.

Once I shuffled us inside, I had her pinned to the wall as I dropped the red duffle bag with the "stuff" inside. I got lost in the kiss and let out a guttural groan as she stroked my cock through my pants.

Fuck.

"Bed. Now," I growled.

As I got off her, she scurried to the room. I grabbed the bag and ran after her. Once in the room, I took in the sight. The bed had metal everywhere, perfect for tying her up. My cock leaked as my imagination got a hold of me.

Fucking perfect.

She growled on the bed, and I retrieved the first items, moving the bag within reach. When I looked up, my cock began leaking like a faucet. She was undressed and wearing the sexiest matching set of underwear.

Holy shit. I practically pounced over her, brushing my bulge against her now dripping kitty.

Fuck, the things I want to do to her.

"Do you trust me?" I moaned against her lips.

"Y-yes," she breathed.

I stripped off the rest of her clothes, taking the time to kiss her skin as the material left it. Then I showed her the metal cuffs and the keys, which got me a squirm.

Gently, I placed the cuffs on her wrists and locked them, making sure the chain was caught on the frame, securing her in place. I pulled out the silk and tied one to each of her ankles, then the post. She was now at my complete mercy, and I was going to devour and worship her whole body.

I put on a show of me taking off my clothes, then I dropped so my mouth was kissing up her thighs, getting close to the sweetness that was her essence. The first time I had a taste, it reminded me of coconuts and I loved it so damn much.

She squirmed against the restraints as I teased her folds with my tongue.

So goddamn delicious.

Her hips thrust up, seeking more of my tongue. I pinned down her thigh.

"Easy there, Dove. Your kitty will get eaten, but first I am going to drive you wild."

Without a word, I plunged my fingers into her, making her

moan. Every part of me wanted to use every toy on her right now, but I knew one at a time was best. Though if you count the restraints, that was three.

Oh well.

I pulled out the purple plug and covered it with a generous amount of lube. Rose's eyes never left me as she bit her bottom lip, and her eyes darkened at the sight.

Hmmm, yes.

I dove down and licked at her folds again as I plunged the plug through her starfish. She arched her back and cried out as I moved the plug in and out until I left it in. The smirk I gave her as I reached into the bag and pulled out the remote was one only a devil should give.

"Fuck," she whispered as I hit the on button.

Her moans drowned out the low vibrations of the plug, and I knew she would come hard. The sight of her toes curling as she fought the restraints told me if I wanted to taste her, I needed to move fast.

I plunged my tongue into her just as she clenched with her orgasm's first wave. I twirled my tongue and thrust my fingers inside her.

"Gah," was all she managed to get out as I showed her kitty no mercy.

Her second orgasm came hard and fast. I sucked up every last drop. Knowing she seemed to like pain, I manipulated my hand so that I could put all of it in, taking it slow.

"Oh fuck," she moaned. Slowly, I moved my hand in and out as she cursed and cried out with her lust for more. "Harder. Faster."

With pleasure.

My tongue kept licking at her clit as my now fisted hand moved in and out of her. She cried out and her walls tightened around my wrist in a vise grip. Her release drowned me in her cum as she squirted.

Fuck me. I actually made her squirt.

The sight was too much and my own orgasm came rushing to the surface, making me spray my load all over her. Some reached her lips, and I watched as she licked my seed into her mouth.

God damn this woman.

Chapter Thirty-Six

ROSE

The pleasure I felt as I squirted, legit squirted, was like nothing I thought I would experience. Hell, I never thought I would be into fisting, but that happened too. Then his own orgasm hit and caked me in his pleasure. The taste was divine, and I wanted more. So much more.

He moved his lips up and down my body as he licked up his juices.

Oh fuck, that's hot as hell.

Every few licks, he gave me a taste. My cum mixed with his, combined with his natural taste, was like nothing I could have imagined.

The need to have him inside me was getting stronger, almost unbearable. He glanced up at me, and the look in his eyes made me think he could hear my thoughts.

"I wasn't planning to fuck you tonight Dove, just this. I don't have a condom." His voice was husky, hungry even, but also disappointed at himself.

Shit.

My body ached for him and needed him.

"I'm on the pill," I said. Which was true. I had been for years.

A growl tried to escape his lips, followed by a twitch of his cock against my thigh.

"Dove, if I fuck you raw, you become *my* slut, and nothing will ever be between us as I devour you again. Can you agree to that?" he gritted out as he seemed to fight against just taking me.

"Yes," I whispered. "I *only* want you."

Without a word, he plunged his bare, hard shaft into my core, making me scream in ecstasy. His thrusts were animalistic and needy. I moved my hips with his as I pulled at the restraints. My body tingled with delight as the pain of the restraint enveloped me.

Oh fuck.

I knew there would be marks, but fuck if I care. Damn, I welcomed it.

Ren pushed the plug further into my ass. My body went numb before I convulsed with my orgasm, making the restraints dig in even more. I fucking loved it. Ren screamed out my name as his cock pulsed inside me, warming me from the inside. The sensation brought me close to orgasm again.

Holy shit.

My body was so limp as Ren pulled out of me. He moved and began to remove my restraints, kissing the red skin left behind. As he pulled out the plug, I whimpered at the empty feeling.

"Hmm. Don't worry, you will be stuffed again," he purred, and I clamped my thighs together.

He chuckled, then moved to the bathroom. I heard sounds of him cleaning off the plug, then he came back with a warm washrag.

Gently, he cleaned up any leftover cum from my body. Then, when I thought he was going to clean the seed dripping from my pussy, he bent down and licked it up.

"Jesus," I breathed as I gripped the sheets.

Once I was clean, he climbed into the bed next to me and I curled into him. My sated body felt completely drained. The things I wanted to talk to him about would have to wait until tomorrow because my mind was too far gone.

Chapter Thirty-Seven

REN

Last night was fucking wild. I was still having a hell of a time wrapping my head around the fact I made her squirt.

Fuck, that was hot as hell.

Now I was satisfied beyond anything I could have imagined. Taking her raw was its own high. Both of us jolted up when there was a knock on the front door.

What the fuck?

She looked at me, and I shrugged. "Seems how you just moved in, I doubt you are expecting anyone."

"No, I'm not," she said as she checked her gun, which was stashed under her pillow. When she turned to get up, she groaned. I couldn't help the smug smile that reached my lips.

Yep, I did that.

"Dove, I know this is your place, but let me get the door while you get dressed," I said, pulling her into me. All she did was nod, her eyes saying her thanks as she slowly moved to get dressed. I had my sweats on in seconds and headed to the door.

I looked through the window and saw a well-built man with a military haircut.

Jesus, he is massive.

Tentatively, I opened the door, and the man looked me up and down. "And who might you be?" the man asked.

"Excuse me, but I should be asking you that, since you knocked on the door of this house," I retorted. The man's lips curled into a slight smile.

"Brave man, not many would answer with your wit to a man of my size."

"Well, I'm not every man." My patience was growing thin. He needed to say who he was or leave before I called the cops.

"Look, I am here to see Rose. Name's R—"

"Babe, who is it?" Rose asked as she rounded the corner.

I stayed silent as she walked up to us, knowing at this point she was armed. Hell, she always was. It also meant if he tried anything, it would be game over. Suddenly she pushed past me and jumped into the man's arms, making jealousy flitter in my core.

What the hell?

"You said soon, but not this soon," she beamed.

"I wanted to surprise you, Fire."

"Color me surprised, Tank. Hey guess who I ran into?" she asked as she led him into the house. I closed the door and pointed to the room, motioning I was changing. She nodded and continued to talk to the strange man in her house. Clearly she knew him, but who the hell was he? I roughly ran my fingers through my hair.

Ugh.

Chapter Thirty-Eight

ROSE

To say I was sore was an understatement, but I fucking loved it. Then I rounded the corner to see Richards at my door. I sat on the couch and Richards sat on the other end. He looked me up and down and grinned.

"Looks like Spokane is treating you well," he said, his tone full of suggestion.

My cheeks heated, and I tucked my loose hair behind my ear. I watched as his eyes darkened with some anger and looked at my wrist, seeing the marks.

Oh shit.

Pretty sure I was as red as a tomato. I could feel his eyes on me, then heard him huff a laugh.

"No shaming from me, but not going to lie. You gave me a damn heart attack."

"Sorry," I mumbled.

"No need. But who did you see?"

Oh, thank God.

Back on topic.

"Charlie," I whispered

"Wait, Charlie, as in…" His words trailed off, his expression only giving minor tells, but I knew them. He was trying to gauge the situation to know how to react, and I respected him for it.

"Yes, the one we saved on my last mission."

He slumped back onto the couch. "Oh wow. How are you holding up?" The concern he had was hard to hide in his voice. We weren't on an op, so he didn't have to have his guard up. But you can't take the training out of the man. At this point, it was just habit.

"Pretty well, actually. It was rough finding out, but Ren, Ren, always seems to know what I need, so he arranged for me to meet him alone in his office. He waited outside, giving us space. Hell, he even asked if I was okay with him being my dad's doctor, fully willing to assign another doctor if I wanted it."

"I'm assuming Ren was the pretty-looking man who answered the door?"

I laughed at the description, but he wasn't wrong. Ren kept his hair long and styled on top, short on the sides, his round face framed with some soft facial hair.

"Yes," I replied.

"Pretty sure that man is jealous. Did you tell him about me?"

Yeah, right. Wait, is he?

Fuck, why does that turn me on?

"Well, yeah, but I didn't show him a damn photo. Do you really think he is jealous?"

"Oh, I know he is, Fire. Let me go talk to him. While I do that, open the garage and have the guys unload. Then maybe we can all go out for breakfast."

"Okay. I'll go help." I headed outside as Richards went to my room to clear the air.

Chapter Thirty-Nine

REN

I heard knocking at the bedroom door as I slipped on my shirt. Obviously, it wasn't Rose, since she would have just walked in.

"Come in." I kept my voice as neutral as I could. The man from before walked in. He had his hands up in surrender.

"I come in peace. Fire said your name is Ren?"

"Rene, actually, but she calls me Ren," I said, my tone a little harsher than I intended. *Oh well.*

"Of course, my apologies. Look Rene, I was about to introduce myself when Rose came around the corner. My name is Richards. I served with her, and I'm the director of the CIA."

Well shit, now I felt like an ass for even being jealous.

"If you are worried how Rose feels about the jealous outburst, she has a tell and it was screaming that she definitely liked it."

I let out a relieved sigh, but my face still warmed up a bit. "I'm sorry if I put you off."

"Don't be. I came unannounced to your home and clearly you two had been up to something."

My mouth dropped open. "I, um, this is her place. I don't live here."

The man smirked. "Oh, you do, whether you know it yet or not. After the still sated look she had, and the marks. You got her wrapped so hard around your…" A smirk spread across his lips. "Around your cock, it's not even funny."

I choked on my spit at the forward comment. *Jesus, this guy is something.*

"Hey man, I am happy for her, and you seem like good people. I mean, if you weren't, Fire is deadly and I doubt you would have lived this long. Now why don't the three of us go grab a bite? I'm going to be around for a bit, helping with some of the back end of Killian's Eye. And I am on a well-deserved vacation."

"Well, if you are on vacation, are you going to stay here?" Rose asked as she came into the room.

"Um. I don't want to hear you two fucking all damn night, so I think I'll get a hotel."

I grimaced, and it didn't go unnoticed. "Yeah, this time of year. Good luck with that," I said.

"I can attest to that. That's how I ended up staying with Ren," Rose said as she wrapped her arm around my waist.

I watched as a lightbulb went off in Rose's mind. She looked at me, "Babe, since I plan to hold you hostage, do you think Richards can use your place?"

Now everyone was looking at me. "I, uh, I can have him there as a house sitter, but despite the crime in the area, there is the matter of the staff, well one in particular."

Richards raised an eyebrow.

"Richards, don't worry about it. It's nothing I can't handle. She is just in love with Ren, and I can't blame her. He is pretty great," Rose said as she placed a gentle kiss on my cheek.

"Okay…but what about the crime part? The man is a doctor,

right? Can he not get a decent place? No judgment, just confused."

I took a deep breath. "No offense taken. My mom is my whole world, and she was terrible with budgeting. She is retired and drowning in debt so I pay her bills. Her health is also failing and she requires special care, so I pay for her to live in a facility that can meet all of her needs and still feels like a home."

Rose moved and wrapped her arms around me, and I pulled her close, knowing she was trying to comfort me. My mom was a hard topic. I long ago tried to move her closer to me, but she refused to leave Seattle. With my position, vacations weren't as easy as I imagined. Even Richards had a rough time getting time off.

"Like Rose said, it isn't much, but you are welcome to it."

"Thanks man, and please call me Declan." He turned to look at Rose. "You still have your rental?"

"Yeah, you need it? I can ride with Ren and take a cab or bus."

"Oh, no, no, no. You can ride with me, yes, but you can also take the car while I'm at work." There was no way I would subject Rose to the public transportation our city had. Not to mention the cost of a cab in this town.

"You haven't bought your bike yet?" Declan asked, his tone full of surprise..

"No. Haven't had the chance yet, hoping to tomorrow, but I would need a ride to that. Because in theory I'm leaving with a bike."

That caught my interest. "I have a short day tomorrow. I'd love to go with you. Shit, I mean my dad used to ride before he passed."

"Did he really?"

"Yes, Dove. I got pictures to prove it."

Declan rolled his eyes. "Look at you, Fire, a temptress getting him all sentimental."

"I'm not going to buy one, if that is what you are implying. I don't need to. My dad's bike is in storage. Just needs some work done to it."

The look of shock and amusement on Declan's face dumb-founded me. Then I glanced at Rose and noticed that her mouth was dropped open. "What, what did I say?"

"Rose has a passion for working on cars and bikes. So you just got yourself a mechanic. Good thing all her stuff is here, including her tools."

"Oh," was all I could say. *Well, damn.*

Chapter Forty

ROSE

I was shocked to find out about the bike he had in storage and his mom. We hadn't had the chance to discuss it yet, but I had long figured out his mom was special to him, just a gut feeling based on how he was about me and my father.

After we finished getting ready, we headed to Molly's, a cute little breakfast place in downtown Spokane. Let's just say the bacon was some of the best I've ever had in my life. It was almost like a family meal, just a few people missing.

Somehow, I needed to help Ren see his mom. It was clear he missed her and by the look Richards gave me, he recognized it and would do his part to help me.

Ren gave Richards the key to his place and let him know how to get there. Even describing the office lady from earlier, just in case. Now we were heading to the hospital.

"Dove, do you want to have lunch with me in my office? I can order in."

"Sure," I said. "I'd love that. Also, can I use your office for a bit when we go inside? I need to look at the potential locations for my office."

"Of course." The way he said it was almost like he was shocked that I felt like I even had to ask, like everything that was his was mine, even at work. That was an amazing feeling and made me feel all warm and shit.

We headed straight to Ren's office, and he grabbed his white coat as I placed the files on his desk, then let my eyes take in the sight before me.

He was hot AF in his doctor attire.

When he caught me looking, well, more like gawking, he smirked and motioned with his finger to come to him. He was now leaning against his desk, and I placed myself between his legs.

"One of these days, Dove, this desk is going to have you bent over as I plunge into you, while my tie is gagging you to keep your screams of ecstasy muffled," he growled in my ear, making my knees go weak. He caught me with ease, still wearing the smug grin on his lips.

Asshole.

"Now, while I go do my rounds, I want you to think about how I will ravish you in this room and at home."

Home. God, I loved the sound of that.

Without another word, he gave me a quick kiss, then left the room, leaving me swooning.

It took me a bit, but I gathered my wits and began looking at the properties. All of them had great potential for sure, but one kept calling to me. It was near downtown, but not in it. The cost was on the higher side but had good parking, easy visibility, and wasn't too far from major roads.

I sent the address to Wes and got a reply.

> Damn, you never fail to amaze me. Again, my favorite as well. I will get the lease today. We can hopefully sign it tomorrow and get some office supplies ordered. Also, I am meeting Richards for lunch. Man scared the fuck out of me when he pulled up to my place. Thanks for the warning. Not.

He had a point. So far, we seemed to agree on everything. And his little tidbit on Richards, complete with emojis, made me smile.

> Not like I had any warning, so bite me. Also, I know a place to get furniture. I'll make it happen.

> Copy that.

Now that business was done, I headed to my dad's room. When I opened the door, I saw Charlie.

"Oh hey," I said.

"Hey, is Rene in?"

"He left to do rounds."

"I'll text him."

"Is it my dad?"

"Oh, no, sorry, didn't mean to worry you. It's another patient he consulted for yesterday. Your dad should be released soon."

"Awesome," I said. As he turned to leave, a thought hit me.

If Richards ever came here, it might get a reaction out of Charlie, and I had a feeling he would at some point.

"Hey um, I wanted to let you know Richards, my SEAL boss, is in town," I said softly. His face turned hard, then sad, before returning to normal. "I just didn't want you taken by surprise if he ever came in."

"Thank you for telling me. Now I can prepare myself for the possibility of seeing another one of my rescuers."

"Come to dinner tonight," I blurted out.

"Um, what?"

"Look, our past is a heavy one, and just as much as seeing me brought some closure to you, I think seeing Richards will do you some good. So come to my place, Ren will be there too."

He seemed to think about it for a bit, then nodded. "Okay, have Ren text me the time and place."

"Will do," I said as he left. I closed the door behind me and headed to my dad's room.

Chapter Forty-One

REN

Once I left my office, I had to palm down my cock. My attempt to torture my girl gave me a hard-on.

Fucking hell.

My phone buzzed with a text from Celeste.

> I got one of yours down here. Didn't see you come in.

I smiled to myself. Today was the first time in a while that I didn't come in through the ER. Honestly, she was probably worried as hell.

> Hey yeah, sorry. I will be there in two seconds.

When I rounded the corner into the ER, Celeste was right there. "Doctor Doux, what the hell?" she yelled at me.

Yep, she was worried.

"Sorry Celeste, I had to unlock my office for my girlfriend," I replied.

Her eyes softened a little. "Okay, fine, but next time, text me, will ya?"

"Deal," I said. "Now, who do you have for me?"

"Walter Williams, he came in with another heart attack."

"Good lord, again?"

"EKG confirmed."

Well, damn.

Despite all available meds, this man was losing his battle. The only thing left was a transplant and with his age, it would not be without a great deal of effort. Honestly, his only hope was the study. I hoped to receive news soon about my selection, then I would bring it up to him and the board. One thing was for sure, I would fight for this man. But for now I had to have a not so fun talk with him.

This man never failed to amaze me. He took the bad news well. His family was back and spent every second they could with him. Hell, half of them were in his room. He elected to be admitted for a couple of days to make sure he didn't immediately have another heart attack, but he wanted to be home. And I didn't blame him one damn bit. As I stepped out of the room, I heard my name called. I looked over to see Declan approaching.

"Hey Declan, what brings you here?"

"Well, I was literally in the area since I have an early lunch with Wes, Rose's business partner, and I am taking care of a few things. So I figured I'd swing by. I, um, wanted to know if you had plans tonight or..."

"Hello, Richards," I heard Charles say.

Oh shit.

It completely escaped me that they knew each other just like Rose. I tensed slightly, uncertain how this would go. It seemed to take Declan a second, but the recognition set in and was visible on his face.

"Don't worry, Commander. We're good. Rose made sure to

warn me, and we are also good," Charlie said calmly with a slight smile on his face.

Oh, thank God.

We both let out our breaths at the same time. "But to answer your question, Rose invited us to dinner tonight at her place."

Well damn, that works.

"Please Charlie, call me Declan or Richards."

"Of course, Richards."

"Doctor Doux, I got the test ordered for Mr.W., should be done first thing. He is also being moved to your floor this afternoon," Celeste said as she walked up to us. When she looked up, she noticed Declan standing next to me. Her mouth formed an O.

My eyes darted back and forth between them.

What the hell was happening?

It was like no one else existed around them. "Pretty sure there are sparks here," Charles whispered.

"I'd say. Hell, Celeste deserves it," I remarked.

"Let's leave them to figure out their connection. I needed to speak to you about Mrs. Thornton."

Oh boy.

She had her tests this morning, and the fact that he seemed to have results already was not good. When they sent them fast, it meant whatever it was, was obvious and didn't need a lot of time to review. They always did, but they would send a preliminary to our tablets ASAP so we could make orders.

Once we were away from the public, I leaned against the wall. "Alright, give it to me."

"Her heart is failing, hard and fast. She needs a transplant stat. Without one, she maybe has months."

Well, damn.

Chapter Forty-Two

ROSE

My dad beamed as I entered his room. We didn't say much. I told him about Richards visiting and the dinner I had planned tonight. He seemed extra interested when I brought up Charlie. I never kept anything from my father unless it was classified, but now he seemed to be the one holding secrets.

Interesting.

After a couple of hours, my dad dozed off, and I headed to Ren's office. I lay down on the couch and covered my eyes. Me and my big mouth made dinner plans, so now after lunch I had to shop and cook, then still be here to pick up Ren after work.

Fuck me.

Technically, I could order in, but where is the fun in that? Plus, my dad raised me better than that. A thought hit me. I wonder if I could get the recipe from Ashley? I met her in a bookstore coffee shop several years ago. Obviously I was rarely stateside, but last time I spent a few days in Seattle. Granted, I was working, checking on a tip about a target. But nothing came of it other than meeting Ashley Searls. She was quite the character for sure and managed to score a CEO while researching her book.

Of course, it didn't surprise me when it did well. We stayed in touch as much as possible, but over the last few years, that was practically nonexistent. Hell, I wouldn't be surprised if she thought I was dead. I opened my phone and shot her a text.

> Hey girl, no I'm not dead. Work has just been a bitch. I'm in the middle of a career change, so you should be hearing from me more. I mean, I'm only a few hours from you now. *wink emoji* But enough about me, we can FaceTime to catch up soon. The reason I am reaching out, well other than to say hi, is I was hoping to get my hands on your lasagna recipe. Some people are coming over tonight and, well, yeah. Can you help a girl out? *prayer hands*

After I hit send, I dropped my phone on my chest and covered my eyes, taking a moment to relax with my earphones in. It had been a while since I listened to some music, so I indulged. I jolted my arm down as I felt the couch shift around me. My muscles relaxed when I noticed it was Ren.

A soft moan escaped my lips as he straddled me on the couch, his blissful weight pressing down on me as his tongue swirled just below my ear, teasing me.

Hmm, yes.

"You ready for lunch, Dove?" he hummed into my neck, the vibrations sending a shiver down my spine.

"I want my dessert first," I said. In a swift move I doubt he saw coming, I had him under me as I crawled down his body until my face was level with his growing cock. He wasn't in scrubs today, so access was easy.

I grasped his shaft and stroked it up and down. His moan sent more desire through me.

Fuck, I loved pleasing him like this.

Using my tongue, I teased his tip. His hand fisted my hair before he slammed his full length into my mouth, making me gag against him.

"Oh fuck, Dove. Your mouth feels so damn good."

I picked up my pace as he thrust into me every now and again. I grazed his cock with my teeth and he bucked hard, ramming himself deep into my throat. His grip on my hair tightened and my hands moved to his balls, kneading them as I moved up and down.

Feeling particularly feisty, I moved my thumb to his ass and pressed down at the opening, pushing through just slightly. A growl erupted as he slammed into my throat, and his cum shot out so hard I struggled to take it all.

"Fuck," he moaned out. I sucked and swallowed until I had every last drop, then looked up to see a look of bliss on Ren's face. He didn't say anything, he just pulled me so I was on top of him, then kissed me. His tongue asked for entrance, asked for a taste, and I gave it to him.

So fucking sexy.

We pulled apart when his phone rang. He looked at the screen. "Celeste is bringing up our food."

I groaned, not wanting to get out of this position, but my stomach growled, reminding me it needed more than his cum to be satisfied. Ren stood and fixed his pants as I attempted to fix my hair, but it had been in a braid, so now I had it in a ponytail. Which, if anyone was paying attention, they could figure out what we just did.

Oh well.

Chapter Forty-Three

REN

To say I was surprised when I managed to sneak up on Rose was an understatement, but I was even more surprised when she swiftly flipped me onto my back and began pleasuring me with her mouth. Her skill was a force to be reckoned with. Then the way she took all my essence, sucking every last drop, almost made my erection return as soon as I came.

Celeste knocked on the door, and I opened it slowly. She looked me up and down and rolled her eyes before handing me the bag.

Well, she knows we just did something.

I understood her well enough to tell when she just knew something, and she never had to say a thing. It was the way her body reacted that told you everything you needed to know. Though it was odd she didn't voice it, seeing how she was a bit of a gossip queen.

Strange.

Oh well, another time's battle. For now, I had a lunch date.

I grabbed some plates from my cabinet and opened the food

containers. Since we only recently met, I didn't know everything she liked, so I ordered a bit of the main things: pepper steak strips, bacon-wrapped onion rings, baked Cougar Gold cheese dip, Pier 51 sampler, French onion soup and a State of the Onion burger.

The Onion was locally owned, and their food was always delicious. So I asked for Celeste to pick us up some and herself a dish for her time. The place was her favorite, so it hadn't taken much convincing.

Rose dished up a bit of each, then ended up adding more of everything except the sampler.

Noted.

I didn't mind though, since she was leaving me with my favorite. Once we ate almost all the food, I thought I might have to roll around the rest of the day. But apart from that, I was impressed she ate everything she did. I placed the leftovers in my mini fridge and sat on the couch.

Within seconds, Rose was straddling me, her lips brushing against mine. My hand immediately moved to her hips.

"Thanks for lunch, babe."

"Of course Dove. I'm glad you liked it. What are your plans?"

"I have to go shopping and cook."

"Hmm. I look forward to it." Before I could say anything else, she ground her hips against my cock, making me groan, and a bulge formed. "Fuck, Dove."

Her playful giggle vibrated my chest. "Well, you said to picture you taking me on your desk, so that's what I did, what I am doing. Fucking take me hard, right here, right now. I need you."

Oh, fuck me.

Chapter Forty-Four

ROSE

Now that Ren was back in the office, the idea of me bent over the desk was all I could think about. Eating could only distract me for so long. I practically begged him to take me, and my panties became soaked when he lifted me up and locked his door before placing me on his immaculately clean desk.

My clothes came off with urgency as his clothes just seemed to fall off. He turned his shirt into a gag and placed it in my mouth, his eyes searching for signs of discomfort, but all he got was desire. He turned me around and forcefully bent me over. I moaned at the dominance.

Fuck yes, just like I like it. He rammed his full length into me all at once. My muffled screams seemed to fuel him as he repeatedly pulled out and then thrust into me, making me take him all at once. The idea that someone could walk by and hear us only seemed to add fuel to the fire. His palm smacked my ass hard as he yanked my head back by my ponytail.

The longer we took, the more likely we would be caught. So this was going to be hard and fast, and I loved it. He nipped along my neck, then clamped down as he pulsed inside me, sending me into my own release, which seemed to give his a second wind.

"Fuck, Dove," he breathed into my ear.

A knock made us both jump and rush to get our clothes back on. I almost lost it in a fit of laughter when he crammed his knotted shirt in a drawer and slipped on a new one. If he thought that wouldn't be obvious, then he must be blind.

I sat on the couch and fixed my hair while Ren moved to open the door.

Chapter Forty-Five

REN

I opened my door to see my boss.
Fuck me.

Luckily, he seemed oblivious to what had just happened here.

"This came for you today. Congrats," he said, handing me a file before turning to leave. As he rounded the corner, he yelled, "Thank you for locking the door, but try not to make a habit of using your office as a love shack."

I coughed back my laugh, and heat warmed my cheeks.

Once the door latched shut, I locked it again. Based on the amused look on Rose's face, she heard that last part.

"Great, my boss knows how I plan to spend my lunches now."

"Maybe next time we can give him more of a show," she mused.

Hmm. There's a thought.

I moved into her and kissed her softly.

"What is in the file?" she asked.

Reluctantly, I pulled back. "I don't know, let's find out."

I sat on the couch. She positioned herself at my side, and I opened the folder, revealing a letter.

Dear Dr. Rene Doux,

Congratulations, you have been selected as the lead doctor for the heart study. We look forward to your knowledge and expertise. You will be working with Doctor Frank Stanson. The study will take place at your location since you are the lead MD. We will be in touch with your chief of surgery and the hospital director soon.

Sincerely,

Abby Lane

Research Specialist

Holy shit!

I fucking got it. Not only that, I was in charge. This was not only huge for me, but for the hospital. To say I had no words was an understatement. Rose kissed my cheek. I turned toward her, seeking more. Which she gave me. Her kiss was like no other congratulations I ever experienced.

My mind spun with hope for several of my patients and the countless others that would be transferring here in the coming months and even years. The hotel just down the hill a bit was going to be fully booked for a while, among some others, I presumed.

There was more in the file, but I didn't care right now. I would look it over in the morning.

"We can celebrate tonight after dinner, but I have to go shopping and then cook," Rose chimed.

"Hmm. I look forward to celebrating with you. Alone, in our room."

"Our room," she whispered.

"Unless you don't want it to be," I breathed, realizing what I just said. Don't get me wrong, I meant it, but still.

"No, I like it."

"Good."

I moved my lips to hers and kissed her hard. Her phone rang, and she pulled away. The smile that took over her face lit up the room.

"Now that I have the menu figured out, I have work to do. I'll be here at five to bring you home."

Home.

Fuck, I liked the sound of that.

"I'll get a ride with Charles. He is coming anyway, so it makes sense."

"True," she said. With one last kiss, she left me to deal with my growing bulge.

Chapter Forty-Six

ROSE

I was so damn happy for Ren. The fact that he was going to be the lead doctor in a study was a huge opportunity and was well deserved. Not to mention, based on the awards and degrees he held, it was a smart decision. To top it off, Ashley texted me back with the recipe and told me the best day to call her was next Friday.

Of course, I thanked her profusely and hurried to the store to get the supplies. And now I didn't have to worry about leaving to pick up Ren in a few hours. Dinner was at seven and the lasagna needed to be in the oven by five.

I headed to Safeway, then Walmart to grab all the supplies. Once I got to my place, I immediately went to work. Making noodles from scratch was not easy, but I managed. I put in the lasagna and started on the bread. As much as I wanted to make it from scratch, there just wasn't enough time. I used the recipe for the butter and put it all over the bread along with the oil.

One thing I loved about this kitchen was the double oven, so I put it in and set the appropriate alarms before starting the fire-place and sitting under a blanket on my couch.

I must have fallen asleep because I jumped when the alarm sounded. Once I recovered, I headed to the kitchen and took out the lasagna, removing the foil before returning it to the oven. Then I took out the bread to cool.

After a while, I looked at the clock and looked around.

Where was Ren? It was six thirty.

I pulled out my phone to text Ren when I heard the front door open.

Richards, Ren, and Charlie had their hands full of my stuff from Ren's place, plus suitcases of what I assumed were Ren's clothes. They said hello and moved everything into our room, then came back down.

"So that's why you're late?"

He buried his face in my neck. "Hmm yes. If I am staying here, then I need my clothes and, well, your clothes were all at my apartment."

"And I needed somewhere to put my clothes," Richards remarked, "and Charlie was Ren's ride, so he got recruited."

"By the way, Dove, it smells absolutely delicious in here," Ren said as he nuzzled deeper into my neck.

"Me or the food?"

"Both," he said, nipping at my ear. I leaned into him and he chuckled. "Easy, Dove. We have company."

Twisting my body, I looked to see if we were alone, and we were. The guys were in the living room messing with the TV.

"What if I want to misbehave?" I teased.

He pinned me to the pantry door.

"Then I will have to punish you," he said, his voice husky with his desire. Without a word, I stroked his cock. He moaned in response. "You are playing with fire, Dove.,"

"I am fire."

"Hmm, that you are." The sound of a voice clearing broke us from our moment. "Later, Dove," he whispered.

"Yes, Alpha," I said as I brushed against his growing bulge.

"Okay, horny rabbits, time to take a timeout. Do you need help with setting up the table?" Richards asked.

"Uh yeah, plates are in the far right cupboard. Silverware is in the drawer by the stove."

Richards moved about and got everything ready. I prepped the salad, then handed it to Ren to place on the table, while Charlie cut the bread. Once the alarm went off, I pulled out the lasagna and placed it on the table. Everything looked perfect and smelled divine.

We all sat around the table and began dishing up the food. When Ren took a bite, his eyes rolled back. I watched as Charlie and Richards did the same.

"Where the fuck did you learn to cook? This is amazing," Richards said. Everyone grunted their agreement as they continued to eat.

"I got the recipe from a friend. It's her family recipe."

"Well, thank her for me," Richards said with his mouth full.

Once we ate our food, everyone helped pick up everything, and I placed the leftovers in the fridge. We gathered around the fire and talked like old friends.

"Where is the little man tonight?" I asked Charlie.

"With my mom. When I called her after you invited me over, she volunteered. She thinks this will be good for me, getting to know the people who saved me. And I have to agree."

"We rescued you, but you've been fighting since. Now you have two more people in your corner, two people who were there with you," Richards chimed in.

"When you're ready, I know I would love to meet the little boy who carries on Jasper's name," I said.

"Of course. His birthday is coming up next month. You are more than welcome to come."

"We'll be there," Richards said.

After another hour, everyone left, leaving me and Ren to ourselves.

"Now I am going to finish what you started in the kitchen." His tone was low and threatening, making me squirm in anticipation.

Oh fuck.

Chapter Forty-Seven

REN

Now that we were alone, I wanted—no, needed—to punish her for teasing me the way she did. I carried her into our room. Our lips met, our breaths quickened as our hands roamed. Her body beneath me was such an amazing sensation. She fit so fucking perfectly. She was my person in every way, and honestly, I was beginning to think I could never function right without her.

My hands tore her clothes, followed by my own. Once fully naked, I moved her so she was level with my cock and my face was buried in her sweet kitty. I plunged my tongue into her, then moaned as she licked my tip.

Her skillful tongue made it hard for me to concentrate on my own task.

"Fuck, Dove," I moaned as she cupped my balls. My hips thrust toward her, seeking more as my tongue swirled around her clit. She moaned out "Alpha" repeatedly, the sound making my balls draw up as I brought her closer to orgasm. The skill of her tongue had me on the brink of release, and I couldn't hold off much longer.

Knowing she enjoyed pain, I bit down on her clit. She screamed out as her coconut juice filled my mouth. She didn't squirt, but she came pretty close based on the amount I swallowed. The taste of her in my mouth brought my own orgasm stumbling to the top. I thrust hard into her throat as my seed exploded out of me. And like the good little slut she is, she swallowed every last drop.

She lay there, limp from her release, but I wasn't done with her yet.

Far from it.

Without a word, I had her under me, face down. My knee separated her legs as my tip brushed against her ass. Since she liked pain, I didn't bother with prepping or lube. I applied pressure to her opening, and she raised her hips, seeking more.

"Hmm. You want my cock deep inside your ass, Dove?"

"Yes," she moaned.

"How do you want it, Dove?"

"Hard, rough," she panted.

"Hmm, good, cause I am going to punish your ass so hard that you will feel me for the next week."

Her responding whimper told me everything I needed to know. Without warning, I rammed my full length into her, making her cry out. "¡Hijo de puta!"

I didn't know what she said or what language it was, but fuck, it was sexy as hell. Her channel had my cock in a vise grip, and I had to grit my teeth to not explode my load right then. Moving my hips just slightly back, I wrapped her hair around my hand, then pulled her back into my cock.

"Scheiße, ja! Gib mir alles."

Oh, fuck me.

She continued to curse me in a multitude of languages, each one better than the next. I didn't need to understand what she said. I could feel it and hear it in her tone. Her ecstasy was fierce, and I relished it.

"Jouir maintenant," I ordered as I felt a shock shoot up my

spine. I was about to cum. I rammed into her with everything I had.

"Alpha," she screamed out.

Her channel tightened around my length as her body convulsed beneath me. My body tingled with the intensity of my own orgasm as jet after jet of my cum filled her perfect ass. When I was finally empty, I flopped down on the bed and pulled her body into mine.

That was intense.

Chapter Forty-Eight

ROSE

When he took my ass hard, my brain short-circuited. For some reason, English wasn't coming to me, so I cursed out my pleasure in Spanish and German and I don't even remember what else. But the way he reacted told me he liked it, not to mention his order for me to cum in his family's language.

Like, damn.

Now I was in his arms, my body still tingling from the two intense orgasms he just inflicted. Honestly, I never wanted him to leave. Every part of me wanted him to live here permanently. Get rid of his apartment and just be here with me.

Is it too soon?

"What are you thinking about so hard, Dove?" he mumbled into my neck.

Fuck, what do I even say?

I refused to lie to this man. My extended silence didn't go unnoticed, and I was flipped to my back as Ren moved his body over mine.

"Dove, you can tell me anything."

"I—" *Fuck, could I say it?* I took a deep breath, taking in his beautiful eyes that were filled with concern. "I don't want you to go back. Honestly, I don't want you to sleep anywhere else," I mumbled as my eyes dropped in shame at how desperate I sounded. His hand cupped my chin and turned me to face him.

"Then I won't," he said, then claimed my lips with his own. My heart soared. He was never going to leave me. When he pulled away, his eyes locked with mine. "Dove, I know it's early, but I need you to know this. I love you with everything I have. Moving in with you is a no-brainer. You don't need to say it back. But this is how I feel, and I want you to know."

My mouth seemed to forget how to work, my voice was gone. No, I couldn't say the words yet. My brain was wild with everything happening recently and I needed time. I have strong feelings for this man, but was it love?

Shit, I don't know.

I pulled him to my lips and kissed him. The kiss said everything I couldn't say. Including I'm sorry. When breathing became necessary, I pulled back.

"I know, Dove. I know," was all he said.

It never failed to amaze me that he seemed to know what I meant without me ever saying a word. What we have is special and I would be stupid to deny that.

"What are the plans for tomorrow?"

"I'm going bike shopping and getting the office set up," I said.

"Sounds good. Now sleep."

Chapter Forty-Nine

REN

Rose didn't say "I love you" to me, but her kiss did. I would wait until she was ready to say it. Tonight she was going bike shopping, so I took the day off to see my mom and pick up my bike from storage. When I told her I might not be able to go with her like I thought, she took it in stride. Especially when I told her I was going to check on my mom. What she didn't know was tonight I would surprise her with my ride.

I left in the very early hours in the morning so I could get there, do what I needed to, and get back. The facility was just as gorgeous as I remembered as I pulled into the property around 7:00 a.m. When I walked in the door, the nurse smiled warmly at me.

"It's been a while, Doctor."

"It has, hasn't it? Work and life have been crazy. How's my mom?"

"She is doing pretty well. Yesterday was tough, but she is doing better this morning."

"That's good," I said, then headed up to her room. I opened the door and my mom's warm smile was immediate.

"Ren, you're here!"

"Yes Mama, I'm here." We spent the next few hours catching up. I told her about Rose and she practically begged me to bring her by soon, which was already the plan. When I left, my mom was bragging to all the nurses that I was in love. Seeing her so happy for me was an amazing feeling.

I was ready to go home, but I had to pick up my bike, a blue 1971 Shovelhead. It technically ran, but it had been sitting for a while, so a tune-up was in order. From the sounds of it, Rose would love to do it, so that was a plus.

Once I loaded it onto the rented trailer, I strapped it down, taking a step back to admire its beauty. When I got back to the house, I wheeled it into the garage. Then returned the trailer and truck to my friend, who gave me a ride to the parts store, then back home. Everything was set up and ready for Rose. I looked at the time, 4:00. I was exhausted but I made it.

My friend brought me to the office Rose rented so I could go with her to shop for her bike. Her smile lit up the room as I entered. I wrapped my arms around her waist and pulled her into a kiss.

"I missed you, Dove."

"Hmm, and I missed you," she purred as her hand brushed over my bulge. Around her I was pretty much always semihard. It was the effect she had on me. I growled low in response. We had company, so I wouldn't fuck her little kitty right now, though the thought was tempting.

"Okay, lovebirds, you two are intense," the man, who I assumed was her business partner, said.

Rose's blush made her look so fucking sexy. I reluctantly pulled away from her, but kept her pulled to my waist.

"I'm Wes. You must be Ren," he said, holding out his hand.

I took it and nodded. "Nice to meet you."

After a while, I sat in one of the chairs and pulled her onto my lap. My hand moved up and down her back while the two of them talked strategy on a missing person case they had already started. She turned in my lap and looked at me.

"Babe, do you think Cobb will give us the case file? I meant to ask the other night but, well, you know."

Oh, I do.

"I can ask," I said as I pulled out my phone and called him.

"Hey man, what's up?" he answered.

"Hey, do you think you can do me a solid?"

"What do you need?"

"Remember my girlfriend Rose?"

"Yeeesss."

"She is opening an investigation business and was asked to work on a missing person's case but needs the official file."

"I'd have to run it by my boss…if she has the credentials, I don't see a problem."

"She is still active CIA, Cobb."

"Oh well, yeah, let me double-check with my boss, but I should be able to make it happen."

"Thanks, man."

"You owe me, R."

"I know," I said, then hung up.

"Hmm, thanks, Alpha," she whispered seductively in my ear. I fought the urge to moan as my cock twitched.

"Always for you," I growled.

I noticed Wes roll his eyes, but he didn't say anything. As they were finishing up, my phone buzzed and I looked down.

> So my boss okayed it. Can you guys meet up tonight? At like 8 for dinner?

I turned the phone to show Rose, and she smiled.

"It shouldn't take too long to get my bike, so that should work," she said. I replied with a thumbs up. Once everything was done for the day, Rose and I headed to the Harley shop.

We walked through the displays hand in hand as she strad-dled multiple bikes before settling on a new red Softail. She looked hot as fuck on the bike and my cock was weeping in my pants. Luckily, I was wearing clothes that wouldn't show the damp spot unless you were really looking, and the only one who should be was Rose.

Oh fuck, that thought was sinful.

She made some customizations so it would be here in about a month. Just enough time to fix up my bike, which now I needed to show her. But first we had dinner plans, so we had to go home and change.

While getting ready, I had a thought. "Hey Dove."

"Yes, babe."

"You know, I might know someone who can help."

"Oh, and who is that?" she asked.

"I served with him in my army days. He moved to special forces after I was discharged but also did some police work before and after his time in the Rangers. The man is massive and a good enforcer, but also a tracker. He is about to retire after twenty years."

"Hmm. I'll consider it."

I scowled.

"Okay, okay. What's his name? I'll talk to Wes about it."

"Liam Perkins."

She pulled out her phone and sent a text. When she got the reply, she turned her phone to me so I could read it.

> He sounds like a perfect addition to our team. Let's do it.

Perfect.

Chapter Fifty

ROSE

I wore work clothes worthy of the CIA since I was getting official files on the prerogative of my agent status. Once I had my weapons secured to my body and my ID, I walked out of the room. Ren had already changed and was filling water bottles.

As I rounded the corner into view, he looked up. I watched as he thoroughly looked me over, a glint of desire in his eyes. "Please tell me that once you leave the CIA, you will still wear this."

"For you, always," I replied. "Besides, depending on the case, this outfit might be needed."

He pulled me to him and tilted my chin up, stealing a kiss. "Good."

We got in the car and headed to a Chinese place called Ming Wah. When we got there, the place was quiet and the only person inside was Cobb and the two staff. I had to admit, the restaurant was beautiful.

Once we were seated, I looked at the menu.
Ooh yummy.

I ended up ordering a No. 7 with sweet and sour chicken instead of fried shrimp. Of course I got soup and extra sauce. Now it was time to talk business.

"I see you are in uniform, as some would call it," Cobb remarked.

"Yes. I figured since you used my active agent status, I would look the part. I see you are also in uniform."

He fidgeted slightly and looked uncomfortable under my gaze.

Odd.

"Yeah, I…um…just got off work."

"I see."

Something was off about Cobb.

What the hell was it?

I glanced at Ren, and he also sported a confused look. This was weird. Ren has known this man for years and now he was acting like he was hiding something. When the waitress came with our food, I turned to look at her. Showing her my ID under the table, I told her to leave us alone for thirty in Chinese. She bowed her head and scurried off to grab the cook and go outside.

Now we were alone.

"Okay, Cobb, what's the deal?" My tone was stern but calm. He didn't speak. "Cobb, you know I am CIA, and that I worked as a Navy SEAL before that. I know when someone is withholding information or is up to something. I also know that you have been around me in my official capacity before, so it's not that I make you nervous. You are also smart enough to know Ren is my partner and because of that, you have my respect. But right now, even he knows something is up. So spill."

"I…do you know anything about 'Red Hawk'?"

What the fuck?!

How the hell?

My back stiffened at the name. The mission I completed four years ago after spending a year in the field trying to get my man. And I did.

"And how would you know anything about it?" I asked, somehow keeping my tone neutral.

CIA training for the win.

He looked really nervous, almost like he would piss his pants if I moved suddenly. Which if he were a bad guy, I would totally use that to my advantage, but he was an ally.

"A guy I know through some friends was talking about it, talking about you. He said he was there, and that you took down his lover."

Now that got my attention.

My mind flooded with images of that day, trying to remember. The only other person on that mission was Agent Kevin Janx. Suddenly, it all made sense. After I killed the target, he went nuts and was removed from duty. If he was compromised and involved, that would explain everything.

Without a word, I pulled my phone from my pocket and called Barks.

"Aren't you on leave? Why are you calling me?" he snarled.

"Barks, this is urgent and important. I know Richards is already here, but this needs you as well. How fast can you get here?" My tone left no room for argument. He knew the tone well, and he damn well knew I wouldn't say anything on an unsecured line.

"I can be there by morning."

"Good, I'll send you my address."

I hung up and shot a text to Richards about breakfast at my place in our code for a meeting. Basically, I misspelled the word. Now to ensure our witness stayed protected. "Cobb, come to my place tonight. You'll be safe there."

He didn't speak, he just nodded. My coded message would have Richards at my place tonight, not tomorrow morning. This was big, and I needed all the help I could get. I wanted Wes, but that was Richards's call since this was CIA related.

I rode with Cobb while we headed to my place. As soon as we

pulled up, Richards was out of his car. Once inside, I locked the doors and set my security system.

"Alright, spill, Fire."

"Red Hawk."

I watched as his face turned cold and he stiffened. "What about it?"

"It seems Kevin was involved with the target and is seeking revenge."

"And what does he have to do with this?" He pointed at Cobb.

"He is our informant and now the man we need to protect."

"On it," he said. I knew he had more questions and he would get his answers, but right now Cobb's protection was at the top of the priority list. "Did you call Barks?"

"Yes, I did. He'll be here in the morning."

Using my secured computer, we pulled up the file. "Richards, can I call in my business partner? This is classified, but we could use his expertise on computers."

"You took the words right out of my mouth. Get him here now."

Without a word, I was on the phone getting Wes to head this way. "It's likely he knows Cobb is connected to you. So I just sent some agents to your dad's room. He will be watched like a hawk." He winced. "Sorry, poor choice of words."

That was a relief. I also knew they wouldn't tell my dad details, but only what he needed to know. Richards asked Cobb questions, finding out everything he knew, while I looked over the case and my notes.

When someone knocked, we all jumped, and our guns were out in seconds. Once I determined it was Wes, I holstered my gun and everyone else followed suit as I let him in. He searched for anything that would prove the connection wasn't just speculation.

No one slept as we worked hard long into the night. Richards had taken care of Cobb's work schedule, putting him on leave.

The only person who knew where he was located was the mayor. Yes, the mayor.

Another knock sounded, and I checked to see if it was Barks. It was. I let him in, and Richards immediately debriefed him. But what really got me was the look he gave Cobb.

Is that interest? Surely not.

"Bingo," Wes called out. We all looked as he spun the computer screen around, showing us messages and photos. To say they were incriminating was an understatement.

"How the hell were these not found before?" I asked.

"The mission was a success. No need to dig further. But I see now that maybe we should have," Barks said.

"Let's go get him," Richards said.

"Wait," Cobb said. We all turned to him. "He is well-connected, and I suspect he is involved in a few cold cases, including the file I was bringing to Agent Conrad."

Wes was now on the computer again, pulling up everything he could on the man. Sure enough, he was tied to some government officials and seemed to have some incriminating timelines with some cold cases. This was something big and needed all hands on deck.

"Looks like Killian's Eye has its first case. You are in charge, Rose. The CIA will help where they can, even the FBI is on your side."

Let's do this.

Chapter Fifty-One

REN

Things had been crazy. Cobb was in protective custody at the house, and I was as well, essentially. Not wanting her dad going home to chaos, I prolonged his stay a bit. Basically, I am weaning him off his meds to see how he does. The idea seemed to thrill him and Charles. Though I didn't know why Charles cared so much. Well, I mean, other than his connection to Rose. I filed papers and got things ready for the study, including enrolling my two patients plus a few others who met the criteria, after asking them, of course.

Richards was always close by. Obviously HIPAA was a thing, so he never came into a room with me, but still. This went on for several weeks and I was getting tired of all of it. My buddy Liam was also doing well, and he and Wes seemed intense, almost like they hated each other. But hey, as long as they would get the job done, right?

"Dove, when will we get our house back?"

"Soon. I promise. We are close to nailing it."

I groaned, flopped onto our bed, and covered my eyes. When

I felt her straddle me, I moved my arm to look at her, placing my hands on her hip, making my cock tease her folds. "Dove," I moaned as she rubbed against me, giving my tip the craved friction. "We still have guests."

"Hmm. I made the room soundproof, Alpha. Only way to hear us is to be directly outside the door or have it open."

Oh, fuck me.

Without a second thought, I had her flipped onto the bed with my body against hers. "So you want me to claim that slutty kitty of yours? I ought to punish you for not telling me sooner about the soundproofing. Making me wait, so goddamn naughty," I growled, nipping at her ear.

"Then punish me Alpha," she breathed.

Lord help me.

I was about to blow my load and I hadn't even touched her yet. We needed supplies. I jolted from the bed and grabbed them. Honestly, I was turned on by the fact that both her bosses were in the house and we were about to ravish each other.

Fuck.

As I secured her wrists and legs, she squirmed in anticipation. My Dove liked pain, so today I would give her just that. I pulled the metal clamps from my bag and clipped them to her dark, erect nipples, watching her as she licked her lips. Then I grabbed the knife and let the devilish grin take over my face. Her whimper made my cock leak in anticipation of her warmth.

Oh, she liked this.

And I was going to deliver.

Chapter Fifty-Two

ROSE

Oh fuck.

Not only was this man mine, but he seemed to know every twisted fantasy I had. The small amount of electricity coursing through my nipples was about to make me cum. Then he pulled the knife. The sound that came out of me sounded like a desperate cry for more.

"Don't move," he ordered.

I fought the urge to squirm as he ran the sharp blade up my leg and body until the tip was sitting under my chin. As the tip poked at my jaw, I all but purred. My body yearned for him to break the skin. When he pulled back the blade, I whimpered, but as the electricity jolted me, it turned into a moan.

The damp sensation of the sheets below me told me I was leaking badly, and based on the random drops I felt on me, so was he. Once the electricity stopped, the knife was back on my breast and the clamp near it was gone. He twisted the tip just to the left of my nipple until blood oozed out.

Oh God, yes.

He dove down and sucked and licked as the knife rested on my chin. The power he emit was so fucking hot. I moaned as his free hand cupped my pussy.

"So fucking wet, Dove."

I fought the urge to move, to speak, but I knew better. The clamp that had been on my nipple was now clipped on my folds. My muscles tightened with anticipation. With the touch of a button, my body jolted from the electricity, sending me on the verge of orgasm. Then his full length drove into me all at once, sending me over the edge.

OH FUCK!

My body convulsed from the intense orgasm that never seemed to end as my cum gushed out of me.

"Fuck, Dove. I love it when you squirt," he growled.

As I came down from my orgasm, I almost felt high. His thrusts were relentless, and I knew with one more jolt I would come undone all over again.

He bit down on my breast hard as more electricity hit my body. His deep, animalistic growl filled the room, and if our room wasn't soundproof, it would have alerted everyone to our activities. I screamed out my own pleasure as my body shook with another orgasm.

His tongue licked the bite mark as he detached everything from me, tossing it off the bed. The exhaustion was evident as he crashed onto the bed beside me, releasing the restraints before pulling me into him as we both lay there in complete bliss.

"Dove, that was just what I needed," he grumbled.

"Hmm, yes," I said as my eyes grew heavy. The intensity of what we just did made my body collapse from exhaustion.

"We have company," Richards's commanding voice came over the earpieces we all had. I jumped from bed and dressed in less than ten seconds.

"Go to the safety room," I barked at Ren, who just put on his sweats. He took off down the hall and caught up to Barks and

Cobb. Barks was to keep them safe while the rest of us took care of this.

This was it.

All our work to lure him into our trap, and now it was showtime.

WITH REN AND COBB SAFE, I had a job to do. Richards was outside, ready to trap our guy. Liam was hiding in my home while Wes was on the computers doing his thing, hiding from view as well. As far as our target knew, I was alone with Cobb.

The front door opened behind me, but I didn't look. Instead, I counted on my senses and training.

"Normally when one comes to another's home uninvited, they knock," I said as I moved the knight on the chessboard. What the man behind me didn't know is this was how I was communicating with my backup. Each piece was a coded beep in our earpieces.

"Oh, don't play like you didn't know I was coming. Cobb was just a ploy in my game. He led me straight to you. But you left the CIA and only one man knows you are here, and I don't see him anywhere."

This man was something if he thought Richards wasn't here. Not only that, but any amount of surveillance would have told him Richards was here. This indicated he was most likely alone. Our plan was built on his performance as an agent, and he hated the ground work. Now it would cost him.

I moved another piece on the board, his piece, as if I was playing myself. "I see you haven't changed. Hate groundwork, just want the action. How many times did I tell you the importance of everything, every step in the mission? Yet here we are. You are standing in my house, knowing I knew you were coming, and you are alone. Not only that, but dumb enough to think I am alone."

He looked around but didn't see anyone. I moved my bishop.

"Check," I said. The man, no, the traitor, took a few steps back, as Liam appeared to materialize into existence. I continued playing the game. To say I was Liam's biggest fan right now was an understatement. "I only have one question. Why?"

"He was my everything. I didn't plan it. But I fell for him."

"No, you fell for his trap," I retorted. "You know the research I did that you didn't want to hear? It would have told you the way he operates. He made you as CIA, though he didn't make me. But he played you and turned you into a traitor. He never loved you."

I tossed a folder in front of him and he bent to look it over. The emails between the target and his second showed plain as day what I said was fact.

"The mission was a success, so we never went through anything until we found out about you, and well, that is only some of what we found."

He was shaking his head now, his breathing erratic, panic in his eyes. I smirked at his deer in headlights eyes watching as I moved my next piece on the board.

"Check mate," I said. He spun around to run out the door but slammed into Richards's chest instead. The impact threw him back, and he landed on his ass.

I stood and gripped his arm, then pushed him to the wall as I gripped his hands behind his back. "Kevin, you are under arrest for treason, breaking and entering, and probably some other things."

As I read him his rights, a patrol vehicle pulled up and Cobb's chief came out. "So this is the guy."

"Yes, Richards will accompany you to the jail. He is very dangerous. We have agents en route to take him."

"Of course. Thank you for protecting my guy."

"It was nothing, sir."

With a quick nod, the three of them left. I helped Wes finish up his part, and he and Liam left. Now to tell Cobb he was safe again.

Chapter Fifty-Three

REN

While we waited for the scene upstairs to unfold, we just talked. Barks really was a good guy, just hurting and not coping well. One thing Cobb said was he needed to have a talk with Rose and also Richards before he returned to Langley. Put everything out there so they could support him in this, in his healing.

When the door opened, I let out a relieved breath to see Rose. She came straight to me and sat in my lap, pulling me into a kiss. Her tongue demanded entrance, and I gave it to her, not caring in the slightest that we were not alone. As the kiss grew heated, I pulled back.

"Dove, we still have company," I whispered. She buried her face in my chest and I could feel the heat in her cheeks, which only made me chuckle. "I'm guessing since you are down here, everything is clear?"

"Yes. He is in custody and being transported now," she said. Cobb let out a breath. "Cobb, you're safe now. Barks will stay with you until he is transported, just in case, but it's over."

Cobb practically jumped into Barks's arms, and I noticed Rose looking curiously at me.

I'll explain later, I mouthed, and she nodded.

We all made our way upstairs, and I headed to the kitchen to prepare some easy food. Nothing like good old Kraft mac n' cheese with corn and chicken.

As I placed the plates on the table, I looked at Rose. "I know my skills aren't as good as yours in the kitchen, but I figured I'd put something together since you just worked."

Her warm smile made my heart flutter in my chest.

"Thank you," she said as she took a bite. "It reminds me of when I was a child. My parents used to make this all the time."

That was not what I was expecting at all.

Though I loved learning something about her childhood, especially something similar to my own. We ate in silence. All of us looked up when the door opened and Richards came inside.

"He has officially been booked and is awaiting our transport agents but is being watched by one who was at the hospital until they get here."

Oh, thank God.

"Barks, let me take you and Cobb to Cobb's place. Rose, the other agent will stay on your dad until Kevin is at Langley."

With that, the three of them left, and I walked up behind Rose and wrapped my arms around her.

"Shall we go take that nap now?" I mumbled into her ear.

"Hmmm yes, but first I need a bath," she said, then turned to look at me. "Want to join me?"

Fuck yes I do.

"Always, Dove. You earned a nice bath, complete with a back rub by some skilled hands."

"Oh, you hired a masseuse. When will they be here?"

I glared at her, and she busted out laughing.

Oh, now she was just being a brat.

The palm of my hand swatted her ass, making an echo as she scurried to the bathroom. I put some essential oils in the tub as I lowered myself into its depths, and she positioned herself between my legs. The jets moved the water against our body as we relaxed into the oasis.

My hands were moving across her neck and shoulders as she closed her eyes, letting out soft moans as I worked her tense muscles.

"Dove, you're so damn tight," I groaned, feeling the knots in her muscles.

"My muscles aren't the only thing that's tight."

Fucking hell.

"Oh, I know, Dove, and I will be claiming that tight little kitty again soon, but first we need to rest."

Chapter Fifty-Four

ROSE

R en spent the next few days at home with me. Including the weekend, it was closer to a week, but his boss said he should take the time off since he had the study starting soon. He still had another couple of weeks of time off left. My dad was finally home, and everything was looking good.

Today I was supposed to have lunch with Barks before he headed back to the office. But first I had to take my dad to his appointment.

"I've had a surprise for you for a bit. Let me show you this afternoon," Ren said.

I moved in close to him. "Oh, really now? Why have you been making me wait, Alpha? I thought I was being a good little pain slut."

The growl that erupted from deep in his chest vibrated me to my core.

Oh, fuck me.

My body was slammed into the wall, causing some pictures to

fall. I whimpered as my arousal made itself known and his hard cock poked at my stomach.

"If you didn't have places to be, I would punish you for being a sassy little thing and make your little kitty so sore you can't walk right. All while making you squirt over and over again until you feel like you need to sleep for days," he growled.

Jesus Christ.

With one last nip at my ear, he pulled back as I desperately tried to catch my breath. I could see the pleased smirk on his face and I couldn't help but roll my eyes.

Bastard.

Before I knew what was happening, my pants were down and I was bent over the couch. The sound of his own pants hitting the floor made me shiver in anticipation. I turned my head in time to see him positioning himself and a strap on to my holes.

Oh fuck.

All at once, my ass and my pussy were filled to the hilt as he thrust into me. I cried out with pleasure as he continued to ram into me. The intensity of being double filled was too much for my body and it went limp.

"Fuck," I moaned.

His hand reached down and circled my clit as his other hand added the much needed pressure to my throat. My orgasm came hard and fast. His own pace quickened and I knew this was about to be over. I rammed back into his thrusts, and his hand tightened on my neck and my clit.

His rough, hard growls filled the room as we both came hard. When he released me, his palm came down hard on my ass.

"I will punish you more later. Now go to your meeting, slut."

Oh God.

My body shivered.

I fucking loved it when he called me that and he damn well knew it, too.

I MADE my way to The Old Spaghetti Factory and gave Barks's name to the hostess. When I got to the table, I sat down.

Shit.

I was so damn sore from the pounding Ren gave me. To say I was thankful that I arrived first was an understatement. No one needed to see my likely comical attempt at sitting down. Hell, I was probably going to sit here until everyone else left first. If the hostess noticed, she didn't utter a word. Richards arrived first, then close behind him was Barks.

We looked over the menu and made our orders before getting down to business.

"When everything went down with Kevin, Rene asked me something while we were waiting in the safe room. We had a good long talk, the three of us, and they said I needed to talk to the two of you, which is why I asked you guys to have lunch with me."

Neither I nor Richards spoke. We just nodded our heads slightly.

"I know I have been an ass as your boss, Rose, and I am truly sorry. You, you look like my sister, and I lost her to a violent man when my identity became compromised while on a mission. He killed her just because she was my family."

My heart ached for the man sitting in front of me.

Shit, I had no clue.

Based on Richards's face, he hadn't either.

"So I responded by making my no family rule, thinking I was protecting agents from the same fate, but in reality I almost cost your father's life since the doctors couldn't reach you."

He paused for a moment as the waitress put down the food.

"Then I met Rene and saw the love he had for you in a short amount of time, and I found someone to stir the dormant lover in me. Cobb told me his story and has been helping me since. Hell, Rene got me a psychiatrist he knows in Langley and I start sessions Monday. I know you are leaving the agency, but I want you to know it really has been an honor working with you and you will be missed dearly. Richards and I will make sure we give you work stateside as it comes and you are able. Hell, I may even consult you on a mission here and there. I just hope you can forgive me for how I treated you over the years."

I remained silent as the words sunk in.

Who did he find?

"I'm happy you are getting help now. I forgive you."

The relieved breath he let out said it all.

Richards patted him on the back. "I guess I dropped the ball too. I never looked at your file. If I had, I would have known this and helped you a long time ago, Barks. For that, I am sorry."

Barks's smile was warm. "Honestly, boss, I wasn't ready. As messed up as this all was, it needed to happen this way. The person who let me see it was in part Rose, but also Cobb. Cobb is the someone who woke me inside."

Well shit.

"You're gay?" Richards asked.

"Fuck, I don't know. I have only ever been with women, but I can't deny the way I feel about the man, the way my body reacts to him. Hell, I hardly want to leave and go back. I'd rather be here with him. But he insists and says if we want to be together then we will figure it out. For now, I have an obligation to the CIA and he is under contract for the next six months, so it will be long distance for a while. Which I can live with."

My head spun with everything he just dropped on us. The cold-hearted boss appeared to be in love and not only that, but wore it well. I was honestly happy for him.

We finished eating our food, and the guys left first. As I went to leave, someone sat across from me. I looked up to see the lady from the apartment. Without a word, I pulled my phone out under the table and texted Barks, Cobb, Wes, Liam, Richards, and Ren in the group chat, knowing it was open from earlier. I typed one word.

Trouble.

This bitch was psycho, and I was not underestimating her. I noticed Wes come in right away and acknowledged him without notice from her. He was likely recording and communicating with the others.

"Look, I don't know what you want or how you knew I was going to be here, but I can assure you I do not care to be ambushed after lunch with my bosses," I said.

"Maybe you should have thought of that before you took my man," she snarled.

What the actual fuck?

"I stole no one's man. Rene is a grown adult who is fully capable of making his own choices. In case it wasn't clear enough, he chose me. If the move out notice wasn't enough, I don't know what would be."

"HE. IS. MINE. I will make sure of it, even if it means taking out a few people along the way."

That made me raise an eyebrow. "And how do you plan to do that?" I asked, knowing the answer but needing her to say it.

The sound of a round being chambered was loud in the restaurant. Luckily no one panicked, likely didn't recognize the sound like I did. I knew Wes heard it and was ready and waiting for me to give the cue.

"So you plan to kill me?"

"If I have to, yes," she said. The bitch seriously thought she stood a chance with her tiny-ass gun. I took a casual sip of my water and laughed.

"Oh sweetheart, you really think you, an apartment manager, can take out a former Navy SEAL and CIA agent? My dear, you are mistaken."

As soon as the words left my lips, I disarmed her using my legs and placed the knife pointing out on my plate. Within seconds, Liam was behind the woman putting her in handcuffs as I kept eye contact with her.

"Hmm, next time, know who you are going up against before you make stupid moves like that. Well, if you are lucky enough to get a second chance," I said, then walked out as Cobb was coming in.

Chapter Fifty-Five

REN

As soon as I got the message "Trouble," my anxiety went through the roof. Even knowing it was pointless, I tried to call her hoping, it was all just a bad dream, dreading that this was real. I called Richards next.

"Hey man. Your apartment manager is here. From what we know so far, she showed up after Barks and I left. Wes is inside doing his thing and Liam is just walking up now. No need to come our way. We got this."

God, I hope so.

"Okay, I have an emergency surgery I am scrubbing in for. But if I need to know anything, get word to Celeste."

"Copy that."

Don't get me wrong, I know Rose can hold her own, but I can't help but worry. My feelings for her are strong and that definitely heightened it. Being that I was by far the least trained of everyone, it was best for me to stay away. But I was going crazy sitting in the house.

Richards told me about some of the issues the manager had

been giving him while he stayed there. The bitch seriously had the nerve to try to enter my place with no notice, saying she smelled smoke. Like, what the actual fuck.

Then I sent my move out notice and removed all my stuff. Shortly after, Richards started staying at the house instead of my apartment since she threw a fit about that too.

Fucking psycho.

Officially, I still had the place until the end of the month, but it was cleaned out and the keys were to be turned in tomorrow. Which would still happen, but now it seemed I wouldn't have to deal with certain staff members when I did.

When the front door opened, Rose strode in, and I let out my breath. I opened my arms, and she walked into them as I just held her. She told me everything that went down, including how the bitch pulled a gun on her. I was fuming so much I'm pretty sure my skin probably resembled a Hot Tamale.

She placed her hand on my chest and leaned into me. "Alpha, I am fine. I was not alone, and my training kept everyone safe."

"I know, I just—"

"You love me and worry about me."

I let out a sigh. "Yeah."

"I know and…" She kissed my lips as I tightened my hold on her. "And I love you too."

My breath hitched and my heart almost jumped out of my chest at the words I longed to hear from her perfect lips.

My Dove loved me.

With immense passion, my lips met hers as I sought to taste her, taste her love. Her mouth opened as she wrapped her legs around me, allowing me to carry her into our room. This time I would cherish her, make love to her. Slow and sensual, allowing my love to pour into her being as hers did mine.

I laid her gently on the bed as I slowly took off my clothes, watching as she did the same. Despite knowing my love for her for a while, I still saw her in a new light. She was mine in every way and soon I would marry this woman. At least, that is what my gut told me.

My hands roamed her body, worshiping her every inch and curve. As I moved up her body, I kissed a trail, pausing over her perfect kitty, giving it some extra love before continuing until my lips met hers again.

Our tongues danced together as my hand cupped her wetness, making slow deliberate circles on her clit while my other hand played with her nipples. Her breathing hitched at the intrusion of my fingers inside her warm channel. The deep moan she let out as I worked myself in and out made my cock leak profusely with pre-cum.

I pressed down on her swollen clit with my thumb and she groaned as her cum covered my fingers. Slowly, I brought my fingers to my lips and licked every last drop. Then I carefully crawled over her and positioned myself at her entrance. As I slid my length into her warmth, my arms wrapped around her head, holding her close and pushing deeper.

Oh fuck.

Her responding moan was so damn erotic. I slowly moved my cock out to the tip before sliding back in. The sweet torture filled me with bliss.

"Je t'aime tellement putain," I whispered in her ear as her walls tightened around my cock and my own release spilled deep inside her.

Once I pushed every last drop back inside her, I slipped out and lay next to her, pulling her into my chest.

"Anch'io ti amo," she whispered into my chest.

"What does that mean, Dove?"

"I love you too."

I moved my lips to hers and we just kissed. After a while, I tilted her chin up and met her gaze with mine.

"I want to show you my surprise. Get dressed," I said.

She slipped out of bed and dressed as I did the same. I took her hand in mine and led her to the garage. Once there, I positioned myself behind her and covered her eyes with my hands.

"Is this really necessary?"

"Yes," I replied. After I guided her down the steps, I uncovered her eyes. Her sharp inhale was the first thing I heard.

"Is this your dad's bike?" she asked as she ran her fingers along the pristine bike.

"Yes. It should run, but I figured since it had been sitting, it might need a tune-up." I motioned to the parts. "I already got the parts for you."

Before I could say any more, she jumped on me and clung to me like a koala before claiming my lips with hers.

God, I loved this woman.

Chapter Fifty-Six

ROSE

When I finally told Ren I loved him, it was so surreal. I was on a high I didn't know was possible. Then he made slow, sweet love to me. And my God, if that orgasm wasn't a new level. I may not have screamed his name or squirted but somehow it was just as fulfilling. Hell, the act of making love only seemed to solidify our bond, and I wouldn't change it for the world.

Then, to top it off, he brought me a pristine 1971 Harley Shovelhead to work on. Not only that, but it was his dad's bike. The man's trust and love for me was like nothing I had ever experienced before. One thing I knew for sure was I loved this man with my whole mind and body, and he was my person. The one I was meant to be with for the rest of my life.

"Marry me," I said without a second thought.

"Wh-what?" he stammered as he pulled back to look at me. His face screamed *did I hear you right?*

"I know it's fast but, but I don't have a single doubt that you are the man I am supposed to be with, my better half, my anchor.

You have shown me how to love, how to be loved, what it's like to be cared for, and so much more I can't even begin to express. I'm not saying let's go to the courthouse and get married right now, just promise me someday we will, promise me forever. Be my fiance."

Chapter Fifty-Seven

REN

H*oly shit.*

I struggled to contain my excitement at her proposal, because that was what it was. It was fast, hell it's only been a little over a month, but she was right. We were each other's other halves. My mouth wouldn't work. I was stunned speechless.

Fuck.

She needed an answer. My mouth claimed hers and ravished her, all of her.

Yes, yes, yes.

All I could do was scream in my mind as I tasted her again. There was never a doubt of my answer, not even for a second. She had me on day one. After a while, I pulled back and nipped at her ear.

"Fiance," I whispered in her ear. "Hmm, I think I like that."

"So, is that a yes?"

"Oh, it most definitely is," I growled.

As I kissed her again, the doorbell rang, and I pulled back, a scowl of irritation on my face. She laughed as she grabbed my ass before heading to the door to see who had shown up. Now I needed to bring her to see my mom and get the family ring to place on her finger, showing the world she was mine.

My Dove.

Chapter Fifty-Eight

ROSE

Containing my excitement was difficult. I had to work hard not to skip to the door. I looked to see who it was. Richards would just come in, and my dad was in his own place and would walk in as well. To say I was surprised to see Charlie only touched the surface of my feelings.

I opened the door and smiled. "Hey Charlie, what's up?"

"Can I talk to you and Rene?"

"Of course, come on in." I opened the door wider so he could come in. "Go ahead and sit wherever in the living room. I'll get Ren."

He nodded as I went back to the garage.

"Who was at the door, Dove?"

"Charlie. He said he wants to talk to us," I said, which got his attention.

"Did he say what about?"

"Nope, so let's go find out."

We both headed to the living room and took our seats across from Charlie, our hands intertwined between us.

"I am here as your subordinate, Rene, and it involves Rose's dad."

Now I was confused.

I looked at Ren, who shrugged. "Alright," I said.

"What's going on, Charles?"

"Rose, we have our history, and I am glad I reconnected with you. Not only that, I am glad you ended up in our hospital. The closure I have found as our relationship grows is enlightening. When the board told me to take your dad's case because of my boss being with you, I was stressed. My patient load was already high, but then I met your dad. Soon I found myself eating lunch with him daily, wanting to get to know him and his story. Even learn more about Jasper."

Where was he going with this?

"Over time, I found myself having feelings. Then we worked him off his meds and now we're in the process of discharging him from our unit. A primary care doctor can continue to wean him off the meds. So, as his daughter and my boss, I am asking permission to see how far my feelings for him can go. I am asking for permission to officially date Dale."

Holy shit.

That was not what I was expecting at all. I was stunned, to say the least.

Shit, was my father even gay?

"As your boss, once he is officially discharged, and it is reported, I am alright with it. But this is not my call to make," Ren said as he squeezed my hand. "I think Rose needs some time, maybe even talk to her father before she gives you an answer."

Oh, thank God.

This man knew how to read me so well. "Of course. I will head home now. Just know no matter what you say, I will respect it."

I didn't utter a word or even spare a glance as he left out the front door, my mind swimming with thoughts.

"Is my dad even gay?" I whispered.

"I don't know, Dove. Why don't we go talk to him? Then let's go on a trip to see my mom. It's time she meets my fiancé."

I KNOCKED LIGHTLY on the door before walking inside my dad's room with Ren by my side. Despite my training, my dad was reading my worry.

"Baby, what is it?" he asked as I flopped unceremoniously on the couch.

Yep, read me like a book.

"Dad, are you gay?" I asked bluntly, not wanting to sugarcoat it. My dad didn't respond right away. I was just about to say something when he spoke.

"I've been bisexual for as long as I can remember. So, in a sense, yes. Why are you all of the sudden asking me this?"

I took a deep breath. "And what are your feelings for Charlie?"

"I'm fascinated by the man but wouldn't dare jeopardize his job to act on anything, Why?"

"He just asked us if we would consent to him asking you out after you're discharged from the Cardiology Department," Ren said.

"Dad, I know you can make your own choices, and Charlie is a good man. I just don't want you to get hurt."

My dad moved close to me and embraced me in a much needed hug. "My darling daughter, you are fiercely protective, and I love that. But just know, I will be careful of my heart just as I taught you to be with yours."

All I could manage was a nod as he squeezed a little tighter. "You have my blessing, not that you actually need it."

"No, I don't *need* it, but I want it and value it."

Well, fuck me, my dad was bisexual.

Definitely was not something I expected, though looking

back, it made complete sense. We hung out for a bit, then let my dad know we were leaving town for a couple of days. I shot Charlie a text, giving him my permission, then Ren and I hit the road.

It was too late to visit his mom tonight, so we settled in the hotel. Not going to lie, it was nice to be away from home for a bit. I was excited to see the city tomorrow and try the local cuisine, not only that, but doing it with my fiance, the love of my life. Oh, and of course, see Ashley if she was free.

We immediately crashed since we were both exhausted from the day's events. That and it was like two in the morning.

The alarm blared, and I groaned in annoyance, which got a chuckle from Ren. "Hmm, groaning, and I didn't even pound that little kitty of yours last night."

I hummed in response as I moved my ass against his morning wood. He growled before biting down on my shoulder, making me whimper in ecstasy.

"So fucking slutty." His deep, husky tone sent a shiver down my spine. "Oh, that little kitty will be mine...tonight, but right now we have places to be."

With a quick swat on my ass, I was up and getting ready, eager to get back here and make sweet love to my man. We were dressed nicely, and I was sporting a dress. Not my usual choice, but every once in a while I wore one. My Navy tattoo showed beautifully on my arm, the color of my dress making it pop more.

When we pulled up to the facility, I was amazed. The place was drop dead gorgeous and definitely did not scream facility but home. Ren took my hand as we made our way inside.

"Oh, back so soon, Doctor?" the woman at the front desk said. "And who is this beauty?"

"This is my fiance, we are here so my mama can meet her."

"Ooh, that's exciting. She is doing well so far today and had a good day yesterday."

Ren gave her a warm smile and started filling out the sign-in log. Once he was done, we made our way down the hall to a room. Ren knocked, then slowly opened the door. "Ma, it's me. Are you decent?"

"Ren baby?! Yes, I am decent."

I followed Ren into the room and watched her smile at him, then her smile seemed to grow when she noticed me. "Oh Ren, is this her?"

Wait what?

She knew about me already?

"Yes Mama, this is the girl I told you about my last visit, except now she is my fiance."

The squeal of joy this woman projected was probably heard all the way at the front desk. "Oh, oh Ren, she needs the ring. Sweetie, it's in the closet in the third shoebox on the right."

Ren was heading that way and following her directions. Meanwhile, my mind was spinning.

Ring?

Damn, I didn't even think about that.

My brain snapped back to reality as foreign arms wrapped me into a hug. I didn't even notice his mom getting up and walking over. Of course, I embraced her back.

"I have been praying for this day for a long time and now here you are, in my house, as real as the pimple on my left ass cheek."

A laugh escaped me and Ren looked over, his expression one of shock and horror at the comment. She let me go and slowly made it back to her seat. It was evident that even that small distance was exhausting. My heart ached knowing her health was failing and time with her was limited.

"Did you find it, dear?" she asked after she was fully settled.

I turned to see Ren down on one knee. My eyes dropped to the beautiful ring he presented. It was perfect. Small diamonds surrounded the giant red stone, the band thin and simple. It was everything I could have asked for and so much more. The value was priceless in every way.

"My Dove. I know you already asked me and I said yes, but please allow me to ask you again and share this moment with the other most important woman in my life. Rosalina Conrad, will you be my wife, my partner in crime for the rest of our lives and into the next?"

"Yes," I breathed. Ren's hand shook slightly as he slipped the ring on my finger before pulling me into a deep kiss.

His mom squealed again and I let out a chuckle. This woman was like the best friend I never had and soon she would be my mother-in-law.

We spent the next several hours talking, well, more like playing twenty questions, but nonetheless, we enjoyed ourselves. With promises to return tomorrow, we headed out to enjoy the city, giving her time to rest.

Chapter Fifty-Nine

REN

The feeling of overwhelming happiness when I slipped the family ring on Rose's finger was like a high I never thought I could feel. She was mine, all mine, and soon she would be my bride and hopefully someday the mother to our children.

First place I wanted to take her was the Space Needle. We made our way to the top, and I stood with my arms wrapped around her waist, her head leaning back into my shoulder as we took in the view.

I'd been up here plenty of times, but with her, it just hit differently somehow. A deep rumbling sound came from her belly, and I let out a chuckle.

"Hmm, sounds like my Dove is hungry. Come on, I know just the place," I said as I took her hand in mine and led her down the tower, then across the street to a Greek place called Grecian Corner.

Whenever I was in town, I found the time to come here. The food was the best, and it was priced well, especially for this area. Once we ordered our food, we sat outside to enjoy the unseasonably warm weather. Christmas had passed us by, but it was still winter. Though the nice weather was well appreciated. Even the pass was clear when we drove up here.

We hit a few shops in town, then headed back to the hotel to order in for dinner. A look of mischief took over Rose's features. I groaned, knowing she was about to tease me. There was not enough time to fuck, but plenty of time for her to drive me wild with lust.

Her hand pressed down on my growing cock as she bit my lower lip.

Oh, fuck me.

Before I knew it, she was on top of me, rubbing herself against my now straining cock.

"Fuck Dove, If you keep that up the food will get cold and I will take you first."

She hummed against my lip, and my cock twitched in response.

Jesus.

When the quick knock sounded, I growled, hating that we got interrupted. Then she ground her hips down on my erection before taking off toward the door as I attempted to swat her ass. I failed.

As soon as she placed the food down on the counter, I was on her, pushing her back into the door as I ripped my belt from its loops, binding her wrists before turning her to face the door with her wrists above her head.

I lifted her dress, exposing her bare ass.

Jesus Christ.

No underwear.

I squeezed her perfect cheeks before slapping my palm down, getting my slutty whimper in response. Moving my hands up her body, I wrapped them on her shoulders. Without warning, I pushed down on her shoulder, ramming her down my length.

The scream of bliss she let out almost made me cum right then. In an attempt to push my orgasm back, I gritted my teeth.

"Hmm, I love it when my little slut screams like that," I growled. Then I continued to ram her up and down my shaft as she cursed me in multiple languages again.

Fuck.

My pace became more animalistic as I felt my balls tighten with my impending release. I wasn't going to be able to stop this one. As I rammed her down again, I bit down on her neck, making her arch her back as her channel strangled my pulsing cock.

Holy fucking shit.

Chapter Sixty

ROSE

I knew when I teased the hell out of Ren that I would pay for it sooner or later, but fuck. What I wasn't expecting with him using his belt and taking me against the door. But I'd be lying if I said I didn't like it.

The punishments this man gave me would probably be better called funishments. Especially since I love pain and the power he exerted over me. He unbound my hands and gave my ass a final swat as I grabbed the food and headed to our bed.

I was pretty impressed with the food. For being hotel restaurant food, it was pretty darn good. As we relaxed, I shot a text to Ashley.

> Hey girl. I'm in town, you and Ezra available for lunch tomorrow?

Her reply was almost instant.

Hell yes. The kids are in daycare so we can for sure meet. How about Potbelly at one?

Sounds good.

Now that we had a plan, I let sleep take over.

AFTER VISITING HIS MOM, we headed to our lunch.

"I am so excited for you to meet them," I said, practically jumping up and down as we walked down the street of the restaurant.

We had to park several blocks away since it was in downtown Seattle and parking was like mining for gold. The whole drive over, I told him how we met and her story. Honestly, the thing that got his attention was the fact that Ezra was a Marine. Ren always had a soft spot for those who served, not to mention mad respect.

When we arrived, I practically ran to Ashley, who eagerly opened her arms for a hug. After we gathered our wits about ourselves we ordered our food and sat down. The guys talked about war and service, mentioning me multiple times. It was cool to hear Ezra had heard of me and my team. The Ghost Watchers was one of the best SEAL teams, and despite the top secret work, we had a reputation that made waves in the military. Now Ashley and I were talking, tuning them out.

"When you said career change, I didn't believe it. But here you are! And of course Liam has been working with Ezra on the equipment for your company, which I love that you came to us," she said.

Um, duh. Who the fuck else would we use?

I don't do second-grade equipment. Only the best, and her husband was just that.

"Of course. I would never dream of going anywhere else."

"Um, excuse me, what the fuck is this?" She grabbed my hand, grabbing the guys' attention.

"My engagement ring."

"Um, bitch, I better be invited."

"Um, bitch, damn right you are, especially since you are the maid of honor."

"No way."

"Yes way."

She stomped her feet below the table in excitement.

"Well congrats, you two," Ezra said.

"Thank you," Ren and I said at the same time.

Lunch lasted over an hour. Then Ezra said he had to go back to the office but we should visit again before we leave, maybe even come meet the kids. Which, of course, we agreed to right away.

The rest of the trip was fun. We spent time on the beach, on a whale cruise, the aquarium and even the zoo. Every morning was spent with his mom and we took her with us on the whale cruise. Over the next couple of weeks, I had grown to love his mom, and she was calling me her daughter already. Then, of course, I visited Ashley, Ezra, and the kids. They were a blast, and I was thrilled she had her happy ending and now I was getting mine. Though meeting her kids made me think about having my own someday.

Unfortunately, it was now time to go back home. Ren had a study to start, and I had a business to run. On the way back, a realization hit me like a ton of bricks. Once we returned home, I had to send my official resignation to Richards. Hard to believe it has been that long. He managed to pull extra time for me based on my performance. Three months had passed in a blink of an eye.

Also, once we got home, I had a wedding to plan. I wanted nothing more than for Ren to have his mom present for our union. And whether he said it or not, I knew he desired it, too. As the beautiful scenery passed by, I found myself dozing off as his hand rubbed small circles on the back of my hand.

As we pulled up to the house, my excitement caught up with me. My bike had been delivered while we were gone, so now I had to tune up his bike so we could go on a ride as soon as possible. I craved the wind in my hair like I craved Ren's cock.

I practically ran to the garage and stopped dead in my tracks.

Fuck, they were sexy beasts.

The sight of them together made my panties wet.

"Hmm, we are going to look so fucking hot riding together," Ren said

"Hmm yes," I agreed.

We made our way to the laundry room, and I put the clothes from our trip inside. We stayed longer than we planned, so the clothes needed to be washed, some items being used more than once.

"You look so damn good, Dove," Ren said, his voice sensual.

The way it made my body purr in response. I bent down seductively, allowing my skirt to ride up.

"Bed now," he growled.

Chapter Sixty-One

REN

The way she teased me as she finished putting the laundry in made my cock turn hard as concrete. Now I was running after her as she scurried to our bed. That sexy ass of hers was about to be mine.

By the time she made it to the bed, she was naked and my pants were dropping to the floor. My shirt, long gone from my body. I flipped her so she was on her belly as I secured her arms and legs to the bed.

I nipped her from her ankle up to her neck, making her squirm beneath me as I pressed my hard length against her thigh. Sitting up slightly, I moved my hand and smacked her ass with brute force, knowing it would leave a mark.

"Fuck yes, harder, Alpha."

Oh, fuck me.

I smacked her ass repeatedly as my cock started to leak like a damn faucet. My handprints made my already concrete cock even harder, the deep purple of my tip begging me for release.

"I am going to punish that sweet little ass of yours so that all you will be able to do tomorrow is feel my cock deep inside you," I growled.

"Fuck yes," she breathed.

Without another word, I thrust my full length into her ass. Her scream of pleasure almost made me cum right then and there. I held myself still for a moment, fighting my orgasm that was teasing the surface. Her unprepped hole was so perfectly tight over my shaft.

"Jesus, Dove. I'm about to blow my load right now."

She rammed herself back, and I growled as my orgasm exploded from my cock.

Oh, she wasn't getting off that easy.

I thrust in and out of her, showing her no mercy. My cock hardened again with ease and I was going to tear up that ass of hers . The palm of my hand came crashing down on her again and again as she cursed me through her pleasure.

The way her muscles tightened, I knew she was getting close. I moved my hand under her and to her throat, adding pressure as I used my other hand to push her hips into mine, driving my cock even deeper.

"Oh my God," she screamed as her walls strangled my pulsing cock as we came together. As soon as that sweet ass of hers milked my cock for every last drop, I released her, then flopped on the bed next to her as she turned into me and snuggled into my chest.

Life was perfect.

Chapter Sixty-Two

ROSE

To say my ass was sore was not doing anything justice. *Fuck.*

How the hell was I supposed to sit down? Between the pounding his cock inflicted and his spankings, I wouldn't be shocked to see a completely bruised ass if I looked in the mirror. Despite the blissful discomfort, I got up and dressed for the day. The roads were clear, and I decided to ride my bike to the office so Ren could use his car since he had a lot to do and might have to stay late.

"What time do you think you will be home from work, Dove?"

"Depends on the cases we've been collecting. All our licenses and permits came in, so we're good to go. My dad will be joining us in a couple of hours for his training. It's weird that Richards is gone now so he won't be there, but from what I was told, he cleared my dad for security clearance, so that's all done."

"Sounds like quite the day."

"Yeah, I might not beat you home, but I will try my best.

Worse case, come have dinner at the office. Then tonight I want to get started on your bike so we can ride together."

"I mean, I can always ride bitch so you can feel my hard cock against your back," he teased.

Oh, fuck me.

I clenched my thighs at the thought and his lip curled up into a knowing smirk. "Oh, I see that slutty little kitty likes the idea."

A whimper of desire escaped my lips and Ren was on me in seconds, pinning me against my bike. "Hmm, and maybe afterwards I will bend you over this sexy bike and punish that little kitty of yours."

Hmm, fuck yes.

"Promise?"

His deep chuckle vibrated my body. "Oh, you know it," he purred, then stood us both upright before kissing me deeply and getting in his car to leave.

Holy shit. The man could make me so damn horny and now I had to go to work.

Fucking Bastard.

Chapter Sixty-Three

REN

"About damn time you come back, Doctor. This hospital was so boring with you gone," Celeste said as I walked into the ER.

God, I missed her.

"Hey sweetheart, I missed you too," I said as I kissed the top of her head.

"We don't have any of your patients down here today. Doctor Stanson should be in your office so you guys can get started with whatever y'all need to. I went ahead and let him in, since I have your key and you still don't have a damn assistant."

"Thank you, Celeste," I said as I headed to my office.

When I opened my door, a tall man stood from the couch.

"You must be Doctor Doux?" he said as he held out his hand for me to shake.

"Please call me Rene. You must be Doctor Stanson."

"Yes, and by all means, call me Frank."

"My apologies for keeping you waiting. I just returned from leave and was a bit slow to rise this morning."

"Oh, I bet. I heard you took over a month off."

"Yeah. It was long overdue and with this study starting, it will be a while before I can do that again. Plus, my mom was dying to meet my fiance."

"Fiance? I heard you had a girlfriend but didn't hear that," he said, shock evident in his tone.

"Yeah, it's new. Just happened. No one except myself and my mom really knows."

"Well damn, congrats, man. My wife is a wedding planner. I would love to put you in touch."

"Wow man, that would be amazing! My fiance will appreciate the help. She is starting her own business, and I already know with her skills she is going to be slammed."

"For sure, here is her card. I'll let her know to expect a call." He handed me a white and gold business card.

"Now let's get to work. How many of the patients have arrived?" I asked.

"All the locals and about 30% of the out-of-town folks. A few are set to check in this afternoon. The ones here are currently getting their final testing done, and the lab is already doing their part."

"Thank you for stepping up while I was away and getting all the pieces moving."

"Of course. Doctor Rain helped a lot, as well. I would love to have him involved as much as we can. And your ER nurse, Celeste, has been great, too."

"Yeah, they are pretty great and I would love for them to be involved if they agree to it."

That reminded me I needed to check in with Charles. I was curious if he ended up asking Rose's dad out or not. But right now, it was time to work.

Let's do this.

Chapter Sixty-Four

ROSE

The amount of paperwork that I had to sign was comparable to signing my damn life away. I mean, holy crap. But the plus was now we were fully operational and our badges arrived yesterday.

I stared at the immaculate design, and a rogue tear ran down my cheek. Jasper would have 100% loved this. Wes patted me on the shoulder.

"I know," he said as I looked up at him, his own tear falling. "Liam is still active duty, so his help will be limited for a bit, but he is a phone call away."

"Alright, sounds good. Did you guys figure out your differences?" I asked, remembering the tension between them. Wes scoffed.

"The man is stubborn and in denial."

I raised an eyebrow.

"He is a closet case," Wes said.

Oh. Well shit.

"Wait, so he likes you but doesn't want to admit it, or…?"

"Something like that."

"Did you ever stop to think that maybe he is scared since he is still serving and not everyone appreciates serving with a gay man for the sole fact that they are gay?"

That got a pause, then a slow shrug. "I guess I didn't consider that."

"Give him time and space. Be a friend, then maybe once he's out in a few months, you can become more. Who knows, maybe sooner as he gets to know you. But don't fuck it up before it starts because you're mad at him for being closed up and closeted when you are doing the same in a different way," I said.

"Okay, Doctor Phil. I hear you. Thanks, though. I needed to hear that."

"Of course, Wes. How about we start with the case we got from Cobb before the other shit went down? We know Kevin is involved, and in that way it's solved, but we still need to find her."

"Brittany Slade. Yes, I have her file right here. While you were gone, I worked some of my own magic and I think I have an idea of where to start."

"Alright, where is that?"

"Well, she was last seen at a party and she attended Eastern Washington University, which is near several lakes, including one called Sprague. Which, if you drive the back roads, you are right on the water. So easy to dump a body."

Well shit.

As a SEAL, I was dive certified, and I kept it up to date even after I left the Navy. It was nice to have, and you never knew when it would come in handy.

"I guess it's time to break out my dive gear."

Wes grinned widely. "Let's go for a swim."

I shot my dad a text to come to the lake instead, and we headed out. Nothing like some on-the-job training. Once we got there, I was in my dive suit and on the boat within fifteen minutes. My dad arrived as we were about to push off.

My dad sat near Wes and they watched the radar for anything to indicate what we were looking for.

"Was she last seen in a car, Dale?" Wes asked.

My dad pulled the file and scanned it. "It says she had a Ford Focus that was never found."

"Well, we have a car here." Wes dropped a magnet that was attached to a buoy.

Show time.

Once I had on my mask, Wes said, "Dive when ready."

I nodded, then went under. The water was clear for the most part, some debris, but nothing that made visibility difficult.

"What is the plate?" I asked on my radio as I made my way to the back of the car.

"C A W nine nine four six."

Well damn.

"This is the car. I repeat, this is the car. Looking inside now." The windows were all up, so I used my light to peek inside. I saw something and tested the back door to get a better look.

Bones.

I closed the door, knowing nothing got out of the car since I only opened it for a second and monitored the area with ease. "Call the police. We have remains. I repeat, we have remains inside the vehicle. I am on my way up with the plate."

Once I had the plate, I made my way onto the boat, my dad already on the phone with the police. The buoy was secured, so we headed back to shore. I didn't get out of my gear fully since, depending on what the police needed, I might be back in the water. This was a multi-county issue. The case was Spokane County, but the body was in Lincoln County.

After about forty minutes, police from both counties arrived and started asking questions, which we answered. Cobb showed up after a while, since he gave us the file. Luckily, I didn't have to dive again since Spokane had a recovery team.

"Who asked you to look into this case?" the sergeant asked.

"Mrs. Slade, her mom," Wes said.

"I see. Have you called them yet?"

"No, sir. We wanted to wait until we had more to tell her. Confirm the find," Wes said.

"DNA will take time, ma'am," the sergeant replied.

"Oh, I know that. I mean, get the car above water and identify the bones as human."

"Of course, my apologies."

The ME pulled up just as the car was fully out of the water. Carefully, the door was opened, and the water spilled onto a tarp to help collect evidence that might fall from the car. Several water samples were taken from the inside. The Sergeant looked at the ME, who was examining a large pile of what I assumed were bones. As soon as he picked up the skull, I knew. He gave a quick nod and started to analyze the evidence.

"Looks like you can make that call," the sergeant said as he handed me a card. I looked to see his name and number. Then I noticed there were two, one for the family, I assumed. I pulled out my phone and dialed Mrs. Slade's number. She answered on the third ring.

"Hello?"

"Mrs. Slade. This is Rose from Killian's Eye."

"Oh yes, are you working on my daughter's case now?"

"Yes ma'am, my partner has been doing some background work while we waited for our licenses, as he told you before."

"Yes, I remember."

"Well, we became active today and got straight to work on a hunch based on that work, and it appears we have found your daughter."

The gut wrenching cry made my heart break. The hurt was powerful, but you could hear the relief that this was over.

"Police are on scene right now and we will be by later with any information we have. Including some business cards to the police involved. DNA will be run for confirmation, but the plate matches."

"Thank you," was all she said before the line went dead. My heart truly broke for her.

Once we had all the important cards and information plus got the official release by police, we headed back to the office. News stations arrived just as we were leaving.

Great.

Now we were going to be on the news.

"Honey, you're the boss, but let me be the public face of the company for press releases," my dad said as the scene disappeared behind us.

"Yeah Dad, I think that would be best, especially with my work history."

We dropped off the documents with Mrs. Slade. Ren's friend, Doctor Ryan Newman, was waiting for us there. He was a psychologist trained in trauma and grief. We employed him for counseling of our victims' families and us if we ever needed it.

It was heart-wrenching to see the devastation battling her relief. But we had brought the torturous chapter to an end, and Mrs. Slade could find some peace, though she would never be the same.

Once back at the office, we continued my dad's brief training since he was already a natural and filled out our own paperwork from the case. I looked up at the time. Four, time to go home.

The ride home was needed, nothing like the feel of a Harley between your thighs to relax you. As soon as I was home, I got to work on Ren's bike. Only thing that would have made the ride home better is with my fiance riding beside me.

So that made getting this done that much more urgent.

Chapter Sixty-Five

REN

When I got home, I found Rose hard at work on my bike. The sight of her on her back as she worked meticulously was hot as hell. Then I noticed the grim look on her face. I saw the news when Celeste came into my office telling me to turn it on. Her company was all over the reports with the finding of a missing person's remains.

Fuck.

I knew she would need me, so I did everything I could to get home to her. Tonight was not going to be a night that I dominated her. No, tonight she needed the control, and I knew just how to give it to her.

After I placed my keys on the hook, I lowered to the ground next to her and rested my hand on her thigh. Her breath caught as she scooted closer. Never stopping the task she was doing, but also seeking my touch. We lay like that as she worked on my bike. Before I knew it, she was done and my bike was ready to go after we got some gas.

"Dove, let's go shower. Then I have a surprise for you," I said as I gave her a gentle kiss.

"Okay," she whispered. She sounded so defeated and my heart ached.

Once I helped her up, we headed inside and showered. I took my time worshiping her body and massaging every muscle, spending extra time on the tense ones by her neck.

I hated she was hurting, and I only hoped that not every case would be like this. The last thing I wanted was for her light to dim.

"How about I tell you some good things that happened today?" I whispered in her ear. She nodded and took a deep breath.

"Well, everything with the study is a go. And my partner gave me his wife's number."

She turned to look at me, a scowl on her face.

"Easy there, Dove, she's a wedding planner."

That got me a smile. "Oh," she said, seeming a little less grim.

"And I talked to Charles. Looks like he and your dad have gone on several dates while we were gone."

"Yeah, he seemed happy today."

I continued to tell her anything positive that happened, even some of the funny things that happened in the ER while I filled in for an hour. She was a bit more relaxed by the time we got out of the shower, but I knew she needed something more and I was going to deliver.

She climbed into bed, not bothering to put anything on. Despite the hurt she exhibited, I could see splashes of lust in her eyes.

If only she knew.

"You don't need me to take your power today. You need to exert power," I said as I pulled the item I wanted from the bag beneath the bed. "Tonight you get to ravish me." I grinned as I revealed the item to my patiently waiting Dove.

Chapter Sixty-Six

ROSE

Holy shit, a fucking strap-on.

The idea of strapping on that massive thing and taking his ass like he did mine was intriguing, to say the least. Hell, it wasn't something I'd ever done, or considered doing. But now that the concept was sitting right in front of me, a waterfall formed between my legs.

He handed me the strap-on and a small bottle of lube before getting on his hands and knees at the edge of the bed. The sight of his ass in the air, his hole twitching, begging to be penetrated, was so fucking sexy. I let out a growl, then coated the shaft after securing it to my waist. The small plug was also in my own ass, which I gave him the remote to.

I slowly inched the dildo in, allowing him time to adjust. His moan filled the room as the full length entered him. "Fuck, Dove, so fucking full."

Starting slow, I moved so that I slid in and out, getting whimpers of pleasure.

"Fuck my ass how you need to, Dove," he growled.

Oh fuck. Now it was on.

I moved my hips back, then slammed into him.

He grunted and cursed, "Fuck yes. Harder, Dove."

With pleasure.

I manipulated the dildo into his sexy ass like my life depended on it, all the stresses of the day leaving my body with every thrust into the man I loved. He took my beating beautifully and with such passion.

Jesus Christ. So fucking sexy.

I moaned out my pleasure as the vibrations hit my system. He had hit the damn button. As my body responded to the sensation, I reached around and flipped him on his back, then plunged back into him.

His responding cursing told me he enjoyed the move. His hand gripped the sheet as his legs wrapped around me. My hands moved with purpose until I was playing with his erect nipple while my other hand was on his rock hard cock, pre-cum leaking in a steady stream.

Oh fuck.

Who would have thought that Rene Doux liked taking it in the ass?

"Now it's my turn to make it so you can't walk right as you feel me inside you tomorrow." I jerked his length with each thrust. His back arched and his eyes rolled back.

"Fuck Dove, I'm fucking com—"

He was unable to finish his words as the first jet of cum shot up his body with such force it hit the pillow above his head, the rest drenching his chest and abs as my own orgasm hit me.

"Fuck," I called out.

As our orgasms slowed, I collapsed onto the bed and we both just lay there, trying to recover. After a minute, I unhooked the strap on, then moved to the tip on his still semihard cock. I licked up every last drop of his essence until he was clean and hard as steel again.

I straddled him, pushing him inside me as I pushed the

button to turn up the vibrations. "Hmmm," was all I managed to say as I rode his cock like a virgin on prom night.

"Oh fuck, Dove," he groaned as he pinched my nipples. "So fucking tight."

He drove up into me, meeting me thrust for thrust until my orgasm came stumbling to the surface.

"Fuck, Alpha, I'm coming." I felt myself squirt, his cock pulsing as he confessed his love to me in French.

Again, I licked up every drop. Then he returned the favor, teasing my clit as he did.

Jesus.

But now we were both spent and unable to do anymore.

We were well fucked.

Very well fucked.

Chapter Sixty-Seven

REN

Fucking hell.

That was intense, and I loved every second of it. Only issue now was my muscles wouldn't allow me to move. I was about to ignore my aching muscles and get a washrag, but Rose beat me to it. I heard the sounds of her cleaning the toys, then she came out with the rag in hand, her own body damp from cleaning herself.

She took care of every inch of me until any remnant of cum was gone. Then she curled up on my chest as we drifted off to sleep.

THE REST of the week she worked until four, then came home while I worked until five. She was working on tracking someone hiding somewhere in the United States. Luckily, her connections made it so she wouldn't have to travel, but she employed veterans to do any out-of-state work, and I loved that.

Having her home every night was the best feeling ever. Not to mention her cooking was on point. Today was Friday, and we had a date with our bikes. Though someday I would need to ride bitch and follow through on my threat the other day.

I got home and was heading to our room when I saw Rose in the kitchen wearing her leathers, looking straight out of a porno.

Holy hell.

My cock twitched at the sight of leather hugging her ass.

Fuck, she was so exotic.

As if she was my prey, I stalked up behind her, then moved to grab her perfect ass.

She spun around and swatted my hand with a wooden spoon covered in white sauce. "No, no. First we ride, then eat the meal I just cooked for us. Then we can play."

"Oh, I will be punishing you for that swat, Dove."

"Hmm, and I look forward to it. Later. Now go get changed while I put this in the oven to stay warm."

Without a word, I was up the stairs and changing into my own leathers. Once I was suited up, I headed to the garage where Rose was waiting. I watched as she took in my outfit, her eyes filled with lust as she bit her lower lip.

I moved into her and brushed my thumb across her lower lip, freeing it from her bite.

"Only I should be biting these lips," I whispered against the base of her ear. Then I nipped at her soft lips before swatting her ass and straddling my bike.

Fuck.

It felt good to sit on her again.

I watched intently as Rose got on her bike, and the sight was one that I would see every time I closed my eyes. It was one of utter beauty.

"Alpha, stop staring and let's ride."

I shook my head and cleared my throat before walking my bike out of the garage and starting her up. She roared to life like she was brand new.

Fuck, I missed this.

Closing my eyes, I said a thank you to my father for taking care of this beauty and entrusting her to me. Our motorcycle helmets had mics in them that connected us so we could talk as we rode. I revved my engine, signaling I was ready to go, and we took off down the street.

Fucking heaven.

Chapter Sixty-Eight

ROSE

The feeling of a Harley vibrating under you was hard to describe. It was one you had to experience to truly understand its power. My job took this love from me, but now I was reclaiming it. Not only that, but doing it alongside the man I loved.

I was in heaven.

We drove, not going anywhere in particular. People definitely gave us looks since it wasn't the normal time of year for bikes, but it was close enough. There was no rain or snow, so neither of us cared.

We rode for two hours before heading home to eat our dinner. This summer, if Ren could get the time off, we would go on a longer ride. When we cut the engines, the quiet unnerved me and the hairs on the back of my neck stood up.

Something wasn't right.

I checked my phone, and my dad wasn't home. He appeared to be at a restaurant.

Ren was looking at me, his helmet already off, so our private communication was cut off. Luckily, I had taught him some hand signals that my team used for Killian's Eye while in the field. They were subtle and unique to us. I tapped my wrist where a watch should be, but I wore mine on the opposite side. He lowered his eyes in recognition. I closed my eyes and took in my surroundings. The threat was inside and likely listening to us.

"Babe. Can you feed the koi in the pond?"

This told him the threat was inside, and we had a pond but no koi. At least not yet. The pond was also near a bunker where he could call my backup.

"Sure, Dove."

He walked away, and I turned to go inside, not knowing what I was about to walk into. As soon as I was in the door, I flipped the lights on, but nothing happened.

Fuck.

They killed the power.

Since my alarm didn't go off, I suspected as much already. I would have to talk to Ezra about getting his system for my home. I had enemies for sure.

"I know you're here, so why don't you show yourself?"

Suddenly, a bright light filled the room, blinding me. After blinking several times, forcing my eyes to adjust and allow fewer spots to fill my vision, I squinted as I tried to focus on the dark figure walking toward me. My phone was in my pocket and already linked to Richards. Ren was calling for local help. I was calling the cavalry.

"You think you are better than me, well, you are mistaken. Cause I got out. I got away and now no one is here to save you. Not even your weak boy toy can save you," the man sneered. Recognition hit me.

Kevin Janx.

Fuck me.

Chapter Sixty-Nine

REN

When Rose taught me the code she used with Wes and her staff, I never thought I would have to actually use it. But here we were and at our own damn house. She told me to feed the nonexistent fish, and I knew. I was in the bunker and on the phone fast.

"Wes, we have an intruder. Rose is inside the house with them. I'm secure."

"On my way," was all he said before the line went dead.

I backed into the wall and lowered myself down to the ground. All I could do now was wait, and I fucking hated it.

Fucking why? Who? Shit.

In an attempt to calm myself, I thought about our wedding and our future family as I sat there, wishing there was more I could do to help.

AFTER WHAT SEEMED LIKE AGES, Wes came and got me. We walked through the house, and he informed me he took photos and cleared the house. He said the power was out but a bright light was on the counter, likely used to blind her temporarily, and there were signs of a struggle. Richards was on his way, and they would get her home safe no matter what. Then he dropped the bombshell.

The attacker was not alone.

Chapter Seventy

ROSE

W hen I saw Janx hadn't destroyed my phone, I knew it was
only a matter of time before Wes made things happen.
The second man appeared to be untrained and somehow famil-
iar. As my eyes began to focus, I immediately recognized him. He
had been the butler for the target, Kevin's lover.

Interesting.

I studied my surroundings and held back a smirk when I saw
all the potential weapons easily reachable. They had my wrists
tied in rope and the knot was not a very good one. Easy to get
out of.

Perfect.

The fact that my hearing was superior to most was helpful. I
heard the sounds of men approaching, men falling. Help was
coming.

Hell yes.

After several minutes, I saw Richards through the window
directly behind the butler. With his hands, he told me the place
was surrounded. I blinked in Morse code, telling him two men,

and I could free my hands. He nodded and held up his hand on my mark.

I ignored the burning feeling as I manipulated the rope. Once free, I held still so as to not cue them in on the fact I was no longer restrained. Their backs were turned to me so I made my move.

My training taught me to go for the bigger threat, so I quickly had Kevin in a chokehold. He struggled against my grasp. As easy as it would be to kill him right now, I wanted to get some of my anger out and have a little bit of fun. I let him loose, and he came at me swinging.

The butler ran out the door but was immediately taken by the people waiting outside. Richards stood at the door, watching. He knew this was my battle, and I was ready for it.

"You are the biggest coward I know. A traitor. Then you try to take me and what? Kill me? If you think for one second Rene would stand by and do nothing, you're wrong. See, I had you the minute I knew you were in my home. Rene wasn't feeding fish. He was calling Wes while I called Richards, who is right behind you."

He spun around to see the man standing in the only exit.

"And if you think he came alone, you are sorely mistaken. The only reason they aren't all in here is because this is my target. You escaped CIA federal custody and kidnaped a former agent who is contracted by the government. This is an act of terrorism. So you signed your death warrant and I am going to execute that sentence. But...I will allow you to fight back, see if you can beat me in a fair fight."

Windows shattered and the army of agents and men came inside to watch and block him from any weapons. Richards took his weapons and pushed him to me.

It was time to fight.

I let him get in a few hits, then I met him punch for punch. When he went for the takedown, I let him, then spun him around into an armlock before snapping his arm. His resulting scream was music to my ears.

Desperate to get the upper hand, he continued to swing kicks my way until I caught one and yanked. The pop of his hip dislocating sent a thrill down my spine.

Ouch.

Too bad I didn't give a shit.

As a child, I did years of martial arts training, and I used it to its full potential. Seeing him writhing in pain after all he had done was a beautiful sight. I hated killing, but this man was a threat that needed to be eliminated. I leaned over him and raised my hand before I let my fist hit his throat, making him unable to breathe or speak.

His windpipe was crushed.

Double, no triple, ouch.

I stepped back and watched as he slowly turned blue and suffocated. A smirk rested on my lips as life drained from the coward in front of me.

Richards checked his pulse and nodded.

He was dead.

Good riddance.

I took a moment to look around at everyone standing in the house. People I had served with, agents I had worked with and even saved, and some new faces. They all came to my aid, hell even Cobb was here.

Holy shit.

"You took a few shots to the head. Let's get you to the hospital. I will have Rene there when we get there," Richards said.

Suddenly, a wave of dizziness hit me and the world went black.

Chapter Seventy-One

REN

This waiting game sucked. There were several cops outside, and I was inside with Wes, waiting. He had an earpiece in, so I knew he would be informed once everything was done, but I was worried.

Fuck a long engagement. This woman was marrying me as soon as possible.

I moved forward in my seat as his hand flew to his ear.

"Copy. We are en route now."

"Well?" I demanded, not even giving him the chance to speak.

"They got her. She took some hits, so they are bringing her to the hospital. Celeste is on the way there now with one of the cops from outside since she was working in the garden. We called ahead to the hospital and your friend is waiting for her arrival."

Thank God.

"Take me to her." I headed to the door.

The drive was torture. All I wanted was to see her, hold her, kiss her. What I wasn't expecting was the number of official vehicles for blocks leading to the hospital. Men and women wearing dark and camo clothes filled the halls like they had just come from a mission.

Were all these people here for Rose?

I looked at Wes with a look of what I could only imagine was utter confusion.

"They are SEALs from her team, an active team, agents she knows and/or saved and even some of Ezra's team. They all aided in her rescue," Wes explained.

The pride I felt for the people who clearly had her back was a beautiful feeling. No one stopped me as we made our way to her room. A few staff shot sympathetic looks my way, but that was it.

When we got to a room, Richards embraced me. "She is going to be okay, man. It's over."

I nodded, then Richards opened the door. The sight of her unconscious on the bed, hooked to wires and an IV, was heart-breaking. I was at her side in a second and took her hand in mine as I kissed the back of it. My hands ran through her hair as I whispered how much I loved her, before resting my head on her chest, letting the tears fall.

My Dove.

When I felt fingers running through my hair, my head snapped up to see Rose smiling at me. Before she could even speak, my lips were on hers, telling her everything with my lips and tongue. She opened up to me as her monitors went crazy. I pulled away breathlessly as Celeste came in.

"Doctor Doux, stop agitating the patient. You know better," she chastised. I rolled my eyes as she hip-checked me, a smile on her face.

"Oh, but Celeste, don't you know my kiss can cure cancer?"

That got a laugh out of all of us. Rose winced, and I was over her, checking her. The doctor in me was unable to help himself. I clinched by teeth at the sight of bruises all over her.

That bastard.

It was a good thing he was dead or I would kill him my damn self. Her hand brushed my cheek and my eyes met hers.

"The only shots he got were the ones I let him get. He was dead long before I gave the fatal blow. But a swift death didn't feel right. So I made sure he was in excruciating pain as he died slowly."

Fuck.

Why did that turn me on?

"Just don't do it again, please, Dove. Seeing you like this breaks me."

"Okay baby, my Alpha."

She scooted over, then patted the bed next to her. I climbed in and took her in my arms as we both drifted off to sleep.

Chapter Seventy-Two

ROSE

For the next several weeks, I healed at home. Since the study started, Ren had to go to work, but Celeste took time off to make sure I was good. My dad's caregiver also came to check on me. Despite my dad's heart being good, she was still around since he was getting older, so why not? Plus, she needed the cash, and we had it. We had grown to like her and honestly considered her part of the family.

Everyday on his lunch, Charlie checked on me, then ate with my dad before going back to the hospital. Hell, even Richards stayed for a few days before he had to leave. Though the tension and chemistry between him and Celeste was noticeable.

When I mentioned it to Celeste, she shrugged. "I can't do long-distance and my home is here. I'd never ask a man to leave a job they love for me."

Little did she know the man had been thinking of leaving since I did, and it seemed he had a reason beyond just a career change.

I looked in the mirror as I got ready for Hannah, the wedding planner. At this point, all that was left of my injuries were a few small bruises. Celeste was downstairs, setting up the table with snacks.

As I got my shirt over my head, I heard the knock on my front door. My stomach flopped with nerves. Planning a surprise wedding that everyone knew about except the groom was not going to be easy, but it would be the best surprise I could ever give him, especially since he was now talking about a shorter engagement.

I came down the hall and sat at the dining room table, ready to start planning. We spent hours going through menus, venues, flowers, DJs, photographers, videographers, yadda yadda yadda. Now all I needed to do was to find a dress.

That was tomorrow's issue.

Hannah was leaving from here to go pick up his mom and I was taking her dress shopping with me. She would room with Hannah and her husband, and at the end of the week, I would marry Ren.

The idea of Ren finally being my husband gave me a feeling so intense it was like a drug.

Hmm. Yes, please.

Everyone made sure to clean up and leave before Ren got home. I had just sat on the couch when the front door opened. Ren leaned over me from the back of the couch. I tipped my head back, allowing him access to my lips.

"Dove, seeing you look at me like that makes me want to fuck your pretty little mouth as you hang off the bed," he growled.

Oh fuck.

"Tempting."

My gaze locked on his bulge that twitched in response.

"Fuck, Dove. I need you so damn bad."

Oh, how I know.

I had been too sore for more than oral and I was missing him deeply, well, deep inside me. But I was feeling better, so I was going to have him right here, right now.

With a smirk spreading over my lips, I reached back and grasped his erection through his scrubs. The responding moan soaked my panties.

"Then take me," I whispered. Without a word, I was scooped up and carried upstairs, faintly hearing Celeste laugh before she left.

It was time for my Alpha to claim me again.

Chapter Seventy-Three

REN

As soon as she was on the bed, I slowly stripped off her clothes, worshiping every inch of her body with my kisses.

Fucking hell.

She was so damn beautiful, her body perfect. Only a few marks were left from that bastard, and I fucking hated it. Every time I saw them, my temper would flare. After she was fully naked, I ripped off my clothes and climbed over her.

My lips met hers. She let out a moan as I pressed my body to hers, allowing my stiffening cock to touch her thigh. I swallowed her sweet moan, and it went straight to my cock, making it twitch in anticipation of taking her again.

Oh fuck.

I was fighting for control. The weeks she spent recovering were torture. Obviously, I would do it all again, but I certainly hoped I wouldn't have to. I needed to know if she wanted me, slow or hard.

Fuck.

I wanted both, but this wasn't about me. No, this was about her and how she wanted to take me.

"How do you want me, Dove?"

"Claim me," she pleaded.

"With pleasure," I growled as I slammed into her, making her take me all at once. Her responding moan of pleasure was exhilarating.

It felt so fucking good being inside her again. Her tightness never failed to amaze me as her channel hugged my cock perfectly. If I wasn't careful, I was going to explode right there. I gritted my teeth, taking a deep breath before I leaned down and bit her nipple, making her arch her back.

"Fuck," she yelled. The sound of her pleasure somehow made my cock even harder, which I had no clue was even possible. My tip was throbbing and I could only imagine how much pre-cum was leaking into her heat.

As I pounded in and out of her, my teeth and hands showed her breasts no mercy. Her responding moans only made me go harder and faster. Her eyes sparkled with her desire and shone brighter with every ounce of pain I inflicted.

The only bruises I wanted on her were the ones of our passion. When her nails dug into my back as she scratched me, an animalistic growl vibrated my whole body as my orgasm shot to the surface with such force I saw spots behind my eyes.

Holy fuck.

Now it was her turn. I bit down on her neck as I felt her walls tighten, her legs shaking against my back.

I didn't want it to be over that fast, but holy shit. Slowing my pace, I refused to pull out. I wasn't done with her yet. Not in the slightest. Now I was going to make sweet love to her. I brought my lips down to hers. As we kissed, her hands roamed my body, digging into my back. Which made my cock hard all over again and told me she too wanted more.

"Hmm," I hummed into her ear.

This time I moved my hips slowly, loving the feeling of my

cum around my cock. Our eye contact never broke as we made sweet love. When I knew my orgasm was coming, I reached between us and pressed on her clit, making her scream out as her body convulsed beneath me, my cock pulsing as I filled her again.

"Dove, I will love you forever," I whispered into her ear.

"Forever," she replied.

Chapter Seventy-Four

ROSE

Fucking Ren after so long was like finding my soul again. I knew before everything worked out the way it needed to, but I seemed lost, my soul just wandering aimlessly, not feeling complete. But now it seemed all I needed was Ren's cock.

When I woke up, I felt like a whole new person.

"How are you feeling, Dove?"

The sound of Ren's morning post-sex voice made my pussy leak.

Good Lord, this man is my weakness.

"Hmm, perfect," I whispered into his chest.

"You know, Dove, you are invincible. With everything that happened, you shouldn't be as tame as you are."

I pushed back so I could look him in his eye. "The minute you think that you are invincible, you become a target," I said in a serious tone. "Yes, I am good at what I do. I have loads of training from martial arts to the military to the CIA, but I can be beat by the right person. There is always someone out there better than you. Richards knows I could most likely handle everything on my own with Kevin, but he also knew there was a chance, hence the army. So no, not invincible, hard to beat maybe, but not invincible."

My eyes studied his expression after I said what I needed to. He seemed proud and a little embarrassed at his naïve comment. I raised my hand and brushed his cheek as I touched our foreheads together.

"I love you," I said against his lips.

"I love you too," he breathed.

I teased his lips with my tongue, asking for entry, which he immediately gave. After a few minutes, I pulled back.

"You have work and so do I. Get up, it's time to get ready," I said. His responding groan made me chuckle. "Don't be a big baby. We will continue that kiss when we get home."

"Oh, damn right we will," he growled as he pulled me closer to him, his erection poking me in the thigh as he gripped my ass hard. I moaned out my pleasure from the sweet pain.

"Later," I whispered, my breath catching as he moved his hips against me.

"Or maybe now." His dominating tone sent a shiver down my spine.

Oh, fuck me.

I was like putty when he used his Alpha tone and he damn well knew he had me and was now sporting a smirk that said *I knew I could get you to cave.*

Well yeah, because you are my damn kryptonite.

Fucker.

Using his hands, he opened my legs and dove down, licking at my folds. My breathing hitched at the pleasure as he nibbled at my clit. When his tongue dove into my core, I thought he was trying to taste what was left of him deep inside me. That thought almost made me cum.

His tongue was like magic as he licked every inch of me, his hand wandering up my seam to my back entrance.

Oh fuck.

I let out a gasp as his finger pressed against it, barely entering. I writhed in pleasure, pushing back, seeking more. He chuckled against my clit. The vibration sent ecstasy through me. He generously gave me more as he continued to work me.

My whimpers and cries of pleasure filled the room, my orgasm fast approaching. I reached down and gripped the long part of his hair as I bucked my hips.

"Alpha," I screamed as my body shook violently with my orgasm. I came hard but did not squirt.

Using my legs, I maneuvered him onto his back and got between his legs, taking his full length all at once, getting me a grunt, then a deep moan that I felt through his cock. I moved up and down his length, licking the rim of his head and running my tongue and teeth across the sensitive spot on his shaft.

He tensed and gripped the sheet as he cursed me in French. I moved my hand to his seam and slowly moved to his hole. The same one I devoured and would do it again when given the opportunity.

Hmmm.

Using my thumb, I pressed into him.

"Fuck," he moaned as he sought more, and I gave it to him.

Just like him working my ass and pussy, I was working his ass and cock. His hand gripped my hair, and I knew he was getting close. On my next up stroke, I grazed my teeth against the bulging vein.

"Dove!" he screamed out as the first jet of his cum hit the back of my throat. I swallowed as I added more suction and moved my hand faster. For a minute, I thought I would drown on his seed, but I managed to get every last drop.

"Now will you let us get ready, Alpha?" I asked and watched as his cock twitched.

"Perhaps," he teased as he swatted my now retreating ass.

Now who's being the brat?

Chapter Seventy-Five

REN

Being with Rose again gave me an intense high. It was like I had gone through withdrawal and got my first taste again, and I wanted more, so much more. Honestly, if it wasn't for the study, I would insist on us staying home to fuck for a week. But people depend on me and even her, with her job.

I did enjoy getting each other off this morning. With the hard-on I had, I desperately needed it. But tonight, tonight I would tear up that little kitty of hers until I was coated in her squirt.

I loved that I had a squirter.

I palmed my dick, desperately trying to get my growing cock to calm the fuck down so I could go in for my shift. When I lifted my head, I noticed movement across the parking garage.

What the hell?

It was Celeste's car, but who was the man inside the car with her? Whoever it was, they were being naughty, judging by the fog-covered windows. Her eyes met mine, and she winked at me.

What the fuck?

I shook my head, trying to clear it. Honestly, it wasn't my business who the man was. But I also knew Celeste would tell me, especially since I essentially caught her.

Once I made it to my office, I spent the morning reviewing files of the study participants. So far, everything was going well. Today was the lunch meeting with all the staff participating in the study. It was something I implemented since I wanted everyone to bounce ideas off each other and be on the same page. Most patients were doing well, a few were having some setbacks, but overall, everything was going to plan.

I got up to head to the conference room for lunch when Celeste walked in. "Good afternoon Celeste. I was just about to head to the study lunch."

"Which is why I came now, to catch you before you leave."

"Oookay?"

"About what you saw this morning. I—um," Her eyes darted around a bit as she fidgeted.

Why was she so nervous?

"Celeste, you know you can tell me anything, right? Fuck, you're like a damn sister to me," I said, trying to ease her nervousness.

Her shoulders relaxed as I spoke. "Richards and I like each other a lot, and well, we are seeing where it goes. He comes to see me any chance he gets."

Well, I'll be damned.

"As long as he treats you right and makes you happy, that's all I care about, and you know it."

"How do you think Rose will feel about it?"

As the question left her lips, Rose walked around the door frame, standing directly behind her.

"I think she feels the same way," Rose said.

Celeste jumped, clutching at her chest.

"Jesus Christ," she huffed before her eyes glared into mine. "You could have warned me."

I let out a chuckle. "I didn't have time to. She materialized, then answered you."

"Celeste, if you are seeking my blessing, you have it. Hell, maybe if you two hit it off, he will come here and work for me. But don't make him choose. Let him make the choice on his own."

"I can respect that. I'll get out of your hair now."

Once she was gone, I pulled Rose to me.

"Now what brings you here, Dove? Cause I know it's not me since I have my lunch," I whispered in her ear as I nipped it.

"Well, like you said, I'm not here for pleasure. We had a case, we found the missing person, and we escorted her here. Wes is with her now."

"I'm glad this one is having a more positive outcome."

"Me too. And I figured while I was here, I'd steal a kiss," she teased.

Oh, she didn't have to tell me twice.

My lips met hers with wild abandon.

Fuck.

It was like I was having my dessert before lunch. When she bit my lip, my head spun from the pleasure she awoke inside me.

Goddamn this woman.

When she pulled away, she held an evil smirk, her eyes filled with mischief. As she turned to leave, I grabbed her by the waist and slammed her into my body, before swatting her ass and squeezing, probably leaving marks.

"Tsk, tsk, tsk, such a naughty Dove. When I get home tonight, that little kitty is mine. I will punish you until I physically can't move anymore," I growled.

With one last swat, I let her leave and I headed to my lunch meeting.

Fucking brat.

Chapter Seventy-Six

ROSE

As I was getting close to Ren's office, I heard him and Celeste talking, so I slowed to allow them time to finish. I wasn't, however, expecting who it was about and why. In the time I've known Celeste, she seems like a great match for Richards.

Then the threat of punishment sounded so divine I wanted to drag the man in front of me home here, strip him naked, and take advantage of his cock in every way imaginable. After a quick goodbye, I headed back to our victim.

When we got the case this morning, we dropped everything. She had been missing less than twenty-four hours. Thank God my future mother-in-law was understanding when I sent her a text moving the dress shopping to tomorrow instead.

I was shocked to see no cops waiting for us, and now that we had been here for a while, none had shown up.

Odd.

I pulled out my phone and texted Cobb.

> Hey. We had a case and found a victim
> so we called the police to meet us at the
> hospital but no one is here yet and it's
> been half an hour.

His reply was instant.

> I'll look into it.

Thank God for the contacts I've made here.

The nurses carefully took photos of and samples from every inch of our victim. Poor thing was malnourished and badly beaten. Honestly, I was ready to kill the man, but we needed him. It seemed this was a human trafficking ring, and I would not stop until it was destroyed and the man in charge was dead or in prison by any means necessary.

Within ten minutes, Cobb was at the hospital with three detectives. I waved him over when he looked in my direction.

Cobb introduced his colleagues, I reached out and shook their hands, as did Wes.

"Thank you for coming. The doctors have been treating her and taking photos. We also took our own at the scene and one of our guys is still there preserving it," I said.

"Yes, we have our partners heading that way right now along with the forensic team," the one introduced as Harrison said. I gave a slight nod.

One of the other detectives went into the room with one of the nurses, while the last talked to the doctors and Harrison stayed with me and Cobb. I gave my statement and handed them my card before leaving.

By the time Liam joined us at the office, we were more than halfway through the paperwork. We kept very detailed records just in case we ever had to testify in court and to look back on for future cases.

Once everything was done, I looked at the time. It was six

already. I stood and stretched, trying to work out the kinks I developed after sitting for hours.

"Do you still have the meeting with the wedding planner tomorrow?" Wes asked.

"Sure do. We can work in the morning and start the next case."

"Sounds good to me. See you tomorrow."

The wedding was mostly planned at this point, just the dresses and suits needed to be done. Which was tomorrow's job. Then I would be married to the man I love. But for right now, I just wanted to go home and lie next to him.

Chapter Seventy-Seven

REN

Lunch had gone well and from the sounds of what Cobb said, Rose was back at her office doing paperwork. On the way home, I stopped by the store and grabbed a few things. I may not prefer to cook, but I knew how. And my mom had a recipe that I had a feeling Rose would like.

Lamb shank navarin was my favorite growing up, and now I wanted to share it with the love of my life. It took several hours to prep and cook everything while I listened to French music. Since I got off at three today, this was the perfect thing to do to pass the time. Plus, I had been craving the dish since I went to visit my mom with Rose.

As I finished dishing the food, the front door opened and the warmth of her arms wrapping around me was delightful. "Hmm, what smells so good, babe?"

"Lamb shank navarin," I replied.

"Oh shit. I haven't had that in ages. Not since my last mission in France."

I turned to face her, leaning back against the counter. "And how did you like it?"

"It was amazing, though somehow I think yours will be better."

"Well, I certainly hope so. I made my mom's recipe and, of course, made it with love." I hummed into her neck and I sought her perfect scent. She let out a slight giggle before pushing back.

"Let me get changed and showered so we can eat."

Reluctantly, I pulled back. I preferred my showers at night before bed, but she liked them as soon as she got home to de-stress, though she sometimes joined me again at night. My cock twitched at the thought of her using her hands to wash every inch of me before I did the same for her.

I'd just set the table when she came back down wrapped in her red silk robe.

Fucking hell, was she naked under that?

I mean, I'm not dumb. I knew she was, but fuck, this was torture, and judging by the smirk on her lips, she damn well knew what she was doing to me. She sat at the table and took a bite of the food sitting in front of her.

"Babe, this is really good. Brings back memories."

"Good ones I hope?"

"Yeah, good ones. Ones I long ago pushed away but am glad to have them back now."

My lips curved up slightly. "Glad I could be of service."

"Oh, you most certainly are of service in more ways than one."

I raised my eyebrow. "Oh, really now?" When she winked her reply, my cock twitched, and I dropped my fork..

Fuck me.

She placed her fork down and stood. When she got close, she spun my chair around, despite me being in it, and straddled me. I moaned as she sank her hips down and felt her against my hard-ness. In seconds, I had my hands on her hips, pressing her down more, needing that contact.

"You fed my stomach, but now my kitty needs to eat," she whispered in my ear before flicking it with her tongue. "Or be eaten."

Without a word, I stood up, holding her to me as I made my way down the hall to our room.

That little kitty was going to be eaten, then fed like the royalty it was.

Chapter Seventy-Eight

ROSE

His speed while he carried me to our room was impressive as hell. I wasn't sure if it was my words or if he was already there before I teased him. Either way, I knew I was about to get pounded and I fucking loved it.

He placed me on the bed, stripped me, and tied me up. Once I was secured to the bed, he pulled out a blindfold and asked permission with his eyes, looking for signs of discomfort.

"Hmm yes, blindfold me, Alpha. Make me feel more of you than I can imagine."

A deep growl vibrated through him and into me as he straddled my hips. His erection looked painful against his pants. Before I could say another word, the fabric was over my eyes and I was in darkness.

It didn't take long for my ears to acclimate to the loss of sight. When I heard his pants being undone and dropping, I shivered. The anticipation of what was going to happen next made me leak. This was always something I wanted to try, but never trusted anyone enough to actually do it. But now I did, and I knew he would make it the best experience of my life.

My skin quivered when something soft touched me. It tickled a trail all over my very naked body. I squirmed in my restraints, wanting desperately to know what was coming next, what he was doing to me.

Fuck.

More sensations moved over my body, and I loved every second of this sweet torture. I squirmed as his breath moved over my kitty.

Before I could react or even squirm, his tongue plunged into me and I let out a groan. His tongue moved in and out, making sure to eat every last drop of the wetness I gave him. I jolted when I felt his fingers enter me, his tongue still working its own magic.

Good God.

Every sensation was heightened, and I was on the verge of coming undone already.

It wasn't long before he was moving his fist in and out of me, my body writhing in ecstasy. I felt something cold and wet pressed against my back hole and let out a moan as it pressed slowly inside me.

Oh fuck.

He moved it in and out a bit before leaving it inside.

When the vibrations started, I knew what it was, and my eyes rolled back at the sensation. His hand and tongue were still working my kitty within an inch of my life. There were multiple times I thought for sure I would cum, but somehow it never happened.

How the hell?

It was like he ordered it away with his touch.

On the next thrust of his fist, my body went numb before every muscle in my body tightened. The amount of cum that gushed out of me was impressive. Pretty sure it soaked him. His growl against me only seemed to fuel my orgasm.

"I swear, when you squirt, I have to stop myself from coming right then and there. So fucking sexy." He licked me some more, cleaning me. "And now I am bathed in it, you naughty little Dove."

Next, I felt his tip pressed against my entrance before he slammed into me. I cried out with pleasure.

"Hmmm, you like my cock in that sexy little kitty, don't you? You like the feeling of your Alpha inside you."

"Yes," I moaned.

"Good, cause I am far from done with you, Dove. You are mine and you are going to feel me forever."

Oh God, yes.

Chapter Seventy-Nine

REN

My hair and face were soaked in her cum, and I fucking loved it. Now my cock was begging for its release. Every muscle in my body begged for my orgasm to ripple through. With every thrust, I ground my hips, trying to go deeper and deeper. The vibrations from the butt plug traveled through me and combined with her channel quivering against my length.

Fuck.

Each thrust was powerful and created a loud smack of our skin. I was sure she would be sore, and fuck if that thought didn't turn me on.

Now that I wasn't fisting her, I was able to use my hands to squeeze her breasts and pinch roughly on her nipples. She squirmed beneath me as she called out every version of my name, adding fuel to the fire brewing inside me.

My orgasm came hard and with no warning as I moved inside her, a growl ripping through me and filling the room.

Goddamn.

My growl of pleasure nearly drowned out hers as her body

convulsed beneath me. Once I drained every last drop from my cock, I moved in and out a few more times, pushing my seed deeper inside her, not wanting any to escape.

Slowly, I pulled my sated cock out of her warmth and untied her, leaving her eyes for last. When I removed the blindfold, her eyes sparkled with her love. She moved her arms around my neck and pulled me in for a kiss, which I gave her.

After a minute she pulled back, then used her tongue to lick her drying cum off my face. The only place she didn't lick was my hair. I relished the feeling of her tongue on me.

"Fuck, that feels good," I breathed.

"Hmm, well, you taste good."

"You mean you taste good cause that is your cum all over me."

"We mix well together, then," she purred. My cock stiffened slightly and she let out a chuckle. "You are insatiable."

"Only for you."

I moved her up on the bed before removing the plug and cleaning it. Once I was done, I climbed in and held her close as we fell asleep.

I WOKE to the sound of water running. When I rolled out of bed, my muscles protested. If I was sore, I could only imagine how sore she was. I made my way to the bathroom and wasn't surprised to find her in the tub soaking.

A chuckle escaped my lips as I shook my head. Rose looked up at me and smirked.

"Hey, it's your fault."

I couldn't help the smile that spread across my lips. Damn right it was, and I'd do it again.

"Oh, you know you loved every second of it."

She huffed. "Well yeah, but that's besides the point."

"Is it though?"

Her response was priceless. I was now soaked as she splashed me with the water from the tub. My floor was now wet.

I was bent over laughing when I felt a hand grip my ankle before my foot slipped out from under me and I fell with a splash on my ass.

Oh, she was going to pay for that.

I got up and moved to lift her from the tub when my phone rang.

Fucking hell, every damn time.

Chapter Eighty

ROSE

I lost it when the water splashed as he fell. It was straight out of the cartoon. My stomach ached from the laughter. He moved in with determination to punish me, but his phone rang and I almost growled my annoyance.

Always interrupted.

While he took the call in our room, I finished my bath and got out, not bothering with a towel since they were now all on the floor soaking up the water. I was combing my hair when my ass stung from Ren's hand.

I leaked from the impact.

Oh yes, please.

"You get off for now. There is a situation at the hospital. I got to shower quickly, then go. But you will pay for that little stunt later, Dove. Just you wait."

The threat was clear, and I fucking loved it. With a quick kiss, he got in the shower and I dressed.

REN'S MOM smiled at me as I pulled into the parking lot of the dress shop.

"I'm so glad you could make it today," she said in greeting.

"Me too, Mrs. Doux."

"Please honey, you are marrying my son. Call me Mom, Mama, or any variation."

"How about Maman?"

She beamed at the French word for mom. "Tu parles français?"

"Oui, flient."

Her smile was contagious, and I was happy that my knowing French brought her so much joy. I vowed to use it around her more often.

We walked inside, and I was immediately overwhelmed. There were so many dresses, and I had no clue where to start. Thank God we had a dress specialist there to help.

"You must be Rose. My name is Raven. I will be your assistant today. Do you have any preferences you want to keep in mind while we shop?"

"Honestly, no. Other than the fact that I need to be able to wear it as is, since I am getting married later this week."

"Of course. I will grab a few dresses I think will fit."

She settled us on a small couch before disappearing into the sea of dresses. When she came back, she had six dresses with her and ushered me into a changing room.

Oh boy. Here we go.

The first few dresses were way too blingy for my taste. I didn't want plain, but also didn't want fully covered in fucking sparkles. Based on my feedback, the lady left the room to grab another dress. I was impressed by the fact that she knew my size just from looking at me. When she came out, she had a beautiful dress.

I slipped it on and felt tears threaten to escape at the way it looked. It was plain except for a flower at the waist and a slightly ruffled top. The rest was smooth and flared out toward the bottom, but my movement wasn't restricted. She wrapped a mesh piece around me and it turned into a gorgeous ball gown.

"You can wear it like this for the ceremony, then slip it off for the reception."

My reply was lost on my lips. All I managed to do was smile. She grabbed a veil and placed it on my head before we walked out to show my maman.

God, I loved that.

When she saw me, her face beamed, and she began to cry, my tears also escaping.

"You look like a queen," my maman breathed.

"I feel like one."

The sales lady took off the ball gown, and a gasp came from Maman.

"Stunning," was all she said.

"So, is this your dress?" the lady asked.

"Yes," I said.

She looked me over in the dress and everything fit perfectly. No alterations needed. I picked out the bridesmaid dresses from the rentals and we headed out, dresses in hand. All that was left were tuxes, and Cobb and Charlie were doing that.

Hannah and Maman were just leaving the parking lot when my phone rang. When I looked at the screen, I was surprised to see it was Barks.

"Hey Barks, what's up?"

"Hey Rose, sorry to bother you, but I need your help on a case."

"How do you mean?"

"I mean, I am about to get on a plane and fly to you. Richards is coming with."

"ETA?" was all I asked. I knew they couldn't say more than that, so I wouldn't ask.

"Zero three hundred. We will come to you."

"Copy," I said, then hung up.

I am supposed to get married in two days and now it appears

we have had a problem. To say I was going to solve this fast was an understatement, cause come hell or high water, I was marrying my Alpha on Friday.

After I placed the dresses in the back, I drove home. I knocked on my dad's door and he answered right away. He took the dresses from me and winked.

"I'll hide them nice and good."

"Thanks, Dad."

"You know I will do anything for you, dear." He placed them securely in his closet. When he turned to look at me, his expression told me I was wearing the concern about the call from Barks all over my face. "What's wrong?"

"Nothing is wrong. Just got an odd call from Barks. They are coming in early and need my help with something. Don't know anything else."

He nodded in understanding. "I'll make sure you and the guys have clear schedules."

"Thanks."

"Always. Now go to your place before Ren sees you down here. He should be home soon, according to Charles," he said, shoving me out the door. I couldn't help but laugh at the childish antics.

Once outside, I took a deep breath. It was my turn to cook dinner, and tonight we were having my dad's meatloaf.

Chapter Eighty-One

REN

The delicious smell of garlic and meat filled the house as I walked in.

I placed my bags and stuff by the door before looking for the source of the smell. A smile spread across my lips when I saw Rose at the stove in her short shorts and a tank top. I walked up behind her and wrapped my arms around her waist. She leaned back into me and I kissed her neck, making sure to tease her with my tongue.

"What are you cooking, Dove? It smells delicious."

"Meatloaf, mashed potatoes, corn, and green bean casserole."

"Well, it smells divine."

"It better, it's a family recipe."

While she finished up the last-minute things, I set the table before sitting down. Rose placed my plate in front of me, and my mouth watered. The food looked like something off the Food Network.

Using my fork, I cut off a piece of the meatloaf and brought it to my mouth.

Holy shit.

The amount of flavor in the meat was almost overwhelming. My mouth watered so much I thought I would start drooling like a damn boxer puppy. I closed my eyes and took in every single flavor it gave me as I chewed.

When I opened my eyes, Rose was looking at me with an amused smirk and a raised eyebrow.

"What?" I said with my mouth still full.

"You were moaning like I was on my knees, taking your cock in my mouth."

I stopped chewing and swallowed roughly.

Wait, what?

Now it was my turn to look confused.

"You telling me you were so entranced by my dad's meat that you didn't hear your own moans?"

"Apparently."

I held back a laugh at her dad's meat comment and felt my cheeks heat with my embarrassment. She stood and moved over to me, sitting in my lap. Her hands on either side of my face, she leaned in until our foreheads were touching.

"You are something else, babe," she said between giggles. "But that is why I fucking love you."

"That and my dick," I deadpanned. She threw her head back while she laughed hard. Her hand smacked my shoulder in a teasing manner.

"You are such a horny bastard."

"Maybe so, but your kitty is greedy for my cock and you know it."

She rolled her eyes, and I pulled her into me, covering her lips with my own. My cock twitched and she let out a low moan.

No amount of sex with this woman would ever be enough. She woke up my inner slut, and I fucking loved it. I was getting used to being constantly semi or fully hard.

Something was off. She seemed distracted.

I pulled back and looked her in the eye. "What's on your mind, Dove?"

She took a deep breath and looked me in the eye. "Barks and Richards are coming. Something about a case they need me for."

Well, damn.

My stomach flipped from nerves. Last case she had, she got hurt, and I don't know if I could survive that again. Almost like she could sense my unease, she leaned down and kissed me before pulling back.

"I will be careful, babe. I have skills they may need. If it was dangerous, they would have given the code word."

I relaxed a bit hearing that it was likely not danger related. But I was still worried. Don't get me wrong, I know she can handle herself, but I wanted to keep her safe and at home. I buried my face in her neck and she rubbed my back, working out the burgeoning tension. Her touch told me everything. She understood my concern but knew I would be here for her. Her body also told me it would be okay and that she would come home to me no matter what. I lost myself in her touch, and my cock grew at the friction of her hips as she worked my muscles.

My body shuttered with barely contained desire as her hand wandered up my shirt until her fingers were flicking my nipple. I leaned my head back as she worked her skills on my chest.

"Hmm, Dove. Feels so damn good."

"You know what also feels good?" She said as one of her hands moved to my rock hard erection. She tugged and twisted as she moved her hand over my cock.

"Fuck," I moaned.

"I want you to tie me up and fuck me until I squirt again," she growled in my ear.

Oh fuck.

Without a word, I scooped her up and carried her to our bedroom. Within seconds, I had her fully naked and tied to the bed. Her eyes locked on me, watching as I took off my own clothes. When she licked her lips, her eyes sparkled with her lust.

I took a moment to look at her lying on our bed tied up and vulnerable.

Jesus Christ, she was stunning.

Chapter Eighty-Two

ROSE

Watching him as he practically eyefucked me was intense and erotic. The amount this man wanted me and loved me practically made my pussy leak constantly. I was about to marry him and we had all weekend to devour each other all day long.

Our honeymoon was scheduled for after the study, and that made me even happier. We would be gone for six weeks, traveling Europe and spending time in France where his family was from. Everything was already paid for and now it was a waiting game.

His mom was coming with us if she could, but she also knew that her health was not doing as good as she wanted. She made a detailed guide of the places to go, just in case.

I moaned and arched my back as he bit the inside of my thigh.

Oh fuck.

"Hmm, I love how you squirm when I do that."

I heard him rustling in his bag, then felt as the pad of a crop slapped my ass.

Fucking hell.

"You worried me, so now you will be punished."

Oh, dear God.

Even if I wanted to, I would not have been able to speak. I loved his dominating side and relished it. My punishments were more of funishments. The sensation the whip left behind sent electricity through my body. He bent down so he could whisper in my ear.

"I will only use my cock to make you squirt tonight, Dove. But for now, I am going to tease you and give you the pain you desire."

He bit my neck, then worked his way down my body, biting me every few inches, leaving his marks behind. Honestly, if I ever ended up in the hospital, the doctor may have some questions.

Oh fuck.

That thought turned me on. Love marks can be nasty looking, but it was all consensual and people shouldn't judge.

When he bit down on my clit, I almost lurched off the bed. If I hadn't been tied, I may have. The pain was intense, but immediately my body responded with desire.

"Fucking fuck me, dammit," I growled.

"Tsk, tsk, tsk, so impatient." Swat. "You are not in charge, Dove." Swat. "I decide when you get my cock." Swat.

This was sweet torture, and I was relishing it.

"If you want my cock, then take it," he growled as he yanked my head up by my hair until I was face to face with his cock. He was on his knees in front of me. I opened my mouth, and he rammed his length into my throat, making me gag.

I hummed my desire and satisfaction. He pulled out slightly, then snapped his hips, forcing the shaft to the back of my throat. My tongue flicked and licked the sensitive spots, and he pounded into my mouth like his life depended on it. Every time I gagged, it only seemed to fuel his need.

On the next upward stroke, I grazed his vein with my teeth.

He roared as his cum erupted from his cock, almost drowning me with the sheer volume. Smack.

Oh fuck.

"So fucking naughty Dove. Making me come before I was finished with you, tsk, tsk, tsk." Smack. "Now you will pay for that."

Before I could utter a response, he rammed his still semi hard cock inside me. I let out a moan and felt him harden instantly.

Fucking hell.

Chapter Eighty-Three

REN

She took me by surprise when she brought me to the most intense orgasm I had ever experienced. This was supposed to be about her, but damn if she didn't make it about me. But now it was my turn to make her cum, make her squirt.

I slammed into her, angling myself to hit maximum depth and her sweet spot. She yelled out my name or Alpha with every thrust. Her legs twitched with ecstasy. As soon as I felt her getting close, I would slow down, then start right back up. Her growls told me I was torturing her.

Good.

Her channel began to quiver, and I knew she was about to blow. This time, I pounded into her sweet spot.

"Fuck!" she yelled as she convulsed beneath me.

The wetness seeped out, my thrusts creating a splash telling me she did, in fact, squirt.

Oh, fuck yes.

A smug smirk spread over my face. Made her squirt with just my cock, no toys or fists. Just me.

My orgasm slammed into me like a freight train, and I growled as I shot my load deep inside her. Once I was sure she took every last drop, I pulled out of her and untied her. She moved off the towel we always had on the bed for instances like this. It was soaked, and the bed was slightly damp with her essence.

"So fucking messy, Dove."

"Hey, it was your fault," she retorted, and I chuckled.

"Not my fault you are so damn sexy."

She rolled her eyes, and I swatted her ass as she pulled the damp cover and replaced it with a clean one. I lay down, and she wasted no time climbing in bed and curling into me, her head resting on my chest.

"I love you," she whispered.

"I love you too."

My ALARM BLARED, telling me I had to get up. I groaned, reluctant to leave the bed. Rose was in my arms and I was comfortable. Ignoring the alarm, I snuggled into Rose and she chuckled.

"You, sir, have work to do."

I moaned my displeasure and pressed my hard cock against her ass.

She rolled to face me, then climbed onto me while she silenced the blaring noise. "As much as I want you right now, you have an important meeting, and you can't be late."

Ugh. Why did she have to be right?

Today I was meeting with the person in charge of the study, the FDA, and the Institutional Review Board. It was an audit, and it was critical that I got there early to make sure everyone and everything was ready.

"Your ass is mine later," I growled.

"Always," she breathed.

My cock leaked at the promise.
Oh God, give me strength.

Chapter Eighty-Four

ROSE

When Ren rutted against me like a horny teenage boy, I almost lost it.

Fuck.

I wanted him so bad, but he had a meeting to get to and I was not about to be the reason the study got derailed. And I knew he would make me pay for it later, but fuck if that didn't turn me on.

While he got ready for work, I made him a breakfast burrito and packed him leftovers for lunch. When he came down, he grabbed his lunch bag and breakfast before pressing me against the counter.

"When I get home tonight. I am going to eat you, then my cock is going to fill that tight ass of yours."

"Don't keep me waiting too long," I said as I flicked his ear with my tongue. His mouth crashed into mine as he kissed me. It was early, it was already past 3:30 in the morning, so any minute Richards and Barks would be here.

Ren left, and I quickly changed into something more suitable for work. I made a few more burritos for the guys and just placed them on the table when the front door opened. Of course I knew who it was, so I didn't look up, just motioned to the dining room table.

"Okay, what brings you here?" I asked as I looked both of them in the eye.

"We need your skills. You are the fastest translator we have, and you know tracking and decoding. We need all of it for this one," Barks said as he pulled out a file and tossed it in front of me.

I opened the file and looked at its contents. My eyes read through the documents. No wonder they called me. They used at least fifteen languages with words that didn't make sense in the order they were. To me, that made me think that the meaning was the opposite or within the word itself.

"What do we know?" I asked, my eyes still glued to the file, my brain working a mile a minute, trying to decode and translate.

"This file came from an undercover. He found it but could only upload it. His language skills were limited to French and English. Obviously this is more than that," Barks said.

"We also know this came from a target to another target, so our concern is they are planning something big. All things considered, our agents might be in danger," Richards added.

"Give me a few hours, maybe less," I said.

"Of course. We will go to our hotel and see if they have any rooms available yet." Barks said.

As they were about to leave, Richards added, "Yes, you can use your business partners if you need."

Well, that was good to know. Once they left, I went up to the bedroom and spread out everything on the bed. After several hours, I had every word translated but was stumped on the next move.

"What are you working on so intently, Dove?" Ren asked. I

almost jumped out of the bed. I was so entranced by my work I didn't hear him come in.

"Just the thing Barks and Richards needed help with. I'm stumped. Was about to text the guys to see what they thought. I hadn't realized the time or I would have cooked something."

"I'll order some pizzas for us," he said as he went toward the kitchen, giving me a kiss first. I pulled out my phone and sent a text to Barks and Richards.

Pizza at my place.

I gathered up the files and my decoding before heading downstairs to wait for the pizza and my former bosses.

Chapter Eighty-Five

REN

I hung up the phone from ordering pizza as she plopped down on the couch with a sigh.

"Is everything alright, Dove?"

"I just can't figure this one out. Normally, I am faster than this."

"May I see?"

She looked like she was contemplating, then handed me a single page, only part of what she was working on. I wasn't a coder by any stretch of the imagination, but one of my buddies was and he taught me some of the harder but easy-to-spot ones, if you know about their tactics. My favorite was evens and odds with a scatter.

Head dead dogsound dicks with dead shot now kill

Evens were *dead, dicks, handsome, dead, now*. Add odds were *head, dogsound, with, shot, kill*. My mind spun with the order several times. The best I could come up with was "Handsome wants dicks dead now Kill dogsound with headshot."

This was a hit, but on who?

Handsome is the shot caller but who is dogsound? My eyes bulged as it hit me. "Dove, where are Barks and Richards?"

"On their way here."

I didn't say a word. I just called Richards.

"Hey man, we are a few minutes from your place. What's up?"

My mind spun, trying to remember the code work for Kevin. "Pluto. Meet at the office instead."

"Copy."

I hung up and looked at Rose, who was tilting her head in confusion. "I had a buddy who did codes for the Army. He taught me a few things. It says 'Handsome wants dicks dead now.' Handsome is the meaning of Kevin in Irish, which is what you translated that word from. Dick is short for Richard and add the S you get Richards. The next part says Kill dog sound with head shot. Barking is a dog's sound. This is a hit on your bosses. I'll text your dad to grab the food and bring it in. You need to call your staff and anyone who owes you a favor because Kevin is calling shots from the grave. Someone was working for him."

Chapter Eighty-Six

ROSE

Holy shit.

First off, I was impressed as fuck that Ren decoded the message. Second off, Kevin was dead but clearly had someone following his corrupt cause and now we needed to figure out who. We hopped on our bikes and sped off to the office while I made calls. This was going to be big, and we needed all the help we could get.

I called Cobb, and he answered on the second ring. "Cobb, come to my office. We have a Pluto issue."

"On my way," he said, then the line went dead.

I must have been wearing my stress cause Ren brushed his hand on my arm at a stoplight, trying to soothe me. We pulled the bikes into the office and went into the back, to the secured room. Despite the street being empty, everyone was there and waiting.

Now it was time to figure this shit out.

Everyone sat around the conference table and looked at me, waiting.

"Richards and Barks called me asking for help with a multi-lingual coded message. I translated everything and was struggling to decode it. There is more to this message than what I let Ren look at. But what we have so far is a target on Barks and Richards."

Richards looked at Ren. "Do you think you can help with the rest?"

"Yes. Give me the rest of the file and I will get on it while you guys talk."

With a quick nod from Richards, I handed over the complete file, and he moved to a small desk in the back and got to work. I needed to know who this friend was that taught him this cause right now I could kiss him.

"We need a plan. But you two are not in charge. You're the targets."

"Agreed," Richards said.

"We came to you for help, Rose. You are in charge, you and your team," Barks said, and Richards nodded his agreement.

"Alright then. I made some calls and more agents are on their way. We also have Cobb and some of his staff since he was promoted to lieutenant."

"How did you…" he started.

I huffed. "You really think I don't have my ways of knowing things. Like my eyes? The silver bar is a dead giveaway."

"True."

"Let's talk about safe house placement. We need undercovers, no obvious agents or cops."

"Consider it done. I have several cops I'd trust with the task," Cobb said.

"Good, you have a location?"

"Yes, we have one in a small town in the middle of nowhere. Open viewing two-way-mirror-style windows. You will see anyone coming, no matter the direction."

"Awesome."

We continued to talk for several hours while more agents

arrived from Langley. Everyone had their assignments and now it was show time. Even Ren had his part with the code. He handed me a piece of paper with the full message.

Kevin is dead. Killed by the traitor who calls herself righteous. His death was torture. He was ambushed and that will not do. She killed his lover before me and now she has killed mine. For this, she will pay. Kevin wants Richards dead now. Kill Barks with head shot. That is the only way. Then I will get my revenge as I kill her lover.

My eyes snapped up to Ren's as my heart clinched. They wanted him too.

"I know you are about to tell me to go to the safe house, but I can't. It could jeopardize the study. Send some agents to watch me. I will only see my study patients, no one else."

"Then I will be with you. The other agents got Barks and Richards. I will take my men and protect you."

His hand cupped my chin, and he kissed me softly. "Okay."

This plan also made it seem more like we had no clue what was happening and could give us the upper hand.

Chapter Eighty-Seven

REN

After the last incident with Kevin, I felt so helpless, but this time I was able to contribute. For that, I was thankful. I hated being on the sidelines, unable to help. My time in the Army was short, and I spent most of it behind a medical desk, but I still went to boot camp. I still trained with my fellow soldiers. But I was a peaceful man, so I had elected out of the more violent jobs.

Now Rose would be with me all day, and I honestly looked forward to it. After everything was settled, we headed home. Rose texted her dad to stay with Charlie tonight, and that was all he needed to hear. Everyone was safe and protected, and now it was time to eat the pizza and go to bed. We needed our rest.

WHEN I WOKE UP, Rose was curled to my chest, still snoring softly. I pulled her tighter and kissed the top of her head.

"Morning," she mumbled.

"Morning, Dove."

She shifted so she was straddling me. My cock responded immediately. When she pressed her hips down on my erection, I growled out my pleasure. We never slept with clothes on anymore, so all it would take is one move and I would be buried deep inside her.

Her body practically begged for my penetration. I placed my hands on her hips, trying to keep my head. "Fuck Dove, you make me so crazy with lust."

"Then fuck me," she said as she sat back, my tip just barely running between her folds, teasing her entrance.

Jesus, fuck.

I needed to get ready for work, but our bodies had other ideas. A groan escaped my lips as I tossed my head back. The warmth of her wetness drove me wild.

"Dove, we have to get ready for work."

"Hmm. We have time for a quickie," she whispered against my lips as she rolled her hips, her entrance practically swallowing my length.

"Fuck," I moaned. She smirked, knowing she had me and I would bend to her will.

I mean, who the fuck could blame me?

She felt so damn good wrapped around my cock. The way she rocked and circled her hips was drawing my balls up quickly.

"Jesus, Dove. Keep doing that and I'll come right now."

She drove down harder and faster, and I tightened my grip on her hip as I thrust into her. Her responding curses made my body tingle with the start of my orgasm. I wrapped my arms around her shoulders and pushed her down onto me, penetrating deep as she screamed out.

My orgasm was right on the edge, waiting for one more thing to break it through the surface. She bit down on my nipple, and the first jet of cum exploded from my cock. My eyes rolled back as I held her down on my shaft. Her moans filled the room, competing with my growl as her walls tightened blissfully around my length, milking every drop from me.

"Fuck Dove," I said between winded breaths.

"Hmm. So fucking warm."

We lay there for a few as we tried to get our breathing under control. She was lying on her stomach when I finally got up. My palm made a smacking sound as it met her perfect ass. Her responding yelp made my cock twitch back to life.

Good Lord.

Chapter Eighty-Eight

ROSE

I knew we needed to get ready, but I woke up horny as hell. More than normal. Maybe it was the fact that, yet again, I was being targeted. I mean, could we not catch a damn break?

My mind whirled with what-ifs and would-hes. The amount of things that have barrelled in our path would break a lot of couples, but somehow we were still good, hell maybe even stronger for it.

As I stood up, a wave of nausea swayed me a bit.

Odd.

I shook my head and headed to the bathroom to wash up for the day. Since I was an acting agent, I wore my CIA suit. Once dressed, I headed to the kitchen to heat up our breakfast. I smiled slightly when I heard his footsteps coming down the hall.

When they stopped, I looked up to see him leaning against the doorframe, looking at me while he licked his lips.

"Fuck, I've missed that outfit."

I stalked toward him, pressed my body against him, and

looked into his eyes. "Hmm. So I should wear this before bed so you can take it off of me to play the role of bed agent," I teased.

The moan that came from Ren told me the idea was very much something he would enjoy, that and the erection currently making itself known between us. I grasped his shaft and squeezed, earning me a groan.

"Later I will suck your cock until you coat my throat with your cum, then I will take your cock hard until you cum again," I whispered in his ear before pulling back. "Now come grab your food so we can go."

I heard him huff in frustration as he palmed his bulge, and I couldn't help but chuckle. Which only got louder when he glared at me. As we walked out the door, he grabbed my ass and squeezed before giving it a hard smack.

"I will punish you hard for that later, Dove," he growled.

Oh, fuck me.

THE MORNING WENT by without any issues. Everything was calm, but something told me it wouldn't last much longer. Security knew there was something going on and was informed to alert me or one of my men if they noticed anything out of the ordinary.

We sat in his office while he did paperwork. Wes was bringing up some food, and I was growing impatient. I was hungry as hell. As soon as the smell hit me, I got nauseous again and ran to the bathroom down the hall.

I barely made it to the toilet before I was throwing up.

What the hell?

I stood and a wave of dizziness hit me, making me fall and hit my head on the door. My head spun, and I leaned forward in time to throw up again.

Was I poisoned somehow?

Slowly, I managed to get up, wincing at the pain in my temple. I stepped into the hall as Celeste passed by.

"Rose, what the hell happened?" she asked as she rushed to help me.

"I got nauseous, then dizzy. Fell, then hit my head." My sentences were choppy as my head continued to spin.

"I'm taking you downstairs. You don't look good. You are pale and bleeding."

I had no strength to fight her as she pulled out her nurse phone and got security to bring up a wheelchair. Exhausted, I dropped into it like a sack of potatoes. The officer was moving past Ren's office when Wes noticed us and came out. His hand reached toward his weapon as he took in my current state.

"What the hell happened?" he yelled. Ren came out from behind his desk and took in my pale appearance.

"Dove, are you okay?"

"Just dizzy, nauseous," I managed to say.

"I'm taking her to Thompson. You stay here," Celeste said before we took off down the hall.

Within seconds of entering the ER, Thompson was there and taking blood and vitals. Celeste cleaned my head and sighed before saying, "Just a small cut."

They gave me Zofran and ran all my tests under stat when Liam whispered to the doctor. I knew he was informing him there was a target on me, and I may have been poisoned.

I was resting in my room when Liam called Ren to tell him I was okay and they were running tests. And he would notify him immediately of any changes. Cobb came in as well, looking like he rushed here from the safe house.

"Do we know anything?" he asked, looking at Liam.

"No, still waiting on tests."

"Which just came back," Celeste said as she walked in, a wide grin on her face.

What the hell?

"Rose, are you alright with me saying the results in front of these two?"

"Yes."

"The tests are negative for poisons, but positive for pregnancy. Rose, you are six weeks pregnant."

Holy shit.

On instinct, my hand flew to my stomach, and my eyes welled up with tears.

Pregnant.

So many emotions swirled in my head. Happiness, fear, shock. But it made sense. We never used condoms and birth control can fail. I was on antibiotics after the attack and even then we had sex like rabbits, so it was only a matter of time.

"Do you want me to tell Rene?" Celeste asked.

"No, I'll tell him when we get married. For now, I'll just tell him low iron."

"Well, your iron is low, so it makes sense. Thank God the wedding is in two days. This will be a hard secret to keep."

I nodded, laid my head back, and closed my eyes.

I was going to be a mom.

Chapter Eighty-Nine

REN

Seeing Rose so pale and bleeding sent my mind spiraling as anger made the hairs on the back of my neck stand up.

Did someone hurt her?

She said she was nauseous and dizzy, but why? The doctor in me was already trying to figure it all out. Liam reported she was fine and her color was back. Nothing serious, just low iron, which made sense based on her symptoms.

But I would not—no, could not—stop worrying until I laid my eyes on her. I wrapped up everything I was doing and went for the door, Wes close behind me. I liked it better when Rose was following me, but hey I can't be too picky right now since she is out of commission. As soon as I got in the hall, the hair on the back of my neck stood up again.

Something wasn't right.

Wes patted my shoulder twice, which told me he felt it too. I noted he had an earpiece earlier, so I wasn't surprised when he didn't pull out his phone, just hit a button on his watch. All he said was one word. "Pizza."

Knowing my job was to stay hidden, I moved back into my office and hid behind the desk. I refused to corner myself by getting under the desk. That just seemed dumb. I worked in a hospital so obviously I didn't have a gun, but I did have a very heavy gold-plated plaque I received years ago.

Waiting was rough. All my mind could think about was if Rose was okay? After several minutes, I stood up and moved toward the door, peeking out the one-way glass. Wes was on the ground, unconscious.

What the hell?

The door swung open. I moved back so it hid me. A woman charged in.

"Where are you, Doctor? I'm having an emergency," she sneered.

I thought Kevin was gay. Guess he was bi or lying to her.

"I know you are here. This is your department, after all."

I still didn't speak or move. I studied her for signs of drug use or patterns. I saw none.

"If you don't come out, I might have to pay your patients a visit. Their lives will be on your hands, doctor. Your bitch of a bride signed your death warrant, so come out now."

With slow and determined steps, I moved out from behind the door and swung the award at the back of her head, knocking her off her feet. She recovered and growled her displeasure before she came at me.

Every punch she threw, I blocked with ease. She was not weak, to say the least, but I was trained by the best. Not only the government, but I did years of martial arts as a child. After several minutes, I gained the upper hand. I remembered the quote Rose said about someone was always better than you and some will fake you out like she did to Kevin. She got in a kick, and I heard my rib pop.

Fuck.

I knew it wasn't broken, but the cartilage definitely was not happy. When I heard Wes groan, I called out to him, "Sheep."

Our code word for "backup needed." The mumbled sound I heard after that was hard to make out, but it sounded like he said the word.

I looked over and saw a scalpel given to me by my mom when I graduated from med school. In a quick movement, I dove across my desk and grabbed it, the bitch right on my heels. I twisted and threw the blade, hitting her right in the neck, severing her carotid. A look of shock etched on her face as her blood spewed out of her and her body hit the ground. As she did, the door swung back open, Rose and Cobb right behind. I could see Liam bent over Wes, checking on him. Cobb dropped to the now lifeless body of the woman, who had a gun by her. Rose was in front of me, looking me over. Her relieved sigh at realizing the blood wasn't mine was audible to everyone.

Security and cops rushed in next. Wes was taken to the ER and Rose helped me downstairs to be looked at. Cobb took my statement while Thompson looked me over. Just some bruised ribs, one dislocated, so it had to be reset. But overall I was unhurt.

As I rested, Rose curled in next to me, and I held her close. Today I proved I could do more, but now my mind spun with the bitch's words.

My bride.

Who was this bitch? How did she know we were engaged? When I got a text from Cobb, it was short, but answered my question.

She has been working at the hospital in the ER for a couple of weeks. Celeste identified her.

Fucking hell.

Chapter Ninety

ROSE

When I barged into Ren's office after Wes's weak distress call, I was so damn relieved to see him standing. A woman lay on the ground, unmoving. I knew Cobb would handle her. All I cared about was Ren, the man I loved.

Thank God he had no serious injuries. His decorative scalpel was evidence for now, but Cobb assured us it would be released to him once they fully cleared him for the incident. Now we were home and resting. The Zofran worked wonders on my nausea. Everything was back to normal, and I was relieved. Tomorrow, I would marry this man in front of everyone we care about.

He was sore as hell after the fight, so I decided to give him a treat. Slowly, I wiggled my way down and swallowed his length, and his cock hardened the rest of the way while I moved up and down. His hand gripped my hair, and he pulled me deeper.

"Fuck, Dove," he moaned.

I moved with purpose as I licked and sucked every inch of his rock-hard erection. He thrust his hips up, and I pinned him down, stopping the motion.

"Nuh-uh, you just lay there and enjoy my mouth on your cock."

"Oh fuck," he said, slamming his head back.

I knew my tone was dominant, and I'd be damned if he didn't seem to like that. The amount of pre-cum leaking into my throat was insane. I cupped his balls into my hand and gently moved them around as I continued to work his length.

"Dove I—" His words cut off as his orgasm shot up to the surface and his cum exploded down my throat.

I sucked hard, seeking every last drop of his release, not wanting to waste any of it. When I finally released him, he pulled me back up to him and just held me.

"I fucking love you, Dove."

"I love you Alpha."

CELESTE FINISHED my makeup and hair, and it was time to get in my dress. It slid on like a glove and I had to fan my face to stop myself from crying. I looked like a queen. After all we went through, I was finally marrying my man. Maman came in the door and smiled so hard I thought her lips would fall off.

"Ma fille, tu es magnifique."

"Merci, Maman."

She placed an old gold coronet with blue stones on my head. "This was mine, my mother's, and grandmother's. We are distant cousins to the crown, and now this is yours. Something old and blue, ma fille."

I felt like my heart would explode with the love I had for this woman and her son. My dad walked in as I pulled her into a hug.

"And I have the something new," he said as he brought in a brooch with two realistic hearts held together by a pair of handcuffs.

The detail was stunning and beyond perfect for me and Ren.

He clipped it to the left side of my dress and took a step back and smiled.

Time to marry the man of my dreams.

Chapter Ninety-One

REN

When Charles and Cobb practically dragged me out of the hospital saying I had somewhere to be, I was confused as fuck. Then they brought me to Celeste's house and forced me into a tux. My mind was spinning.

What the hell is happening?

Once I was fully in a penguin suit, I was led outside, where I could take in my surroundings. My jaw dropped as I took everything in. Flowers covered a yard filled with chairs, and a brick aisle led to a canopy strung with lights.

"Welcome to your wedding, Rene," Charles said.

"My what?"

Charles laughed. I knew I sounded shocked and confused, so I likely looked the part as well. "Your wedding. Well, surprise wedding. Rose planned it, with help, of course. After everything that happened, she didn't want to wait to be your wife. So here we are."

Holy shit.

She did all this for me?

My lips curved up into a smile. My little Dove did all this and I never even had a clue. I took my place at the altar and waited eagerly for my bride. As Celeste came down the aisle, I saw she was walking with my mom.

Even my mom was in on this.

When the music changed, I knew my Rose was next. Charles practically had to catch me when I saw her standing next to her father. She looked like a queen, no, a goddess. My cock twitched slightly at the thought of stripping that sexy dress off her later, as my wife.

The wedding was a blur as I stared into her eyes, getting lost. I managed to say my vows by some miracle.

"You may kiss the bride," Richards said.

Shit.

You don't have to tell me twice.

I leaned down and kissed her with passion, forgetting we were not alone in the slightest. After a while, Richards cleared his throat, and I reluctantly pulled away.

"Mr. and Mrs. Doux," he yelled, and everyone clapped.

Celeste ushered us to a quiet area, and we had photos taken before Celeste unclipped part of Rose's dress, revealing a hidden beauty beneath.

Holy shit.

She looked even sexier in this version. After a few more photos, we headed to the reception. The tables were decorated beautifully and fit us just right, cuffs and hearts everywhere. Perfect representations of both of us.

We sat at the head of the table and ate a lovely dinner. Now it was time for toasts.

Oh boy.

"When I first met Rene, I wasn't sure what to think of him, but as I got to know him, I realized he was perfect for my best agent and soldier. Now I consider him one of us. Take care of my agent, Doctor," Richards said.

"When Rose left the agency, I lost my best agent. I was mad

as hell, but when I got the call that she needed my help, I came. Because of her, I met someone special to me and for that I thank you both," Barks said.

"When I realized my daughter was crushing on my doctor, I worried a bit, but then I saw them together and I knew, probably before they did, that this day would come. Congrats, son, on getting married to my daughter, and thank you for all you did for me medically and personally. Even before you met my girl, you were family," Dale said.

"You two are insane and seem to attract trouble, but I wouldn't change any of it for the world. So Ren, since you married my boss, does that mean you are also my boss or is she yours too?" Wes said. Everyone laughed, and I threw a piece of bread at him.

"When I met Rose for the first time, I was in shock. For years we called and got no answer, but then there she was. When Ren seemed to change all of a sudden, I knew something had sparked. Congrats you two," Celeste said.

A few more people said their congratulations, then my mom stood up to speak. "Mon fil et ma fille, merci pour cette belle journée. Félicitations pour votre famille."

I was shocked when Rose stood.

"Thank you all for coming and keeping the secret. Three of you know another secret. The other day I felt unwell and ended up in the ER after I hit my head while I was dizzy. There was a threat to my and Ren's lives at the time, so everyone assumed the worst. The results came in at the worst time, but today is the right time to share with all of you, especially my husband." She turned to look at me. "Ren, today you became my husband, and in just over seven months, you will become a father."

Wait, what?

I sat there in silence. My brain spinning in shock, words lost on my tongue.

"You're pregnant," I managed to whisper. She nodded and

placed my hand on her belly. The contact seemed to make it click. "I'm going to be a dad?"

"Yes," she breathed.

I stood up and picked her up, spinning her around before kissing her.

Holy shit. I was going to be a dad.

Chapter Ninety-Two

ROSE

I had to fight the wave of nausea from him spinning me, but I was excited and clearly he was too. We cut into the beautiful cake and completed the process by smashing pieces in each other's faces. As per tradition, right?

Now it was time to dance. When I dragged him to the makeshift dance floor, he laughed. "I can't believe you did all this."

A soft smile spread across my lips. "I can't believe you didn't figure it out."

He let out a slight chuckle. "True. But I'm glad you did. This was the best surprise I could have ever asked for, Dove."

"I'm glad you like it and so is little bear."

Ren chuckled, then placed his hand on my belly. "I still can't believe I'm going to be a dad."

"Same." We stayed like that for the rest of the song before my dad stepped in for his dance.

"You did good, dear."

"Thanks, Dad," I said with a smile.

"You know my grandchild will be spoiled, right?"

I rolled my eyes. Oh, how I knew.

When I was finally done dancing, I sat at the table.

"How's the bride?" Ashley said as she sat next to me. I turned to her and gave her a hug.

"I'm so glad you could make it."

"Are you kidding? I wouldn't miss it for the world, and now you and I are having babies together."

"Wait, you're pregnant again?" I exclaimed.

"Yep. It's almost like the man can't keep his hands off me." She laughed.

"Oh, so you're telling me I am going to be constantly pregnant?"

"I mean, hopefully not. It gets exhausting. After this one, he is getting snipped. No more for us."

"Probably wise."

We talked some more before I let out a yawn.

"Uh-oh, the bride is tired. Best get the husband to take you home," Ashley said as she waved her husband over, who was talking to Ren, my husband.

Fuck, *I loved the sound of that.*

"Rene, it appears your wife is tired," Ashley said.

"I'll get her home."

Everyone cheered as we said our goodbyes and headed home.

Chapter Ninety-Three

REN

Rose slept in my arms as I reflected back on the day.

A surprise wedding.

I never saw that coming. Even as we talked about moving up the date, I had no clue. She gave absolutely no detectable signs.

Figures. She is a trained agent, after all.

My mom looked amazing, and I was so happy she could make it. Turns out she was in town for a while, just enjoying herself. Tomorrow afternoon she was leaving, but we would have lunch with her first.

Having her at my wedding meant everything, and she told me she confided in Rose that she wanted to be here for this and Rose made it happen. That only made me love her more. Yes, she wanted to be with me, but we all knew my mom's health was getting worse and so my wife moved everything up for her, for me.

When I talked to Ezra, I was impressed with everything he did and how he had and will continue to help Rose. The man had five kids and another on the way.

A friend for our baby.

Our baby.

My mind was having a hard time wrapping itself around being a dad. Soon the study would be over and we could go on a proper honeymoon. Now she would be pregnant, but we would make the best of it.

I enjoyed watching everyone who came to celebrate with us. Her dad, well, our dad, and Charles. They seemed to be hitting it off. Celeste was dancing with Richards the entire time while Barks and Cobb seemed stuck to each other. Then Liam and Wes gave off vibes, though neither of them made a move. It seemed we had all found someone and were in various stages in the love journey. That made the already amazing day just that much better.

Family.

$$-\!\!\sim\!\!\sim\!\!\heartsuit2\!\sim\!\!\sim\!-$$

I HADN'T REALIZED I'd fallen asleep until I woke up to an amazing warm feeling on my cock. A moan escaped my lips as I opened my eyes. Rose had my cock in her mouth and was looking up at me.

Oh fuck.

I gripped her chin and guided her to her back as I maneuvered over her, pressing my erection against her thigh.

"Does my Dove want my cock?" I whispered in her ear.

"Yes," she breathed.

"Yes, what?" I growled.

"Yes, Alpha."

"Hmm, better."

Today was about making love, finishing our marriage vows with our bodies. I slowly pressed myself into her, watching as she swallowed my length. Seeing our connection was hot as hell, and I closed my eyes and breathed so I wouldn't come right then and there.

I glided in and out of her smoothly, taking my time, enjoying the sensations of her wrapped around me in every way.

"I fucking love you so damn much," I said into her ear as I snapped my hips forward.

"I love you so damn much," she replied.

I moved a little faster as my hand reached down to play with her clit. She cursed and writhed beneath me, and I felt myself getting close.

"Oh fuck, your kitty is so fucking tight." I looked down to see our connection again just as she rolled her hips into my thrust.

Oh fuck.

My orgasm exploded from me so hard I lost my balance and almost fell on top of Rose, who was now soaking me with her waterfall of cum. I knew she didn't squirt, but that in-between of the normal cum amount and her squirt was just as heavenly.

This was my forever with my Dove. My wife and I couldn't be happier.

Fucking perfection.

Chapter Ninety-Four

ROSE

As per my new norm, I woke up horny as hell, so I got what I wanted and then some. Sex with my Alpha, my husband would never get old. I was thankful it was the weekend cause we had nothing to do but each other, and I was all about that. The pregnancy was starting to make itself known. Morning sickness had really kicked in.

We had lunch plans with his mom before she left, so we dressed and headed out. Ren was off until Tuesday, so we even had an extended weekend.

"Maman, it's good to see you," I said as she sat across from us.

"You too, ma fille."

Throughout lunch, she told me all the stories about Ren, and I could see his embarrassment all over his face. My hand rested on his thigh as I made small circles to keep him calm. Not that he would do anything, but the touch was likely still comforting. So regardless of whether he needed it or not, he was getting it.

Hannah met us there to take Maman home. "Mon fil, you take care of her and my grandbaby."

"Avec ma vie."

Once she was gone, I turned to face my husband and wrapped my hand behind his neck, pulling him in.

"Let's go home," I said as I bit his bottom lip, rubbing my thigh against his bulge. He didn't say a word, just growled before practically dragging me out of the restaurant with a huge grin on his face.

The rest of our mini honeymoon was spent in our room. Between fuck sessions, we planned out the rest of our trip with his mom. To say we were all excited was an understatement. Every meal was cooked and made to accommodate the weird cravings I was developing and always in bed. I felt like a queen, but unfortunately, we both had to return to work.

"Hmm, I don't want to go back to work," he mumbled.

"Neither do I, but duty calls."

He grumbled some more before repositioning himself between my legs. "I'll just have to make sure you feel me tomorrow."

Oh, fuck me.

I had no idea what this man was about to do, but something told me it was going to be hard and rough. Some things were forbidden for the safety of our unborn child, but there were plenty of safe ways to satisfy a pain slut, and I looked forward to just how this man would do that for me.

"Fucking hurt me, Alpha," I growled.

In the blink of an eye, his hand was around my throat.

"Hmm yes, choke me harder, Alpha," I pleaded.

Chapter Ninety-Five

REN

When she begged me to choke her harder, I obliged, quickly earning me a deep moan. The amount this woman loved pain was exhilarating and a major turn-on. I rammed my length into her, making her scream. I angled myself and snapped my hips like my life depended on it.

She wanted to be sore and hurting. I would give that to her and then some. And while I did it, I would pour my love into everything I did. I raised my hand, poised to swat her perfect ass when she ground her hips, making my head spin.

Jesus Christ.

I gritted my teeth, trying desperately not to cum. The loud smack that sounded as my hand met her ass was intoxicating. And the slutty moan that followed made my balls draw up, ready to explode. Never missing a beat, I had her handcuffed to the bed. She pulled against them as I thrust into her with everything I had.

Wanting more, I put her legs on my shoulder as I moved in

and out of her sweet channel. One hand moved to her tight back hole and pressed down while my other pressed on her clit.

"Oh putain, qui. Plus, donne-moi plus."

Hearing her beg for more in my native language was enough to send my orgasm loose and rushing to the surface. I thrust harder while I pressed down more. Her hips bucked into me as her back arched.

"Je jouis," she yelled as her legs shook so hard I thought she was seizing.

The way her walls tightened around my cock as it exploded was the most euphoric feeling I've ever experienced. As I filled her heat, I slowed my pace, kissing her whole body, worshiping her beauty.

"J'aime quand tu me parles salement en français, Dove."

I kissed her some more, wanting to savor this feeling. But we had to work, I had a study to get to, and she had her business to tend to. More would have to wait until tonight. And there most definitely would be more tonight, a lot more. In a swift motion, I uncuffed her.

Plus, this afternoon we had our first ultrasound appointment with Doctor Barron Archambeau. Or as I call him Arch. He was a damn good OB-GYN, and I was not about to let my wife have second best. Not only was he the best but also he was always on top of cutting-edge technology and, like me, top of his class.

"Dove, as much as I want to continue our honeymoon, we both have work to do."

She let out a moan and grumbled, "I know." Then rolled over to sit up.

"Don't forget you'll see me this afternoon at our appointment."

She hummed and turned to look at me. "We get to see our little gummy bear."

The smile on her lips as she talked about our child was breathtaking, and all I could do was nod. Even the word yes was too much for me to say.

I couldn't help but picture her with a huge belly as our child grew.

Fuck, that's hot.

She was going to be the best mother out there.

Chapter Ninety-Six

ROSE

The way Ren looked at me when we talked about our child was one of utter hunger and adoration. It took a while and a lot more steamy make-out sessions, but we were now both heading to work.

I walked in the door and Wes looked up and smiled at me.

"Glad you're back, boss," he said as the door closed behind me.

"Good to be back." I noticed the stack of files on his desk and cocked an eyebrow. "New cases?"

"Yeah. Some are simple enough. Plus a few missing people. A lot of translating and decoding, though. Some for the FBI, DEA, and, of course, the CIA."

"Figures. I'll handle those while you and Liam do the missing persons cases."

"Sounds fair."

"Any word on his discharge?"

"Should be out in three months."

"Awesome. He still planning to work full time here?"

"Yep."

Thank God.

He was a damn good asset, and I did not want to lose him. I grabbed my stack and headed to my office and got to work. When my door opened, I looked up and smiled when I saw it was my dad.

"Hey, Dad."

"Hey dear. How was your mini honeymoon?"

My cheeks heated as I looked back up to him. "Do you really want me to answer that?"

He grimaced. "Now that you mention it, probably not."

"That's what I thought."

"Okay then, are you excited about your appointment?"

Now that was a safer question. "God yes. I can't wait."

"I can't wait to meet the little one. Just wanted to say hi since I haven't seen you since your wedding. I'll let you do your thing while I do my job."

My dad left my office, and I got to work.

—∿∿♡2∿∿—

AFTER SEVERAL HOURS, it was time for me to head to my appointment. It didn't take long to get there, and Ren waited at the doors for me. He pulled me into him and gave me a sweet kiss as he wrapped his arms around me.

"After this we are going to the Social Security office and finishing the name change and then getting your ID at the DMV."

"Hmm. Sounds good to me. Then afterward we can have a little fun," I said as I nipped his neck just below his ear. He growled as he pulled me closer, doing the same thing to my jaw. I let out a chuckle, then pushed against him. "Let's go see our gummy bear."

He took my hand in his and we headed to the OB-GYN's office. The receptionist smiled as we walked in.

"Doctor and Mrs. Doux, I will get you checked in, go ahead and have a seat."

"This is so surreal," Ren whispered.

"I know the feeling."

"Doux," the nurse called out. We both stood and followed her into the room. Once inside, she took my blood pressure and weight. "Please change into this gown for the ultrasound."

"Top only or bottoms as well?" Ren asked.

"Both. Depending on the baby's position, we may need to do a vaginal ultrasound."

I nodded and the nurse left. When I looked at Ren, there was a fire of lust in his eyes and I felt the wetness forming.

"Stop looking at me like that," I huffed.

"Like what?" he asked, moving closer.

"Like I'm something to eat."

My breath caught as he pressed against me.

"Oh, but you are," he growled.

Oh, fuck me.

I swatted at his shoulder. "Later."

He pulled my shirt over my head, then unclasped my bra.

Was he seriously about to take me right here?

He dropped to his knees and pulled my pants and panties down until I was fully naked in front of him. He placed gentle kisses at the start of my kitty and worked his way up until his lips were on mine. My breathing was erratic, and I wanted so much more.

Fucking hell.

Just as I was about to grab his length, which was poking me and telling me of its need to be inside me, he placed the gown on me and tied it on. Gently, he sat me back on the table to wait. When he sat down, he palmed his cock, and I couldn't help but smirk.

"Let me help you with that," I whispered.

"And how will you do that?"

I didn't speak. I motioned with my finger for him to come

over. When he did, I unfastened his pants and freed his very purple erection. My tongue swirled his tip, and he grunted.

"What are you doing, Dove? Arch will be here any second."

"Then I'll be fast," I said before taking him fully.

"Oh fuck," he moaned.

I worked quickly, hitting all the spots I knew would drive him wild. He pulled my hair hard, and I loved watching him as his knees buckled from the ecstasy.

"I'm going to cum," he moaned right before he shook as his cum jetted down my throat. I hummed my pleasure as I milked every last drop from him.

A knock sounded, and Ren hurried to right himself, though his face said it all. I turned to see the doctor Ren called Arch and to say the man was hot as hell was an understatement.

"Jesus." I whispered, which got me a look from Ren that I ignored. As I looked the man over, I swear he seemed flushed.

Had he heard us? Was he turned on by it?

Chapter Ninety-Seven

REN

I wasn't sure what to think about Rose's comment when Arch came in, but we could talk about it later. I mean, the man was hot. In my military days, we would hook up from time to time. Not many women to satisfy a man's needs, but then we both caught feelings and struggled with that. We broke it off, though we stayed friends.

If Rose knew what he was packing, she would say a lot more than Jesus.

"Alright Doctor and Mrs. Doux, let's get some eyes on your little one," he said as he squeezed some gel on her belly. "Ah, found them."

My eyes filled up with tears at the sight of our baby.

Wait.

Babies?

"Um Arch, are there two?" I asked shakily.

"Hmm. It does appear that there are two separate sacs. Congrats, you are having twins."

Holy shit. Fucking twins.

Pretty sure my eyes were wide when I met Rose's gaze. The shock was evident in her own face. I was faintly aware of Arch taking photos and then we heard it, a heartbeat, then another. Hearing that sweet sound confirmed everything. We were going to have two babies.

"I'll give you two some time to process the news," Arch said as he placed the ultrasound photos on the bed. When the door shut, I let out a breath I didn't realize I was holding.

"Twins," she whispered. "Holy shit."

"This is insane. Do twins run in your family?"

"No."

"So you being on birth control is to blame," I teased.

"Ha, apparently. Blame the pregnant lady. You are just as much to blame."

"True," I said as I kissed her.

"Fucking twins."

"Twice the work, twice the diapers."

"I'm going to look like a damn whale."

"Oh, but you will be a sexy whale."

She rolled her eyes, and I laughed. I picked up the photos, and we just stared at them. Our precious babies, our world.

WITH THE NEWS OF TWINS, we pushed the trip to a year after the due date. We knew with two we were likely to have complications and an early birth, and the last thing we wanted was to go into labor or have a problem in another country.

She was now twenty weeks, and we were supposed to find out the gender today. To say I was excited was an understatement. The study prevented me from making the appointment. Things were wrapping up, and I had an important meeting. But Rose would tell me later what we were having.

Apparently, she had a whole thing planned, and that made me a bit nervous.

Chapter Ninety-Eight

ROSE

As I left Arch's office, I paused in the hall. That man was sinful to say the least. But I was in love and married, so I would never do anything. Now I had the results in my hands, the gender of our two beautiful babies.

Some of the results were concerning for Baby A. So we had to do more testing, including blood work, which he ordered already. I went to a balloon shop and handed them the envelope with the results, and they got to work as I headed out to the car.

Once they loaded the balloons and returned the envelope, I crossed the parking lot to Tomato Street and picked up our favorites. When I got home, my dad came outside and helped me carry everything in.

"Thanks, Dad," I said as he placed everything down.

"Of course."

My dad sat with me for a while as he waited on me hand and foot. I rolled my eyes. The men in my life were so damn crazy about the babies that I was treated like a fragile doll. Sometimes it was annoying, but it was also kinda cute.

Ren came in the door and smiled widely when he saw me sitting at the bar. He came over to me and kissed me, resting his hand on my belly before giving it two kisses as well, then back to me.

"How did the appointment go?"

"Pretty good. They are running tests on Baby A. But Baby B is perfect."

"What are they testing for?"

"Trisomy something," I said, not quite remembering.

"Trisomy 21?"

"That sounds right," I mumbled. He took a deep breath. "What is it? I didn't ask."

"Down syndrome."

My heart dropped, and I felt my eyes water. He was holding my face and looking at me in seconds.

"Dove, it's okay. Little one will be okay. Just might need extra help and some medical issues, but they will be okay. I am a heart doctor, after all."

I nodded and took a deep breath. Ren was smart and resourceful and would make damn sure Baby A had everything they needed and more. And, of course, only the best.

"Are those filled with confetti?" he asked, pointing at the two large black balloons.

"Yep."

"Can I pop them now?" he whined.

"You sound like a child."

"And your point?"

I rolled my eyes. "Let my dad set up the camera so everyone can see."

In a flash, my dad had my phone in his hands, ready to go. I grabbed the balloon labeled A. Together we poked the balloon, popping it. Blue confetti filled the room. *Our special boy.*

I was pulled into a strong kiss. "He will be perfect, no matter what."

Next it was Baby B. Simultaneously, we popped the balloon. This time, pink confetti filled the room. *A girl.*

A perfect family.

Chapter Ninety-Nine

REN

One of each.

Fuck, that was perfect.

My heart clinched when she said our boy might have Down syndrome, but I also knew he would be okay. No matter what, he was going to be well-loved. Now we just needed names. But that was for later.

My phone rang, and I saw it was the center my mom was at. A feeling of dread hit me as I swiped to answer the call.

"Hello," I said as calmly as I could. Rose snapped her head up, telling me I had failed.

"Doctor Doux. Your mom, she has hours left."

I dropped the phone and was faintly aware of Rose grabbing it from the floor and telling them we were on our way. She knew, and no one even had to tell her. Next thing I knew, she was on the phone while pushing me toward the car. She drove fast as she talked on the phone.

When she pulled into a private airstrip, I looked at her, confused. "Ezra is in town. He is loaning his jet, now get in."

She didn't have to tell me twice. I took the steps two at a time, and we were in the air in minutes. A man named Travis was waiting for us when we landed and drove us to her facility like his life depended on it.

When we pulled up, I practically jumped from the car before running inside, my wife right behind me. I clutched my chest at the sight of my mom. She looked so damn sick, nothing like she did only a couple months ago.

Rose sat on my knee as we held my mom, crying. She was in and out, but when she saw us, she smiled.

"Mes enfants. Je vivrai à travers tes jeunes. Grand-mère regarde, toujours," she said as her hand fell to Rose's stomach and her eyes glazed over.

A sob exploded from me as I clutched my mom. She was gone, and I had no idea how to live without her. Rose turned and straddled me. It wasn't sexual, it was purely a comfort, as she just held me while I cried. She never said anything, just kissed my head, and she rubbed small circles on my back.

Honestly, she didn't need to speak, her touch did all the talking. My mom's words replayed in my head. I pulled back and looked at Rose.

"Can we name our daughter Esme after my mother?"

She smiled. "I was thinking Esme Estelle."

Loved Star. *Beautiful.*

My breath caught. "Perfect. And for a boy?"

"Valentin Orson."

Strong Bear.

Gummy bear. Perfect.

Chapter One Hundred

ROSE

Ren struggled after his mom died. He would work and sleep. To be honest, I was worried about him. Even sex was the last thing on his mind. The study would be done in a few weeks, then we would make the trip to spread his mom's ashes as soon as the babies were old enough to travel and we felt comfortable.

Today was a mini celebration of her life, and it seemed to take everything out of Ren. I hated seeing him so damn broken. Yet again, I was at my appointment alone.

"You know, honestly, I think the man just needs a good release. A good fucking," Arch said, and I laughed.

"Yeah, if I could get him in the mood."

"Look, I lost my mom while I served with Ren. He was the only one able to get through to me. And he did it with sex."

Wait, what?

My facial expression must have been hilarious cause he laughed.

"I don't know how much you know about our past, but we were friends with benefits. There weren't any women around to get our release, so we used each other. Then feelings got involved and, well, you know how the military is. We cut it off and stayed friends."

Holy shit. Well, that explained the reaction to the pegging. He might be bi.

"Go home, get him out of his head."

"Thanks, Doc," I said as I stood.

"Please call me Arch, not Doc."

I smirked and rolled my eyes. "Yeah, yeah, yeah, I know."

Over the weeks, I had grown to like this man. We became friends quickly, and he always told me embarrassing things about Ren. Now I was thirty-five weeks pregnant.

"You know this could put me into labor, right?" I quipped.

"Yep, I'll be by my cell."

"Jackass," I said as I left the room, leaving him laughing. I was supposed to be induced in three days, so it wasn't that big of an issue. I'd already had my injections and everything, so we were good to go.

I thought about going home and ambushing Ren there, but then I remembered how much he was turned on when he fucked me in his office. If I was doing this, I needed a lookout, so I pulled out my phone and texted Charlie.

> Hey, is Ren in his office?

> Yeah, he just got there.

> Can you make sure he isn't disturbed?

> Oh shit. You are going for it. Hell yeah. I'll keep watch.

I let out a chuckle. Charlie knew everything, as did my father.

318

We all were worried since we knew how much the man loved to fuck me any chance he got.

Thanks.

No problem.

I put my phone back in my pocket and made my way to his office.

Chapter One Hundred One

REN

F *uck.*
      Losing my mom was doing wonders for my mental health. It was like I used all my energy on my job and had nothing left. My heart was broken, and I didn't see the way out. I pushed everyone away, even my wife.

Shit.

I knew it was unhealthy, but I was drowning inside.

I drove my fist into the filing cabinet and lined up to do it again when a hand caught mine and spun me around. My anger fell flat when my eyes locked onto Rose's, which were filled with sadness and worry.

She cupped my face in her hands, and my hands fell to her stomach. Her lips met mine, and I let myself get lost in the kiss. My cock twitched, screaming its desire to be in her again. Her touch seemed to bring my mind back to reality.

My wife was the key to this the whole time, and I pushed her away. Not only that, but I did it while she was pregnant.

What the fuck was wrong with me?

My mom was probably rolling in her grave at my childish behavior. I maneuvered us so she was sitting on my desk, which I quickly cleared off. I took a step back and took in the beautiful woman in front of me. Her huge belly reminded me of our love and that I had plenty to live for and a little girl who would carry my mom's name for another generation.

"I'm so sorry," I whispered, pulling her into me.

"I know. It's not your fault. You lost your mother."

"That's no excuse to treat you like I have been, leaving you to prepare for our kids alone. It's fucked up."

"But I wasn't alone. The people I met because of you, our chosen family, they stepped in. They helped me so I could focus on growing our babies and being there for you."

"It should have been me. I should have…"

She silenced me with her lips.

"Don't. What is done is done. Just be here now. Show me how much you love me with your actions, not your words."

Fuck.

She was amazing. Most women would have likely given up and left, but not my Dove. She stayed through it all.

I moved in and kissed her again, spreading her legs. A deep growl escaped my lips as I found no underwear. My hand moved to her wetness and my knees went weak when I felt just how ready she was for me.

"Fuck Dove, so goddamn wet for me."

"Need you," she whined.

"You have me," I said as I unfastened my pants and let them drop to the ground. Right now, I gave zero shits we were in my office. We both needed this. Our love connection was hanging on by a thread and we needed to repair it.

I plunged into her heat and gritted my teeth, my orgasm already trying to come to the surface. "Fuck Dove, I'm about to cum already."

"Fill me up," she moaned.

Oh God.

As much as I wanted to prolong this. I knew it was no use. I pulled out and drove my length back in with a snap of my hips. Her moan was porn worthy and made my already hard cock even more so.

"Fuck," I growled as I moved in and out of her. "Feel so damn good. So fucking tight."

I sped up, looking into her eyes filled with love, happiness, and lust. The entire time I was feeling depressed, all I needed was her.

Fuck.

I missed her slutty kitty, and I had been depriving it for months. Right then, I vowed to make up for it every day for the rest of our lives. I didn't know how, but I would.

"Dove, I love you," I whispered into her ear.

"I love you too, Alpha."

My orgasm rushed to the surface, and I bit down on her breast, getting some wetness on my tongue.

The fuck?

I looked, and her breasts were leaking. The sight seemed to give my orgasm a second wind.

Jesus Christ.

Once I was drained, I pulled out of her. Her groan made my cock twitch. I fixed my pants, then helped her off the desk.

As soon as her feet hit the floor, a pop filled the room, and we both got wet. I looked down and realized it was her water.

Oh shit.

Chapter One Hundred Two

ROSE

Well, I was not expecting my water to break in his office. But hey at least I didn't have far to go. Ren stepped outside the door and yelled for Charlie.

"Get me a wheelchair and call Arch."

Within minutes, I was in a wheelchair and heading to the Labor and Delivery floor.

It was baby time.

The pain was definitely not a pleasant one. I've been shot, stabbed, beaten, waterboarded, and everything else under the damn sun, and this was worse than all of those combined.

Fuck me.

Ren was amazing. He fed me ice chips, rubbed my back through the contractions, let me practically break his hands as I gripped them for dear life, begging for relief. The ultrasound showed both babies were in the correct position for a natural birth. Though once the first baby was out, that could change quickly.

The contractions were getting stronger and longer, and I felt like my vagina was going to explode. Arch came in after a while and checked me.

"Looks like it's time to push."

Oh, thank God.

We had been at this for twelve hours, and I was ready to be done. The nurse and Ren moved me to the tub. Ren entered first and I got between his legs. I leaned back into him as I pushed with my next contraction. Arch talked me through it, though I barely heard him.

"Okay, one big push and we will have the shoulders, then the baby will slide right out."

I bore down hard, pushing with everything I had as I screamed and cursed in every language I knew. The wave of relief I felt as the baby came out gave me a floating feeling. Then the cries of our baby filled the room.

"She is beautiful." Arch said. Ren cut the cord before the nurse ran off to check vitals.

My daughter.

So precious.

Another contraction hit, and I screamed with the pain. This one seemed to move faster, everything already stretched for him. After just five pushes, his cries filled the room, joining his sister's.

"He is a hunk." Arch said. I watched as Ren cut his chord.

My special baby.

So beautiful.

He had Down syndrome, but Arch educated me about every-thing I needed to know, including all the potential medical issues. We also knew that he would have a longer NICU stay than his sister because of it.

Arch had introduced me to the NICU staff, and we had become friends over the weeks. I knew he would be taken care of not only by us, but by everyone here.

"Would you look at that, two seven-pound babies, and you didn't even tear. Just have to get the placentas out and you are done," Arch said as he stood up.

The nurses walked over to us. "You can hold them for a minute before they go to the NICU. They are stable."

Both were placed in my arms, and I looked up to meet Ren's eyes. They mirrored my own with the tears sitting just at the surface.

My life was perfect.

Chapter One Hundred Three

REN

Seeing my wife holding our babies was breathtaking.
So fucking perfect.

My heart was full. The loss of my mother was still there, not as dread, but as a reminder. She lived on in Esme. Watching Rose breastfeed our babies was one of the most beautiful sights, more beautiful than a sunset in the mountains.

Though I may be a little biased.

When the nurses took them to the NICU, I wanted to follow but knew her dad was there waiting. I needed to be here with my beautiful wife and the mother of my precious children.

After she delivered her placentas, we got her out of the tub and into the bed. I crawled onto the bed and just held her as we both took a well-needed nap. Her more than me, of course. She did all the work, I was just her support.

The only thing that would make this perfect was if our beautiful littles were snuggling with us. But Valentin needed tests on his heart and lungs, and Rose needed her sleep before she went down to see them again.

My eyes opened when I felt her moving in my arms.

"How did you sleep, Dove?" I asked.

"Like a rock."

"Good, you needed it. Now let's go for a walk and see our babies."

She nodded, and I got up and grabbed the wheelchair just in case she needed it, per hospital protocol. If I got caught breaking the rules, my boss would have my ass.

The nurses smiled as we walked in, greeting Rose by name. She must have made friends with the NICU staff while I was in my head.

"Both babies are doing fine. Little Bear is not back from his last test yet, but our little Star is."

The fact that they knew the meaning behind their names made me smile.

Plus, the nicknames were cute as fuck.

Once in the private room, Rose sat down, wincing slightly at the discomfort. I was so damn proud of her. She delivered twins with no meds and even now has yet to take a pain med. But I worried about her. I wanted her to be comfortable.

Her dad walked over to Rose and placed a crying Star in her arms. When she started singing to her, my mind flooded with memories. Rose would walk around the house singing to our unborn children, making sure they knew her voice. The sound would bring me out of my fog even if just for a minute.

As soon as Esme heard her, it calmed her just like it did for me, whether I knew it or not. She sat there for a while, holding our daughter while she slept in her arms.

"Hey. You should hold our daughter," Rose whispered as she held out our child. I took her, and she wiggled but stayed asleep. Her tiny hand wrapped around my finger.

"That's right, baby girl. You are wrapped around my finger. Daddy's girl. But your mama will make sure you can hold your own in any fight, that's for sure."

Rose let out a chuckle. "Damn right I will. Just like your Papa did for me."

We both looked up when our son came back. The nurse wasted no time handing him to Rose. "Now you, my special Bear, will be a mama's boy that also knows how to kick ass and take names."

I barked a laugh, and so did everyone else.

Oh, how I knew.

And despite being younger, he would fight off all the boys to protect his sister.

ALL HIS TESTS WERE GOOD. He had a small hole in his heart, but they didn't see it needing an operation in the near future, maybe in a few years if it didn't resolve itself. They stayed in the NICU for just over three weeks. Everyone made sure the house was ready for the two additions, including bassinets on either side of the bed. We each had a baby to tend to each night and alternated them. She breastfed and pumped so I could help with feeding.

Luckily, she produced enough milk to feed both, and for that we were thankful. Life was now feeding, changing diapers, tummy time, sleep and repeat, but neither of us would change a damn thing.

Our family was perfect.

I was the luckiest man on earth, and I knew my mom was smiling down on us.

Epilogue

REN

Traveling with two small children who were under a year old was a bitch, but I knew my mama would roll in her grave if we didn't include them on this trip. We delayed it to ensure Valentin was good to go and now it was go time. Obviously, we would do it again when they were older and could appreciate the meaning more. Charles and Dale joined us so that we could get some time together at some point.

I was shocked when Ezra let us use his jet for the trip. His reasoning, babies' first flight can be rough and why fly commercial when he had a jet?

This trip was needed in so many ways. Not only was my mom's wish to have her ashes spread all over France and her hometown, but also to see my extended family. Our first stop was to a town called Saint-Jean-en-Royans, my mom's birthplace.

The landscape was gorgeous, with horses and rock cliffs everywhere. Most of my family now lived in Lyons, but my aunt still lived in their childhood home. We knocked on the door and were greeted by a young man.

"Puis-je vous aider?"

"Oui. Nous sommes ici pour voir Juliette. Nous sommes la famille de sa sœur Esme," I said.

"Ah, oui. Entrez, s'il-vous-plaît."

The four of us walked inside and were immediately greeted by my aunt. "You came, neveu."

"Of course I did, Tata. This is my wife Rose, our son Valentin, and our daughter Esme."

She gasped at her sister's name. "Belle."

"This is Rose's pere, Dale, and his partner, my coworker and Rose's comrade, Charles."

"Nice to meet all of you. My name is Julliette, but you may call me Juli."

"The pleasure is ours," Dale said, and everyone agreed.

"Thank you for having us," Rose added.

"Of course. Please eat and get some rest. We have a life to remember tomorrow."

Dinner was divine. I missed the family cooking. The man who answered the door was my cousin Benoit or Ben. He seemed like a great kid. Apparently he was in high school and asked about us hosting him to study in the US, which, of course, we agreed to. He had dreams of becoming a doctor, though he wanted to specialize in pulmonology. I promised I wouldn't hold it against him. When Rose invited his mom to come as well, she beamed but declined.

"I will visit, yes, but my home is here."

"Of course," Rose said.

The next night at sunset we spread most of my mom's ashes on the family's land. The sunset was one of the brightest I've seen in a long time. "You inherited your mom's part of this land. A house is already there for vacations. If you want, we can get it fixed up," my aunt said.

"Thank you, Tata."

The next day we headed to Lyons to see the rest of the family and spread some of the remaining ashes before taking a drive to spread the rest. Everyone was so happy to see us. It was insane. They had a whole reunion planned, and we were at the center of it.

It felt good to have Rose meet my family. Granted, no one else lived in the States, but we had a second home here. My family accepted everyone and every way and between that and the successful study, my life was better than ever.

Heaven on earth.

Who would have thought the former Navy SEAL turned CIA agent would fall for and start a family with the nerdy cardiologist?

Not me, that's for sure.

THE END

BONUS SCENES CAN BE FOUND in paperback editions available only at special events.

Acknowledgments

To Good Girl Author Services: Thank you so much for all you have done for me. I can't thank you enough. Even after every set back I have had with this book, you always come through for me.

To Emily Michel: Thank you for being this book's saving grace. Your TikTok video saved me from panic after losing my previous editor. I can't thank you enough.

To Kellie Cover Designs: Thank you for coming through for a new cover when I needed a backup option due to unforeseen circumstances.

To S.P. Stavros: Thank you for giving me the idea for the word funishments. I loved it and had to use it. Thank you for all the nights on TikTok and Discord. You are the best.

To Ruby Spark: Thank you so much for all that you do. Between helping with the hardback cover for this book and other covers for other books and just dealing with ADHD moments, you have been amazing through it all. I am so glad BookTok brought me to you. Keep being you.

To everyone else who's helped: There are many others who I have met on BookTok and Facebook that have been amazing and helped with small little things along the way. There are so many I can't possibly list them all. Just know you are appreciated.

About the Author

Between her part-time job in the security industry, her full-time job in healthcare admin, and being a mom of three boys, Cierra finds the time to write all things smut. At any given time, she can have multiple books in progress and the list of future books could be its own novella. She's loved writing from a young age, and with her mom being a reporter, you could argue it's in her blood. While sitting in the hospital with one of her boys after his brain surgery, she wrote her first book. Next thing she knew, she was five books deep and editing her debut from those five. She dabbles in shifters, vampires, humans, fairies, witches, first responders, and so much more. Pay careful attention while reading—she leaves Easter eggs for future books.